A Dying Fall

A Dying Fall

JUNE THOMSON

PUBLISHED FOR THE CRIME CLUB BY

DOUBLEDAY & COMPANY, INC.

GARDEN CITY, NEW YORK

1986

All of the characters in this book
are fictitious, and any resemblance
to actual persons, living or dead,
is purely coincidental.

Library of Congress Cataloging in Publication Data
Thomson, June.
A dying fall.
I. Title.
PR6070.H679D8   1986   823'.914   85-12931
ISBN 0-385-23159-8

First Edition in the United States of America

For Chas, whose idea it was. With affection.

CHAPTER ONE

Driving back to Barnsfield was for Martin Holt more than just a physical return to that part of the countryside where he had spent his childhood; it was a journey into the past which, since the death of his mother and his quarrel with his father, he preferred not to make. Those memories were still too painful.

They always began for him at Welham, the market town, ten miles from his family home. The place had changed over the years, of course, but not enough to make it indistinguishable from his recollection of it. The tea-shop, Gentle's, where his mother had taken him for ice-cream sundaes on school holiday treats was now an optician's. But the clock tower still dominated the market square, where it faced the one hotel the town boasted of, the Red Lion, its classical eighteenth-century façade repainted since the last occasion he had returned home two months before.

Its bar had been his father's lunchtime habitat. It was there he had met his business acquaintances and where, in the unquestioning assumption that his son would take over the family firm, he had introduced him to those laconic, slow-speaking, hard-headed farmers and builders who made up his clientele.

"You'll be dealing with him when I retire."

What price betrayal?

He could only thank God that his route didn't take him past the actual premises, situated behind the town centre, where, no doubt, that façade, too, had been repainted; no longer Holt and Son, Haulage Contractors, but Dalby's Limited, the consortium which had bought Rex Holt out of his retirement five years earlier.

After the roundabout, where he turned left, he was in more familiar territory, those few square miles of north-east Essex which, as a boy, he had walked or cycled across and which, despite everything that had happened since, he still thought of as home. It lay resplendent on that late July morning under a light golden haze which promised another hot day, the woods and hedgerows dark green, the blond harvest fields full to the brim, it seemed, with the richness of the grain.

At the top of Fair Mile Hill, he drew the car into a gateway and, as he had done as a boy, climbed the bars, following the footpath to the edge of the meadow, where he looked across to Barnsfield, which lay below in the folds of the low valley.

It was the landscape he loved most, although he would have found it difficult to say exactly why. There was nothing spectacular about it; it was simply farmland, pasture and arable, the small fields pieced together with hawthorn and bramble, with great trees standing solitary or gathered together in woodlands.

Perhaps it was the sense of continuity that appealed to him, an awareness that men had tilled this land for generations and would, God willing, go on cultivating them. It was the reason why, on breaking with his father, he had set up on his own in a smallholding on the other side of the county. To grow things, to handle earth and plants, was for him one of the greatest pleasures in life.

The village itself was partly hidden by the surrounding trees, only the church towers visible above them, riding the green foliage like a stone galleon, the pennant of its gilded weather-vane catching the sun and, to the left of it, the high gable end of the mill. Although he could not see the river, he could trace its course by the double row of willows lining its bank until, once clear of the village, it ran between open water-meadows, where its surface glittered like a sword.

And then reluctantly, he looked to the right towards the house which stood a little apart from the village on its own sweep of lawn so that its façade faced him—outfaced him, it seemed to him—in a manner which was typical of his father, bold, solid, four-square, its brick façade with its many white-painted windows stating a little too obviously that here was money, power and prestige.

It was Queen Anne period, built, he imagined, for some portly, fox-hunting country gentleman. His father, a shrewd business man where land and property were concerned, had bought it twenty-five years before at a rock-bottom price when its owner had bankrupted himself trying to live up to the same image of the local squire.

So it was an investment merely but beautiful all the same and, despite everything, the place he still thought of as home. It was not easy to dig out all the roots. Some went on clinging deep into the soil of the past.

Turning away, he walked back to the car, noticing as he did so the patches of wild flowers growing in the turf nibbled short by rabbits. In childhood he could have named them all. Now, stooping to examine them, he recognised only a few: eyebright, agrimony, yellow toadflax and harebells, their blue caps balanced above the others on long, fragile stems, trembling with the faint vibration of his footsteps on the ground.

The colour of the sky. His mother's description.

Fumbling a little, he picked one, crouching awkwardly on his heels, his expression intent.

He rarely smiled and, although still a relatively young man, only in his early thirties, his serious, almost sardonic air gave him the impression of someone older; middle-aged, disillusioned, already a little world-weary, as if, finding life a disappointment, he viewed it with a distant, ironic gaze, not giving a damn about anyone else's opinion.

This negligence was apparent in his appearance, his dark hair untrimmed, the plaid shirt and jeans worn carelessly. Even his manner of walking expressed this indifference as, getting to his feet, he strolled at an easy, nonchalant pace back to the car, where, as if losing interest, he laid the harebell he had picked so carefully only a few moments ago on the passenger seat beside him before driving down the hill into the village.

The entrance to Barnsfield Hall, his father's house, was on his right, a small, single-storey gatehouse standing beside it, where the Drewetts, his father's gardener and housekeeper, lived. The gates to the driveway were set open but Martin Holt made no attempt to turn into them. Instead, he continued on down the road towards the village, where he drew up outside the first in a row of four cottages.

Biddy must have heard the car because she was at the door to meet him, a small, indomitable figure standing in the porch at the end of the long front garden where flowers and vegetables grew side by side with that practical, profuse generosity which was so characteristic of her. Arms folded on her apron, she watched his progress past the roses and the broad beans, the currant bushes tied up in old net curtains, with her head cocked critically, looking for signs of change since the last time she had seen him.

She herself had grown older, more shrunken and frail, so that he had to bend his head further down to kiss her. Her cheek against his had a dry, papery feel, too, as if the tissues were, like pressed flowers, losing their substance, but she still set him back a few inches from her as she used to do when he was a child to give him a good, hard look before letting him inside the cottage.

"You've lost weight," she told him accusingly. "You're not taking proper care of yourself."

"I'm all right, Biddy," he replied, stooping to accommodate the low doorway, which led directly into the tiny sitting-room from the garden.

It was full of the furniture he remembered had stood in her room at the Hall when she had been housekeeper there before his mother's death and her own retirement: the painted vases, the chiming clock, the pair of low armchairs with their worn velvet seats and carved arms, the little round table with the brass tray as a top. Cups and plates were set out in readiness for his arrival and a walnut cake out of which Biddy had already cut a huge slice.

"Eat that up," she told him, passing it to him as he awkwardly folded his long legs to sit down in the low chair. "I'll fetch the teapot."

While she was gone, he took the opportunity to look round the room, his gaze resting longest on the portrait of his mother which stood on the mantelpiece.

He had photographs of his own of her, of course; but not this one. It was a studio portrait taken when his mother had been a girl, before his birth and even her marriage to his father, and had he not known her, he would still have been attracted by the expression of grave innocence. She was looking out of the frame over one shoulder, her lips slightly parted, the light eyes with the dark pupils—eyes which he had inherited—faintly apprehensive, as if she found the world she was contemplating a bewildering and frightening place. They looked directly at him with a gentle appeal which he remembered seeing years later when she lay dying and to which he had not known how to respond.

Biddy came back with the teapot and he averted his gaze.

"So you've not been to see your father yet?" she asked, her own eyes intent on the cups as she poured tea for them both.

"No, not yet," he replied, watching her face closely. He was aware of an uncharacteristic reticence about her. Biddy had something on her mind which under normal circumstances she would not have hesitated to express. Now, she folded her lips in an expression of disapproval.

"Then I think I ought to tell you that Mrs. Chilton's moved into the village. She's bought that house in Mill Lane. You remember it? The one where old Agnes Hope used to live."

"Bea?" he asked sharply. "When?"

"Two days ago. Your father's said nothing to you about it?"

"No, but we haven't been in touch recently except for the note he sent asking me to lunch today. There was nothing in it about Bea."

As he spoke, he wondered if the invitation hadn't been deliberately timed in order to contrive a meeting between himself and his father's mistress. It wouldn't surprise him. His father was adept at manipulating events to suit himself.

"Well," Biddy said, summing it all up in the one word.

There was no need for her to add anything more. They both understood the situation perfectly: the minimal communication between Martin and his father, the lack of frankness on Rex Holt's part over the arrival in the village of his mistress of many years' standing, the uneasy relationship which existed between all of them, including Biddy herself.

"I suppose," Martin said ironically, "that I ought to be grateful that she hasn't moved in with him. At least they've shown that much sensitivity. Are they going to get married?"

"Nothing's been said to me," Biddy retorted, reluctant to discuss the matter further. "Eat your cake up."

"But my father told you himself that Bea would be moving down here?" Martin persisted, anxious to have this point quite clear.

"Yes. He called here about a month ago; said the lease on Mrs. Chilton's flat in London was running out, so she'd decided to buy Agnes Hope's place." She gave him one of her quick, shrewd glances. "But it was fixed up long before that, wasn't it? Even I know that much. Besides, I've seen the SOLD notice up in the front garden for the past two months at least. Still, it's *his* business when all's said and done. They've known each other for years."

"Old friends," Martin said and smiled sarcastically. That was how his father had first introduced Bea to him years before. "An old friend of mine."

Good God! Young as he was, he had been aware of the exact nature of the relationship between them and the reason for his father's frequent "business" trips to London.

The "business" was a small, neat, dark woman with a fashionable, self-assured gloss about her which, at thirteen, he had found intimidating and whose easy intimacy with his father he had bitterly resented.

He wasn't sure now what his reactions were. He hadn't seen her for years and rarely thought about her, merely assuming that she and his father still met. At least, from time to time Rex Holt referred to her in an oblique, half-bold, half-ashamed manner.

But, as Biddy would have said, it was *his* business.

Having unburdened herself of that particular piece of family news, Biddy seemed relieved to change the subject.

"You'll call at the churchyard before you go up to the Hall, won't you?" she asked. "You can take some fresh flowers with you. I weeded on Monday and did the vase but, in this heat, it won't have lasted."

"All right," Martin agreed reluctantly.

He had not intended visiting his mother's grave. But, as Biddy expected it, he didn't like to disappoint her.

"I've cut some roses," she continued, fetching them from the kitchen, their stems wet from standing in the sink. Wrapping a sheet of newspaper round them, she added, "You ought to get married."

Used to her *non sequiturs*, he asked with amusement, "You recommend it, Biddy?"

"Me?" she said sharply. "I never found anyone I fancied."

"Neither have I."

"Then you ought to look more carefully. You're too choosy, that's your trouble. When all's said and done, a man needs a woman to look after him."

"Are we so incompetent?"

"Men are fools," Biddy replied as if she meant it. "Here, take the flowers. I've crushed the stems so they'll last. And mind you arrange them nicely."

"I'll do my best," he promised.

At the door, she voiced the last concern which had been on her mind.

"If he does marry her . . . ," she began.

"I know," Martin said quietly.

He understood exactly what she meant. It could affect his inheritance. Biddy was practical and shrewd enough to see the implications of such a possibility. If Rex Holt married again, the bulk of his fortune would go to his second wife, who, in Bea's case, had a daughter of her own. Not all of it, of course. Rex Holt was a rich man and, even in a revised will, there would no doubt be provision made for an only son.

His inheritance was a subject he preferred not to consider but it always remained on the edge of his thoughts, never totally banished.

Aware of her concern, he added, trying to set her mind at rest, "It doesn't matter, Biddy. I can manage."

"You shouldn't have to," Biddy retorted tartly.

He bent down quickly to kiss her before she could say any more.

"Take care of yourself," he said.

Laying down the roses on the passenger seat, he turned to wave to her before driving off. She was standing in the doorway, hands clasped in front of her, refusing, as she always did, to wave back but whether out of a dislike for farewells or a reluctance herself to make the obvious, conventional gesture he wasn't sure.

She disapproved of the gravestone; he knew that.

"Too showy" had been her comment when it was first erected.

He agreed with her. It was one of the reasons why he disliked visiting it. It reflected his father's taste, which suggested not only a desire to be seen making the obvious gesture but spending money in doing so.

A white marble angel, wings folded forwards, leaned over the graveplot, which, surrounded by stone kerbs, had its centre filled with marble chippings.

Chips off the old block, Martin had thought irreverently when he had first seen it. It had been the only way he could contain his anger.

SACRED TO THE MEMORY OF ELIZABETH HOLT, BELOVED WIFE OF REX HOLT, read the inscription cut into the plinth at the angel's feet.

Beloved wife! Christ, when all the time his father had been paying regular visits to his mistress in London.

Below the inscription and the dates, another line of words had been cut; a quotation, judging by the inverted commas round it:

'REMEMBER ME, IF AT ALL, WITHOUT REGRET.'

It had been his mother's choice, Martin had learnt from Biddy.

"She asked for it to be put on her grave before she died," Biddy had explained.

Well, she certainly had had enough time to think about it, Martin thought bitterly. Two years' dying of cancer had given her plenty of opportunity.

He had wondered if it were a line from one of Edward Voyte's poems but had been unable to trace it either in the one volume of his collected works or in the three unpublished poems which Voyte had sent to his mother many years ago when she had been a girl; possibly at about the same age when the photograph of her in Biddy's sitting-room had been taken.

Like one of the Greek myths or a fairy story, the account of his mother's love affair with Edward Voyte had been part of the fabric of his childhood memories, casting a spell over his mind with its tale of young, doomed lovers, parted by others, of secret meetings and early death.

Analysed and stripped of its associations with childhood, it became more prosaic, as most fairy stories are when subjected to adult criticism.

His mother had met Edward Voyte when she was sixteen, staying with an uncle and aunt, the local baker and his wife, in a market town in Suffolk. Voyte was then twenty-one, an undergraduate from Oxford, spending the long summer vacation with his mother in the same town. They had met and fallen in love. But his mother, the well-to-do widow of a solicitor, had disapproved of the relationship. They were too young; there was too much difference in their social backgrounds. Mrs. Voyte had other plans for her only son than marriage to Elizabeth Renfrew, as she then was, the niece of a local tradesman and the daughter of an impoverished farmer scratching out a living on a few acres near Welham. She forbade them to meet.

So they met secretly by a lake, hiding messages for each other in a hollow tree in the lane which led to it, Voyte's letters containing the poems which together with his photograph were still among her possessions when she died.

That image of the lake was still powerfully evocative and Martin Holt could not even now see a stretch of inland water without associating it with the idea of lost love.

But it was 1939, the summer just before the war. Voyte, a member of the Oxford University Air Squadron, had abandoned his studies and joined the RAF. While he was under training, a small volume of his poems had been printed privately, a copy of which he had sent to Elizabeth before he died a year later, shot down over Kent in the Battle of Britain. He had been not quite twenty-two.

It was the only time she heard from him after he left Suffolk. When recounting this part of the story, his mother had still been too affected by it to give him a rational account. Edward Voyte had not forgotten her. Of that she was convinced. But he had been forced to give her up. "They didn't want us to marry," she had explained and even forty years later the tears had stood in her eyes. "They came between us. But he still loved me. I know that. He told me that, whatever happened, he'd find some way to come back to me. Then he was killed, so it was too late."

Desperately unhappy, Elizabeth had met Rex Holt, who, after several years' courtship, had persuaded her to marry him. Knowing his father, Martin could imagine the persistent, determined pressure he had brought to bear on her. Once he had made up his mind, Rex Holt was a very difficult man to refuse.

The rest he knew from his own experience. As might have been expected, his parents' marriage was a failure. Rex Holt had little understanding of the young, unhappy woman he had married. An ambitious man, his main concern had been to build up the family business which he had inherited from his own father after the war. In that, at least, he had been successful.

> This rose breathes out
> Our summer fragrance,
> Perfumed with the exhalation
> Of its own death and resurrection.

Lines from one of Edward Voyte's poems to his mother.

It was impossible, Martin decided, lifting the marble urn containing the dead flowers from the centre of his mother's grave and carrying it to the incinerator behind the vestry, to disentangle the images. Even Biddy, sensible, prosaic Biddy, seemed to be affected by them.

Why else had she chosen roses, and white ones at that?

There could, of course, be a quite ordinary explanation. Biddy's front garden was full of them. What would be more natural than for her to cut some?

But, as he tipped the dead blooms onto the pile of other fading flowers and refilled the urn with water from the tap, he could not help thinking that Biddy's choice was deliberate.

Roses. Love. Youth. Death. Poetry.

The chain of words went echoing on, evoking other symbols until the reality was buried so deep that it was transformed beyond recognition.

Unwrapping the fresh flowers, he discovered the single harebell which he had picked on Fair Mile Hill had become caught up in the paper. Its stem was bent but the small blue flowers still trembled like a bell on the top of the stalk and, on a sudden whim, he tucked it into the stone vase that held the roses before carrying it back to the grave.

His own symbol, perhaps; but of what? It was a broken flower, for God's sake!

Voyte could no doubt have turned it into a poem, he thought wryly. He himself possessed neither the words nor the understanding. Nor indeed, he added, placing the marble vase among the chippings, the inclination. Turning abruptly, he walked back to the car.

It had been a mistake to come, as he knew it would be. Revisiting his mother's grave had unsettled him. He felt impatient, restless; in no mood to meet his father although he never looked forward to these occasions with any sense of pleasure. They were merely a duty.

Bea's arrival in the village would further complicate the uneasy relationship between himself and his father.

As he started the car, Martin wondered how his father would explain it. Knowing his tactics, he'd probably try to bluff his way out of it. Martin had never known him admit to being in the wrong.

As for himself, it placed him in a dilemma. At the end of the visit, he knew his father would refer to money. He usually did. His parting remark was almost invariably "Are you all right for funds?"

In the past, Martin had always been able to say, "Yes, thank you," turning down the profferred cheque out of pride and a stubborn refusal to admit that he might be in need of help.

When he had left home after three disastrous years spent working in his father's business being trained to take over Rex Holt's place as head of the firm on his retirement, Martin had sworn that he would never ask his father for financial backing. It had been eleven years of hard slog on minimal resources, but so far he had managed to keep to his word. Never once in all those years had he accepted a single penny of his father's money.

It was ironic, therefore, that only that morning before setting off for Barnsfield, Martin had decided for the first time not to refuse. The heating system in one of the greenhouses had broken down earlier in the season. It was too old to be repaired and he had been advised to replace it at a cost of two thousand pounds. There was no chance of raising the money himself. He already had one bank loan which he had guaranteed to pay off the following spring out of the sale of early tomatoes, one of his best-paying crops. But, with no heating in his main greenhouse, this now seemed an impossibility.

It was a Catch-22 situation with no way out that he could see except by accepting a cheque from his father, however much it might hurt his pride to do so; but as a loan only and with interest payable on it as on any borrowed capital. Under those conditions, he could minimise the obligation.

Bea's arrival had given him no choice that he could see except to refuse. He wasn't enough of a hypocrite to accept his father's cheque with one hand while rejecting his mistress with the other. He only hoped to God she wouldn't be at the house. It would be the last bloody turn of the screw if he had to meet her face to face.

There was a car parked outside the front door of the Hall on the semicircular sweep of gravelled forecourt but not hers, he thought as, getting out of his own car, he glanced briefly inside it in passing. A metal case for carrying camera equipment and a tripod lay on the back seat; too professional-looking to belong to her, for, as far as he knew, she had never been interested in photography.

At the top of the steps, he paused before entering the Hall, turning his back on the house and looking across the valley to Fair Mile Hill, the reverse of the view he had looked at earlier that morning.

"It'll all be yours one day, Martin."

His father had spoken those words on his twenty-first birthday, taking him out onto the porch, a little drunk from champagne, one arm across his shoulder.

He had meant, of course, Barnsfield Hall, its grounds and outbuildings, together with the family firm and all that this implied, not the view itself. But it went with them nevertheless—the exclusive ownership of that particular vista of English countryside—and, oddly enough, Martin realised, standing there, it was its loss which he felt the most.

Four months after that occasion, his mother had died and eight months after that he had walked out after a final quarrel with his father.

But, as Biddy would have said, What's gone is gone. He had no real regrets and, shrugging dismissively, he turned away and entered the house.

CHAPTER TWO

After the sunlight outside, the hall seemed dark and more unfamiliar than on his last visit, as if, on each succeeding occasion, the objects it contained became more distanced from his childhood recollection of them.

He still missed Biddy's welcome, too, although it was four years since her retirement. She would have been at the door to meet him. Instead, Mrs. Drewett, her face anxious, appeared from the passage at the end of the hall which led into the kitchen, dressed in a blue overall coat like a canteen manageress.

"Oh, Mr. Martin, I thought I heard a car. Your father's in the drawing-room."

She was never quite sure how to treat him. Aware as she must have been of at least some of the tension between the father and son, she was always uneasy when Martin visited the house.

For his part, he never felt relaxed with her either. She was constantly on the defensive, expecting criticism although he suspected this was largely his father's fault. He was not an easy man to work for, as Martin knew from his own experience. Biddy had stood up to him. Mrs. Drewett was easier to bully. With her genteel mannerisms and sad, drab appearance, ginger hair going unbecomingly grey, she merely worked the harder, assuming any criticism was justified.

Martin had once heard his father say of her, "I wouldn't give her house-room if she wasn't such a damned good cook."

Remembering the comment, Martin smiled as he thanked her, at which she became more flustered.

"He has a gentleman with him," she continued and then stopped, unsure whether or not it was her place to advise him to wait.

Martin made the decision for her.

"That's all right, Mrs. Drewett. My father's expecting me. I'll go straight in."

The drawing-room was at the back of the house, overlooking a terrace from which a flight of stone steps led down to a sunken rose garden in the centre of which stood an ornamental pool with a fountain. During his mother's lifetime, the room had been almost exclusively hers and had borne the stamp of her personality more than any other part of the house. After her death, he had hated going into it, finding it contained too much which reminded him of her and the last painful and lingering years of her illness. He was relieved, therefore, that when his father had suffered a minor stroke the previous spring, he had chosen to turn it into a bed-sitting-room for himself to save the effort of climbing the stairs more than he had to. The furniture had been rearranged, a divan bed replacing the sofa and Rex Holt's own desk replacing the small bureau belonging to his wife, which had been moved to a bedroom.

Rex Holt was standing at this desk as Martin entered, his back to the door, presenting a view of himself which was only too familiar to his son: that solid stance, leaning slightly sideways as he rested his weight on the stick which he now used to help him get about, the end of which was dug into the carpet, his head carried aggressively forward so that even a normal conversation with him took on some of the qualities of a confrontation.

As he opened the door, Martin heard him saying, "You can do what you like with them as far as I'm concerned."

The man he was addressing was in his late thirties, tall, angular, with fair hair cropped short and a clean, sharp outline to his light-weight beige suit, which made Martin suspect that he might be an American even before he spoke.

"That's very generous of you, Mr. Holt. I really appreciate your kindness."

In the few seconds it took him to absorb the pair of them, Martin was aware of something else—the papers which were laid out on top of the desk and which, even from the doorway, were instantly recognisable. He had seen them too often to have any doubts about their identity.

Edward Voyte's letters to his mother were set out individually, together with the poems, his photograph and the volume of his poetry, its thin grey cover of poor-quality wartime paper printed with the emblem which he always associated with Voyte—the figure of a winged man; Icarus, no doubt, and more symbolic than Voyte could have realised when he chose it. He, too, had met his death falling from the sky.

Before he could register his anger at the sight of these possessions belonging to his mother, his father had turned to face him, taking in with that rapid appraisal of his not only Martin's presence in the room and his awareness of the papers on the desk but also his likely response to them, and was already preparing his defence, a quality in his father which Martin had never known how to combat. It was rooted in native wit and an overwhelming need always to have the upper hand. In business dealings it had served him well. In personal relationships it had often proved disastrous.

"Ah, Martin, so you're here at last," he said. "Let me introduce Lawrence Hurst. My son, Martin." As the two men shook hands, he continued, "Mr. Hurst is thinking of writing a book on Edward Voyte. We were in the middle of discussing it as you came in."

In a few brief sentences, Rex Holt had contrived, as he always did, to shift the blame. In this instance, his son's late arrival together with the inference that he had interrupted a private conversation put Martin in the wrong, while the remark about Hurst's book placed most of the responsibility for the Voyte papers' being on display on the American's shoulders, a liability which Hurst seemed uncomfortably aware of, for he said quickly, his craggy features taking on an apologetic expression, "It's only mooted so far, Mr. Holt. Nothing's been written down yet. I'm over in England gathering material at this stage."

In the face of the man's embarrassment, it would be churlish to express his anger openly, Martin realised. Besides, it would hardly help the situation.

Instead, he asked, making his voice pleasant but aware that the point of the question would not be lost on his father, "Were you thinking of using Voyte's letters to my mother as part of your book?"

Hurst looked across at Rex Holt for help but, old fox that he was, he refused to be drawn.

"No, not the letters," Hurst said at last, realising he would get no support from Rex Holt. "Just the unpublished poems. And possibly the photograph as well for a frontispiece. It's the best I've seen of him so far. The book's intended to be a literary appraisal rather than a straightforward biography."

"I didn't realise Voyte had that sort of reputation in the States," Martin replied. "I doubt if anyone in England, apart from the people who knew him personally, has even heard of him."

"Then that's a pity," Hurst replied. "Of course, he's not widely recognised in the States either. But as a minor poet, I mean as a writer whose poetic qualities haven't been fully appreciated and who's been . . ."

He broke off, unable, it seemed, in his embarrassment and eagerness to explain, to complete the sentence.

"Underrated?" Martin suggested in the same pleasant voice and saw the corners of his father's mouth twitch in secret amusement.

"Yes, indeed." Hurst seized on the word gratefully, "Seriously underrated. I hope my book will go some of the way to redress the balance."

The man's earnestness, even his touch of verbal pomposity, made Martin decide to back down. Why go on with the game when it was his father, not Hurst, he should be confronting? It seemed all the more pointless, since he realised Rex Holt was finding a great deal of quiet pleasure in the situation.

"So you've given Mr. Hurst permission to use the poems?" he asked, looking directly at his father.

"Yes, I have," he replied shortly, lifting his head at the challenge. "Have you any objections?"

Never apologise. Never explain. Old adages of his father's. And wherever possible, carry the battle into the enemy's camp.

"Not really," Martin replied easily. Walking casually over to the desk, he picked up the letters, aware that the two men were watching him. He allowed a fraction of a pause before adding, "After all, they're your property now."

He knew by the quality of the silence behind him that the remark had struck home. Then his father said, "And are going to remain so.

Mr. Hurst had asked to photograph them, that's all. If you're ready, Mr. Hurst, you can start setting up your equipment."

"Of course. Straight away." The wretched man was almost gabbling in his anxiety to please. "My camera's outside in the car. If you'll excuse me?"

He backed out, closing the door carefully behind him.

As soon as he had gone, Rex Holt said, "Hurst is here at my invitation. I hope you realise you've thoroughly embarrassed him."

"That wasn't my intention," Martin replied.

"No?" His father raised his eyebrows. "Then all I can say is for someone who wasn't really trying, you made a damned good job of it."

"I'm sorry," Martin said.

He was angry now with himself. Why the hell did he always finish up apologising? He had no intention though of trying to explain his feelings, a lesson he had learned from his father. There would be no point. As far as Rex Holt was concerned, Voyte's letters were part of a past that was over and done with, mementoes of a love affair between his wife and another man which had been finished before he met and married her and in which both participants were now dead.

The papers were normally kept in his mother's bureau, tucked away in a small inner compartment, and it further angered Martin that his father must have gone searching through it in order to find them; more especially since he himself, on discovering them after her death, had hesitated to take them. He wished now he had. That way, they would have been safe from the scrutiny of outsiders. Not that he blamed Hurst. It was his father's high-handed action which he resented and his total lack of sensitivity.

There had always been a coarse-grained quality about him, Martin thought, which, as he grew older, became more apparent. As a younger man, much of his need to dominate had been channelled into his business. Now retired and partially crippled, there were fewer outlets for it and it had taken on a more petty, tyrannical form although the energy was still there. Martin could feel it, smouldering below the surface, as his father, his heavy features still wearing a glowering expression, only partly mollified by his son's apology, said gruffly, "I'd reckoned on Hurst finishing before you arrived."

The remark was intended, Martin supposed, as a form of explanation, the nearest his father was likely to make, and laying down the letters, he moved away from the desk, signalling his own acceptance of the truce.

"I thought," Rex Holt continued, raising his stick to point towards the French windows, beyond which a garden table and chairs had been set up under a sun umbrella on the terrace, "that we'd have lunch in the garden. I want to make the most of this summer. God knows when we'll get another one like it."

The remark, with its hint of mortality, was uncharacteristic of his father and Martin looked at him sharply. Was he thinking of death? It was possible. Although at sixty-seven, Rex Holt could not be considered an old man, he had aged since his stroke, the once floridly handsome features grown puffy and less mobile, settling down into an habitually truculent expression. But before he could follow up the remark, his father added, "Reggie Trimmer's coming to lunch. And Bea Chilton. You know about Bea?"

Any stirring of compassion which Martin might have felt for his father was instantly stifled as he realised that Rex Holt had deliberately set up the situation in order to minimise his own part in it. Not only had he invited Bea to lunch, making it impossible for Martin to avoid meeting her, but by including Reggie Trimmer in the party, his father had guaranteed that the conversation would remain on a politely social level.

Trimmer was an old fool and a toady, a retired estate agent with a taste for gossip and an eye for scandal. Knowing this, Martin would have to guard his tongue, a limitation which he suspected his father was very well aware of and had deliberately used.

As for Bea's arrival in the village, his father had successfully shuffled off all responsibility of acquainting his son of this fact by assuming he already knew about it and for that, of course, he had relied on Biddy, no doubt knowing of his son's habit of calling first at her cottage before coming to the Hall.

To test out this assumption, Martin said, "Yes, I'd heard. Biddy told me."

"Oh, Biddy," his father replied dismissively, confirming Martin's suspicion. Rex Holt always adopted his most abrupt and gruffest manner towards those he was guilty of manipulating.

But Martin had no intention of letting the matter rest there. Determined to force his father into further explanation, he said, "I'm surprised she wanted to leave London. I can't imagine Barnsfield would hold much interest for her."

The remark was intended to be provocative and difficult to answer. In all the years of his relationship with Bea Chilton, Rex Holt had never once admitted that she was his mistress although he must have realised Martin had guessed the truth. Neither of them were fools.

Looking directly at his son from under his heavy eyebrows, Rex Holt took his time before replying, waiting while he summed him up and weighed his own answer.

"Like the rest of us, she's not getting any younger. She wanted a little peace and quiet."

And what the hell am I supposed to read into that? Martin wondered. Was it a veiled appeal for his sympathy and understanding for them both? The aged lovers tottering into the sunset hand in hand?

Hardly. The image struck him as absurd. His father had never shown any sign of that kind of sentimentality. Thank God, he surprised himself by adding.

Just for Bea, then? It seemed more likely. Be kind to her, his father seemed to be saying. Accept her.

Well, he would see. He was not prepared to make any commitments quite yet.

Before he could reply, there was a tap at the door and Lawrence Hurst entered, carrying the case and tripod which Martin had seen on the back seat of the car.

"All right if I come in?" he asked, hesitating on the threshold and looking anxiously from Rex Holt to Martin.

Rex Holt seemed pleased at the interruption, limping quickly forward with the gratified and energetic air of a man who prefers action to talk.

"Of course. Help yourself," he explained, waving a hand expansively towards the desk. "Can I offer you a drink? What'll you have?"

"A whisky and soda, sir, would be fine."

In his turn, the tall American seemed pleased at the hospitality, taking it as a sign of acceptance.

"Martin."

A nod of the head this time directed Martin Holt towards the tray of bottles and glasses which stood on a side-table and, as he crossed towards it, he thought with some amusement how his father, with the minimum of words, had managed to set them both about their tasks.

"I'll have a whisky, too," Rex Holt added, addressing Martin's back as he stood at the table. "Help yourself to what you want."

As he poured the drinks, Martin could hear Hurst setting up his equipment while Rex Holt stood over him, asking questions with that keen curiosity of his which extended to anything mechanical or practical.

"What's that?"

"A close-up lens, Mr. Holt."

"What's the definition like?"

"Pretty good if I use flash."

It was a pity, Martin thought, that he never showed the same interest in people.

Carrying the glasses over to the two men, he was in time to witness the photograph of Voyte being copied. It was propped up on the desk as Hurst, his long, bony frame bent over the tripod, looked through the camera viewfinder. A click. A sudden burst of bright light from the flash bulb in which the face on the piece of paper seemed suddenly to jump forward.

It was several years since Martin had last seen it and, even though it was familiar to him, he felt he had never before been so keenly aware of the features. It was as if that momentary burst of brightness had printed them onto his retina. A thin face. High forehead. Dark hair falling across it. A young, serious look about the eyes. Something oddly dated about the features, too, a face of the thirties, suggesting the proximity of the war and the lean, disillusioned years of the Depression which had preceded it. And also, he realised for the first time, a weak face although he could not say precisely what had given him that impression.

No, not weak, he decided a moment later as the flash faded. Doomed was a better word; the face of a dreamer or a loser; a young man glimpsed standing alone on the corner of an empty street at midnight.

The opportunity had gone when he might have pinned down the impression more accurately and he was aware that he was resorting again to imagery which, if he wasn't careful, would draw him along in its undertow of half-realised associations and emotions.

The facts were Edward Voyte had loved his mother, had written a few poems, had died tragically young. Without that knowledge, would he have given his photograph more than a passing glance?

"Your drinks," he said, handing round the glasses.

Hurst turned to take his, giving Martin a quick, bright look of gratitude.

Gratitude for what, for God's sake? Martin thought. That he was getting through the task without evoking the family row which had seemed impending?

As for his father, he took his drink without glancing up, his eyes looking sideways at the photograph, his expression inscrutable.

It was impossible to gauge what he was thinking. His face had the same closed, heavy, brooding look which he used to wear when he examined the company's accounts—summing them up silently and giving nothing away.

It occurred to Martin to wonder what his father had thought of the love affair between Voyte and his wife. He must have known about it. She had never made any secret of it and, if she hadn't openly discussed it with him, the letters and poems which he must have read were eloquent of at least Voyte's feelings for her.

> In the glassy lake
> Under the summer-vaulted sky,
> I see your image
> Smile back at me,
> Doubly beloved,
> Doubly adored.

Standing by the drinks tray, he remained silent, occupied with his own thoughts, as Hurst finished copying the poems.

The task completed, Hurst turned to his father.

"I can't tell you how much I appreciate your kindness, Mr. Holt. To be able to read some of Voyte's poems in manuscript is a very great privilege indeed."

Rex Holt nodded, accepting the gratitude. At the same time he began slowly folding up the poems and letters and reinserted them in the envelopes. Martin watched his father's large, blunt fingers gather them up into a small bundle which he held for a moment in his hands as if testing their weight before opening the top drawer of the desk and thrusting them away inside. The drawer was then closed with a small, decisive slam.

There was something about the gesture which left Martin trembling with anger. The shutting of the drawer seemed to negate not just the love affair between his mother and Edward Voyte, but all memory of her as well. It seemed more final even than her death.

Had he met his father's eyes, he would have lost his temper. And if that had happened, God alone knew what he might have said. Instead, anticipating the moment when his father would look up, he said, "Do you mind if I use your phone? Mine's out of order and I'd like to report it."

It was a genuine excuse. He had discovered the break the previous evening when he had tried to contact a business acquaintance at home and had found the line was dead. The call hadn't been urgent and, although he had intended stopping on his way to Barnsfield to report the fault from a call-box, it had slipped his mind. Now he was grateful for the chance to distance himself and, as his father said, "Help yourself," indicating the telephone on the desk, he deliberately turned his back as he dialled the operator.

When he replaced the receiver, his father was at the door, speaking to Mrs. Drewett, who had put her head briefly inside the room to announce, "Mrs. Chilton's just arrived, sir."

"You go and meet her, Martin. Bring her round to the terrace and offer her a drink," Rex Holt said in a tone of voice which invited no argument. "I want to have a last word with Hurst before he leaves. That's if you're sure you won't stay for lunch?" he added, addressing the American.

It was an invitation which had evidently already been offered earlier that morning before Martin's arrival, for, as he left the room, he heard the man repeating what must have been the same apology.

"Thank you all the same, Mr. Holt. I appreciate the invitation but, as I said before, I ought to be getting back to the hotel."

As he crossed the hall, Martin was surprised to find that the rage he had felt earlier at that small, decisive slamming of the drawer no longer seemed to matter. The ability to contain his anger by the simple act of turning away had steadied him. It was so damned easy, after all. That was all he had ever needed to do—to distance himself from the relationship by a conscious effort of objectivity. From this standpoint, he could almost admire the skill with which his father had contrived the situation so that he would not be present when his son and mistress met, leaving it to the pair of them to come to their own terms with one another.

As it turned out, Bea wasn't alone. Reggie Trimmer was with her, getting out of the passenger seat of her Renault and coming forward to shake Martin's hand, monopolising his attention while Bea was still at the wheel, turning round to collect her handbag from the back seat.

"My dear Martin, how splendid to see you again!"

The warmth of his handshake, enclosing Martin's hand in both of his, typified the spurious joviality of the man himself. Tall, stooping, desperately English and county with his dapper little brushed-up moustache and blazer, he had all the phoniness of a minor public-school boy turned third-rate entrepreneur.

Martin had often wondered why his father tolerated him. One look at those foolish, inquisitive, pale blue eyes should have warned him of Trimmer's stupidity and untrustworthiness.

He was watching now as Martin stepped forward to meet Bea, curious to know how the son and his father's mistress would greet one another and, aware of his observation, Martin smiled as he held out his hand.

She was uncertain herself how he would receive her. He could tell that by the angle of her head, which was inquiring and tentatively defensive, prepared for his coolness and ready to turn it aside with her own social arts, at which she was practised.

She had aged, of course, since the last time he had seen her, but not enough to make too much difference. Careful about her appearance, she still gave the impression of a well-groomed, attractive woman; intelligent, too; a good match for his father, Martin found himself thinking, observing her with the same objectivity with which he had earlier scrutinised him. Neat and fashionable, dark hair cut stylishly short, a plain green linen dress showing off a slight, trim figure and with those feminine touches to lend an air of softness to the overall impression—jade earrings picking up the colour of her dress and a long green chiffon scarf worn loose about her throat—she could still be taken at a distance for a young woman.

But there was more to Bea than mere surface attractiveness. The little he knew about her told him that. Widowed in her thirties, she had never remarried but had returned to her former job on a woman's magazine, supporting her daughter, Hester, whom Martin had met on the same occasion he had first been introduced to Bea all those years before.

They shook hands under Trimmer's scrutiny.

"How are you?" she asked.

"Fine. And you? I hear you've moved into the village."

He felt he owed her at least that opportunity to ease the situation and was rewarded, as he conducted the pair of them round the side of the house to the terrace, by the look of quick appreciation she gave him.

"Yes. It's a charming little house. I'm delighted with it."

"Better than London?" he suggested.

They were both aware that, under the exchange of social pleasantries, they were testing out each other.

"Oh, London!" she said, dismissing it with a ringed hand. "It's so expensive now and so dreadfully crowded."

"So you've given up your job?" he asked.

"Yes, I'm out to grass at last."

A lifted eyebrow suggested he, too, should see the humour of the situation.

"And how is your daughter?"

"Hester? She's well. As a matter of fact, she'll be joining me later tonight. She's applied for leave to help me with the move. Did you know she's a sister now at Birmingham General Hospital?"

"Really?" He hadn't, in fact, known this, his father's occasional comments about Bea rarely extending to include her daughter. "The only time I met her was when my father took me up to London for a Christmas treat and we all had tea together after the theatre."

He couldn't resist this small jibe to remind her of what the situation had been between them, he at thirteen bewildered and embarrassed at this sudden and unexpected meeting with his father's "friend" whom he had known instinctively he shouldn't discuss with his mother, tea at an expensive hotel—the Ritz, wasn't it?—an unfamiliar, smartly dressed woman asking him about his school while her daughter, aged about ten, dark, fierce and equally embarrassed, had glared at him across the table. It had been a disaster. No wonder his father had not attempted the experiment again.

"She kicked me under the table, I remember," he added.

Her laugh was purely social but the look she gave him held a more complex appeal.

Anxious not to be left out, Trimmer put in, "She sounds as if she can look after herself."

"Oh, Hester certainly can," Bea replied. It was said lightly but not without a touch of pride.

They had arrived on the terrace, where, having seated them at the table and asked what they would drink, Martin reentered the drawing-room through the open French windows. As he was pouring Bea's gin and tonic, his father came into the room from the hall, having presumably seen Hurst off at the front door.

Nodding briefly to Martin, he went out onto the terrace, where Martin saw him greet his guests, shaking hands first with Trimmer before bending down to kiss Bea, who held her cheek up to him.

It was an intimate moment despite the public setting under his own scrutiny as well as Trimmer's and one that Martin found strangely disturbing. They seemed so much a couple, more so than his father and mother had ever been. He had never given their relationship much thought before except on a derisive and dismissive level. Now he found himself wondering how long they had known each other and where they had first met. It was none of his business, of course, more especially since the death of his mother, which had removed any impediment from them to acknowledge their affair openly. Had his mother known about it? he wondered. Probably not. His father had a talent for secrecy and close dealing. And even if she had, he doubted if she would have cared.

It was this sense of being an outsider, observing them, which made him reluctant to join them on the terrace and it was only when his father called out, demanding to know where the drinks were, that he stepped out into the garden.

The same sense of alienation continued throughout lunch, a cold buffet which Mrs. Drewett wheeled out on a serving wagon and left at the side of the table before departing.

The conversation was general although the party was evidently to celebrate Bea's move, judging by the bottles of champagne in the ice bucket and the manner in which Rex Holt lifted his glass towards her in salute. No toast was made, however, perhaps in deference to Martin's presence. He wasn't sure. He felt both he and Trimmer were on the outside of the festivity, invited as spectators to form an audience in order to give the occasion authenticity. Trimmer seemed unaware of it and, quite happy in his role, helped himself generously to the food and champagne, joining in the conversation and offering Bea advice about the house, the planned alterations, the garden, on which, as a retired estate agent, he seemed to feel he was an expert.

Apart from making an occasional remark, Martin was for the most part silent, preferring to listen to the others.

Seeing them together, his father's tolerance of Trimmer was easier to understand. Like Barnard, Rex Holt's former manager, Trimmer was a yes-man, anxious to please and to carry out the more menial tasks which Rex Holt couldn't be bothered to attend to himself.

As for Trimmer, it was reward enough to sit, literally, at the rich man's table.

The relationship between Bea and his father was less easy to define. Martin's presence as well as Trimmer's cast a restraint over their behaviour but, from time to time, in a gesture or a shared glance, Martin was able to read something of their attitude to one another.

On his father's part, Martin was aware of an unexpected reaction—gratitude. It was an emotion he had never seen his father display before. Mixed with it was admiration, more easily understood, and physical desire. Whenever he could do so without drawing too much attention to the contact, Rex Holt touched her, placing a hand on her shoulder when he filled her glass or brushing against her arm as he passed her a dish.

It might have been obscene or ludicrous; Martin found it neither. There was a gentleness and a humility in those brief physical encounters which suggested a deep affection.

Bea's attitude to his father was more enigmatic, her social skills serving her as a better disguise for her real feelings. Even so, it was possible to pick up small signals which Martin thought expressed a tenderness towards him, tempered with a compassionate concern, as if, more objective than Rex Holt, she could regard him for what he was, not so much a lover but a man past his prime who had already suffered one minor stroke and for whose continued well-being she was willing to accept responsibility.

"You haven't much to say for yourself, Martin."

His father's voice, a little abrupt and impatient, cut across his thoughts and he made an effort to rouse himself.

"I'm sorry. I was miles away, I'm afraid."

"Thinking about your smallholding?" Bea suggested, trying to turn away Rex Holt's exasperation. "Rex has told me about it. I imagine you must be very busy at this time of the year. I meant to ask you earlier how it's going."

"It's undercapitalised." His father's comment had the same curt ring to it. "I told him so when he first set up on his own. It's no good starting off any business without the right sort of financial backing."

"I manage," Martin said. It was the same brief response he remembered making to Biddy although he meant it differently on this occasion. For her sake, he had wanted to minimise her anxiety. For his father's, he was more concerned to assert his own independence.

There was a small, uncomfortable silence in which Martin thought how impossible it was to preserve any kind of truce between himself and his father for longer than a few hours.

The lunch was finished and they were sitting over the debris of the meal, empty plates and glasses littering the table.

His father had lit a cigar and had taken up a characteristic pose, one arm flung over the back of his chair, his legs crossed; his boardroom position, Martin thought, feeling his anger return. How often had he seen him seated in this manner, replete with food and wine, ready to give his opinion on politics, business, the arts, any topic which might be under discussion?

He felt in no mood to listen.

To give his father his due, he seemed aware he had bungled the conversation.

"If you're short," he said gruffly, "I could always write you out a cheque."

"I don't need it," Martin replied, aware of Trimmer's eyes on them. Bea had glanced away across the garden, only her profile visible.

Well, that was that, Martin thought. There was no possible way he could now accept his father's financial help. Between them, they'd managed to shut that door pretty effectively.

He rose from the table.

"I ought to be going."

"So soon?"

It was Bea who spoke, looking up into his face with quick appeal.

"It's a long drive back," he replied, "and, as you so rightly said, it's a busy time of the year." Holding out his hand to her, he added, "Goodbye. It's been very pleasant meeting you again."

It sounded more stilted than he had intended. He meant to express more than just a mere social pleasantry—his apology for not being able to accept her more readily, his regret at the abrupt end to the lunch party and his own part in it.

"I hope we'll meet again before too long," she replied. She seemed to mean it quite genuinely.

His father, who had watched this exchange with a morose expression, his chin tucked down on his chest, said, "If you're going, you can give Reggie a lift back to the village."

So they were both dismissed.

Trimmer tried to hide his disappointment. He had clearly expected to stay on and he rose reluctantly, pulling down the cuffs of his blazer.

"If Martin doesn't mind—" he began.

"It's on my way," Martin said, cutting him short.

Despite his anger, Martin found himself half-admiring the ruthlessness with which his father had contrived their departure.

"Goodbye," he said, addressing the parting remark to both Bea and his father before, turning quickly on his heel, he walked away, Trimmer lingering to make a more protracted farewell.

Glancing back as he reached the end of the terrace, where he waited for Trimmer to catch up with him, he saw them sitting at the table, his father sunk down in his chair while Bea leaned towards him, her hand resting on his in an attitude which was strangely supplicatory.

CHAPTER THREE

Bea was saying, "You realise you drove him away?"

"He's too damned touchy, that's his trouble," Rex Holt retorted.

"But you touched him off," Bea persisted.

"Perhaps I did." Rex Holt seemed willing to admit that much. "He annoyed me, that's why; hardly opening his mouth over lunch. I think it was bloody rude of him both to you and Reggie."

"I don't think Reggie noticed," Bea said, smiling. "And I didn't mind all that much. Martin was quite pleasant when he first met me at the car."

Rex Holt gave her one of his long looks from under his eyebrows. "Was he?"

Not at all intimidated, Bea replied, "Yes, he was."

She did not add that, even at that first meeting, she had been aware of Martin Holt's uneasiness in her presence although he had tried to disguise it.

Rex Holt refused either to be satisfied or to let the subject drop.

"He was damned rude, even before you came, to that American."

"What American?" Bea asked, hoping to distract his attention.

"A chap called Hurst. Didn't I tell you about him? He wrote to me from the States several months ago, asking if he could see Voyte's poems. God knows how he knew I'd got them. Anyway, he rang me when he arrived in London about a fortnight ago and I asked him to come over this morning. He's researching for some book or other on Voyte."

"And Martin was there at the time?"

Rex Holt had the grace to look a little ashamed.

"All right, so it was stupid of me," he conceded. "When I fixed up the lunch for today, I'd forgotten Hurst was coming. Anyway, I thought he and Martin would hit it off better. After all, they're both interested in books and poetry; much more than I am."

"Did you ask Martin's permission before letting Hurst see the poems?"

"No. Why the hell should I? They aren't his."

"But they were his mother's. Can't you see, Rex, that he'd feel some sense of ownership, knowing how close he'd been to her?"

"I didn't think of it that way," Rex Holt admitted. "He never knew Voyte. The man was killed before he was born, even before she married me." Leaning forward, he crushed out his cigar in the ashtray, adding bitterly, "I was always second best to her."

"It's over," Bea said quietly. "She's dead."

But he couldn't leave it there.

"She always said I never understood her. God knows I tried, Bea. To begin with, at least. I gave up after a while. I could never get close to her. He's like her. He keeps his distance."

Bea silently agreed with him. There was an aloof quality about Martin Holt which she had noticed all those years before when they had first met over tea and he had been just a schoolboy. She had found it strangely intimidating in one so young. Meeting him again, she saw no reason for changing that original impression.

"I could have done a lot to help him," Rex Holt was continuing. "Even after he walked out, I was prepared to meet him half-way and finance him in any scheme he fancied. Instead of which, he cleared off and bought that tuppenny ha'penny bit of land. And look what he turned his back on! That business of mine in Welham was booming. The profits alone were almost a quarter of a million a year. It could all have been his when I retired. But he wouldn't listen and so I had to sell out to that damned consortium."

"I know, Rex," Bea said gently. She had heard the monologue many times before, the same phrases, the same bitterness, which never seemed to soften.

"That hurt me," Rex Holt went on. "I don't mind admitting, Bea, that cut very deep. Well, I'm damned if he's going to treat you in the same high-handed manner. He'll be polite to you at the very least or he won't be welcome to show his face here again."

"Oh, Rex, don't be so angry about it. And try to see it from his point of view. It can't have been easy for him meeting me again after all this time, especially now I'm practically living on your doorstep."

"It's none of his business."

"Perhaps not," she replied, not sounding very convinced.

He looked at her again from under his eyebrows.

"Is that why you refused to move in here with me—because of what he might think?"

"Partly," Bea admitted. "There's Hester to consider as well, of course. Not that I think either of them would be shocked at the idea of us living together. But it would complicate the relationships and, quite frankly, Rex, I can do without that stress. Besides, as I've already told you, I like my independence. I'm too used to it now. So are you. You wouldn't want me around the place day after day."

"I could marry you, Bea," he replied, ignoring her last remarks. "I keep offering, but you keep turning me down."

It was said half-humorously, as if, knowing what her reactions would be, he had turned it into a joke between them, a form of protection, Bea suspected, for his self-esteem.

Her hand still on his, she said, smiling, "I might accept one day and then what would you do?"

He laughed out loud.

"Give in gracefully, I suppose, and admit defeat. So the answer's still no?"

"For the same reason, my dear, that I haven't moved in with you. I'm too used to running my own life."

"It might be the last time I ask you. Have you ever thought of that?"

She said quickly, "Don't say that!"

"Why not?" he asked, surprised at her reaction.

"You make it sound too final, as if . . ." She broke off, unwilling to continue.

"I might drop dead at any moment?" He completed the sentence for her with a brusqueness which shocked her. More gently, he continued, "I can't live for ever, Bea. The stroke I had last year taught me that lesson. I'm not a young man any more; not even a middle-aged one. That's the main reason why I wanted you to move down here. I need you near me. I'm too old a lover to keep dashing up to town every time I want to see you." Holding out his hand to her, he added, smiling, "Come on. It's too beautiful a day to be gloomy. Walk with me."

She took his arm as he struggled up out of the chair.

"Where to?" she asked. "The rose garden?"

They walked to the top of the steps leading down to the sunken garden, where he paused.

"No, not down there," he said. "It traps the heat like an oven.

Besides, I'm too shaky on my pins these days to manage the steps. Let's walk across the lawn. I like the view of the house from the other side." As they set off, Rex Holt's stick jabbing at the grass, he continued, reverting to his former bitterness, *"She* never liked it, you know—the house, I mean; thought it too big and grand. She preferred the old place we used to have in Welham where Martin was born. Frightened of ambition, that was her trouble. Thought the higher we went, the harder we'd fall. Well, I haven't taken a tumble yet."

Bea was silent, letting him talk himself out of his morose mood and, as she had expected, by the time they had reached the far bank of shrubbery and turned to face the house, his spirits lifted.

"See what I mean?" he asked triumphantly, raising his stick to point at the rear façade of Barnsfield Hall, its brickwork rosy in the afternoon sun.

"It's beautiful," she said.

"Not bad," he agreed, "when you think my grandfather started off life as a farm-labourer's son; nine of them sharing a two-bedroomed cottage; no proper drains; not even water laid on. He was the only one out of the lot of them who made anything of himself; started off with a hand-barrow, then later bought a horse and cart. He even taught himself bookkeeping in the evenings. That's how the business began, Bea, with just one man's enthusiasm and damned hard work and that's why I get so angry when I think of Martin turning his back on it. Three generations of graft and God knows how many working hours, not to mention the hopes and dreams that went into it, just chucked away on a whim."

"No, not a whim," Bea interrupted him quickly. "You mustn't think of it like that, Rex. It's just not true. Martin has his own dreams. He wants to make his own way in the world, not have success handed to him on a plate. Can't you admire him for that? After all, it seems to be a family trait which he's inherited."

"Like my brother, you mean?" Rex asked.

Bea was silent, regretting having spoken. In defending Martin, she had intended that the parallel with the grandfather would be drawn, not with Arthur Holt, Rex's younger brother. It was many years since she had first heard the story from Rex and, as he had never referred to it again, it had slipped her memory. Now, reminded of it, she saw too late that Rex would inevitably make the more recent and valid comparison with his brother. Like Martin, Arthur Holt had quarrelled with his father and had left home, more dramatically in his case, taking with him his portion of the family money, to settle in South Africa, leaving Rex to inherit the family business. At the time, it had been a fair division; only Rex had prospered, while his younger brother, the money invested in a printing firm which had gone bankrupt, had failed.

Was he still alive?

Bea wasn't sure. Apart from that one occasion, Rex had never spoken of him again until now, perhaps out of guilt at his own good fortune. As far as she knew, there had been no contact between the two brothers since Arthur's departure at the age of twenty-one. Pride and stubbornness, those other two inherited qualities, had probably been to blame on the part of both of them.

Rex continued in the same abrupt, bitter tone, "And I can see him finishing up like Arthur, too, without a penny to his name."

"I don't think so," Bea replied. Absurdly, she felt the need to defend Martin even against Rex. "He may be short of capital but he's prepared to work for what he wants. In that respect, he's like you, Rex, and your grandfather. He'll put up a damned good fight."

"You think so?"

Rex seemed gratified by the remark; as if the compliment reflected entirely on himself, Bea thought, touched by his almost naive family pride and, at the same time, exasperated by the sheer cussedness which prevented him from admitting as much to his own son.

"And you think he's short of money?" Rex added, swinging round to look her in the face.

"That's my impression."

"He's only got to ask," Rex growled.

"Oh, Rex, you know very well that's the last thing he'd do! Would you, if you were in his place?"

He considered the question, looking past her to the solid façade of Barnsfield Hall, his expression closed and stubborn.

Then suddenly, taking her by surprise so that she had to hasten to catch up with him, he went stumping off across the lawn towards the open French windows.

"How much?" he asked a few minutes later, standing at his desk, his cheque-book, which he had taken out of the drawer, lying on top of it. As she hesitated, he urged her, "Come on, Bea! It's your idea. How much do you think I ought to send?"

"Five thousand?" she suggested. It seemed a suitable sum, large enough to be useful but not so excessively generous that Martin might feel obliged to return it.

"Five thousand it is, then," he agreed.

He remained standing as he wrote out the cheque, his stick leaning against the desk, his head and shoulders hunched forward as, holding the pen in a schoolboy's fist, he scrawled out the amount.

"I suppose I'd better write a letter to go with it?" he added, peering round at her for her agreement, and when she said, "Yes, of course, Rex" he nodded, pleased with her concurrence.

The letter written, he slipped the cheque inside the envelope before ringing for Mrs. Drewett.

"Tell Drewett to take this straight away to the main post office in Welham," he told her, "and then bring tea for the two of us." As Mrs. Drewett withdrew, he added, his face anxious, "He should get it tomorrow morning, shouldn't he, if Drewett catches the last collection?"

"Of course he will," Bea assured him.

He closed the cheque-book up slowly, as if reluctant to admit that this brief magnanimous episode was over, drumming his fingers on the cover before returning it to the drawer. At the same time, he took out a small bundle of papers and a key which he handed to her, saying at the same time, "Would you do something for me, Bea? Put these papers back in the bureau upstairs. Here's the key. It's in the third room along on the left, the one that overlooks the side lawn. I'd deal with them myself only I find getting up and down those damned stairs a bit of a problem."

"Of course, Rex," she replied.

The upper floor was unfamiliar to her. She had visited the house only once before on the previous day when Rex had taken her on a tour of the downstairs rooms, opening doors briefly to show her the interiors, many unused, before introducing her to the Drewetts. It appeared that, since his stroke, he had retreated to the drawing-room, where he had gathered about him the essentials of the limited life he now led.

On that occasion, they hadn't gone upstairs either, Rex offering the same excuse, that he found the stairs too tiring to climb.

It had been a strange experience seeing the house for the first time, like being a day-tripper conducted briskly from room to room, Rex hardly giving her time to inspect anything except cursorily, as if he were ashamed of possessing so much and embarrassed by her exclamations of admiration. At the same time, she had been struck by its melancholy, which the sunlight had not been able to dispel. The house seemed to be waiting for other presences to occupy it, not just Rex and the Drewetts.

She had understood, once she had seen the village, why he had been
so anxious not to introduce her to the place before, preferring to travel
up to London to visit her.

"I don't want everyone to know my business," he had said in explanation.

His need for secrecy was almost obsessive, which was why she had
given way to it, although she had been amused by his introduction of
her to Mrs. Drewett as "an old family friend." Some pretences, it
seemed, had to be maintained.

She reached the upper landing and, opening the door which Rex had
indicated, found the bedroom beyond unused, the furniture sheeted
apart from a bureau which stood between a pair of long-sash windows.

Unlocking it and letting down the flap, she placed the papers in the
last compartment, noticing as she did so that it contained others; letters mostly, done up into neat bundles, hers to Rex making up the
largest.

She was surprised and touched that he should have kept them. It
revealed a sentimental side to him which he rarely showed but, at the
same time, she wished he hadn't. Knowing they were still in existence
made her feel oddly vulnerable, although they seemed safe enough
locked away.

Returning to the landing, she hesitated, looking down quickly over
the bannisters to check that the hall was empty and the door into the
drawing-room was closed before going quickly along the passage, opening each door in turn.

The day before, during their tour of the house, Rex had said, with
one of his oblique, offhand glances, "If you ever want to stay the night,
there's a room ready for you."

She found it at the point where the landing turned, the only room to
show any signs of preparation for a guest, the bed made up, the furniture uncovered and dusted, towels laid out in the adjoining bathroom.

So it had evidently been Rex's intention that she would eventually
give in and stay the night.

A sense of his loneliness overwhelmed her but, at the same time, she
was exasperated as well as amused by his deviousness and, deciding to
say nothing about the room nor her knowledge of its preparation for
her occupation, she closed the door on it quietly and descended the
stairs.

"You found it all right?" Rex asked as she entered the drawing-room.

"Yes, and I've locked the bureau up," she replied, holding the key out for him to take.

To her surprise, he shook his head.

"No, you keep it," he said. "I've got another one for my own use. I'd like you to have the spare, just in case. My will's up there so you'll know where to find it." Half-turning away, as if embarrassed, he added gruffly, "You'll be all right, Bea; financially, I mean."

"Oh, Rex, please!" she began, distressed by this second reference to his dying.

She was still holding the key out to him on her palm and, with one of his sudden changes of mood, he smiled and folded her fingers over it before raising her hand to his lips.

"Keep it, my dear; at least, for the time being."

"But shouldn't Martin have it?" she asked.

"Later, perhaps. I may ask for it back again to give to him. I'll see."

She thought she understood what he meant. Whatever had been written in the letter, it was some form of test. If Martin responded in the right way, he would be entrusted with the spare key. Meanwhile, it was to remain in her keeping.

"Very well, Rex," she agreed, slipping it inside her handbag. Knowing her letters were in the bureau, she was half-relieved the key was in her possession, although she could see it causing further complications in her relationship with Martin. The last thing she wanted was for him to think that she was usurping his place or taking over responsibilities which were his by rights.

Rex did not refer to the matter again until she was on the point of leaving. It was soon after nine o'clock. They had eaten supper, a light meal which Mrs. Drewett had left in the refrigerator before going off duty. When they had finished, Bea carried the tray back to the kitchen, collecting her long silk scarf, which she had left in the hall, on her way back.

Standing in front of the mirror to arrange it about her throat, she thought how vacant the house seemed, the emptiness and the shadows appearing to gather as a great weight which she could feel pressing down on her, making her uneasy.

Hurrying back to the drawing-room, she found Rex seated in front of the open French windows, looking out over the garden, where the blue dusk was already gathering. The only sound in the room was the faint, tinkling chime of the fountain, which seemed as melancholy as a musical box left playing in a deserted room.

He heard her enter and turned his head.

"You're not going already?" he asked, noticing the scarf about her neck.

"I must, Rex," she said reluctantly, aware of his isolation, seated alone in an empty room in an empty house. "Hester will be arriving later this evening. She's driving down from the hospital as soon as she's off duty and I must have a meal ready for her. What will you do?"

"Oh, I'll watch television for a while," he replied, indicating the set which stood on a trolley at the foot of the bed. "I shall probably have a bath first and then try to catch the ten o'clock news."

"Do you want me to close the windows before I leave?" she asked.

"No, I'll see to them myself before I go to bed. I don't like shutting out the evening yet. It's the best time of the day."

"I'll say goodnight, then, my dear," she said, bending down to kiss him on the forehead. "I don't like leaving you on your own. Are you quite sure you'll be all right?"

"I have the bell by the bed I can ring if I need the Drewetts in the night."

"I wish they lived in. Can't you arrange for them to move in here?"

"It may come to that one day but, until it does, I prefer my privacy. That damned woman fusses about enough as it is. But if you're worried about me, you know what you can do, don't you? You can always stay."

He was looking up at her, his eyes bright with amusement and appeal, that old blackmailing look of his which she found so difficult to resist.

"Perhaps one day I will," she replied, remembering the room upstairs and feeling her resolve weaken. How impossible it had always been to disappoint him!

"Is that a promise?"

"I'll see," she said, knowing that eventually she would give way.

"If you married me—" he continued.

"Sh!" She laid her fingers briefly on his lips. "Not now, Rex."

"But one day?"

She realised he had taken her reply, perhaps deliberately, to mean that she would finally consent. It wouldn't be the first time that he had twisted her words to suit himself.

"I don't know. Perhaps. It's too soon."

He sat back, smiling, pleased at this sign of capitulation.

"Don't lose the key," he said.

The remark seemed inconsequential at the time. It was only after she had let herself out of the front door and crossed the gravelled forecourt to her car that she realised its implications. Rex was hinting that, if she became his wife, she could retain not just the key but all that it symbolised as mistress of his house and the major heir to everything that he possessed.

CHAPTER FOUR

Martin dropped Reggie Trimmer off in the village, refusing his offer to come into the bungalow for a drink. It had been bad enough parrying his questions during the short drive from the Hall. How long since he had last seen Bea? What did he think of her moving down here from London? Was it his father's idea?

Trimmer was not intelligent enough to be subtle, but all the same the cross-examination had been wearying and it was with relief that Martin drove away from Trimmer's gate, hardly acknowledging the man's hand raised in farewell.

Thank God that was over, he thought, not just the drive back with that old fool but the whole visit. It had been an exasperating waste of time. But then it usually was. He hardly ever returned from Barnsfield without some friction developing between himself and his father.

Bea's presence had been a source of added tension, although unexpectedly he felt more guilty about his behaviour towards her than towards his father. She had an honesty and an integrity which, under other circumstances, might have made him feel a genuine affection for her.

In the centre of Welham, he encountered a queue of cars which was waiting at the lights opposite the Red Lion. As he sat with the engine idling, cursing the delay, Martin noticed a man waving to him from the opposite pavement. At first, he didn't recognise him for the tall American, Lawrence Hurst. The next moment, Hurst had threaded his way through the stationary cars and, stooping down, looked in at the open driver's window with that apologetic smile of his, pleased at the encounter but half-expecting to be rebuffed.

"Mr. Holt! I thought it was you. What a lucky coincidence! Is there any chance of you stopping off at the hotel for a drink? I'd be greatly honoured if you'd join me."

Martin's first inclination was to refuse. Although the reason he had given to Bea and his father for cutting short the visit had been largely in the nature of an excuse, he nevertheless had enough work to be done at the smallholding to not want to waste more time in social conversation, especially with a comparative stranger like Hurst.

On the other hand, some of the lingering guilt he felt towards Bea brushed off on the earnest American who was so anxious to please. At least, Martin thought, he could make some sort of amends, if not to her, then to him. His anger over Voyte's letters and Hurst's involvement with them had largely died down, too, to be replaced by a curiosity to find out just how much the American had discovered about Voyte.

The traffic began edging forward and, on the spur of the moment, Martin said, "All right. I'll park round the corner and meet you at the entrance."

He was waiting on the steps when, having parked the car behind the hotel, Martin returned.

"The bar's closed," Hurst said as he approached. "I'm sorry I didn't think of that when I offered you a drink. But I've got a bottle of whisky in my room."

"That'll do fine," Martin replied, following Hurst into the foyer.

It had changed remarkably little since the last time he had been there with his father. The same comfortable, country-house atmosphere was still evident in the deep, dark red carpets, the panelling, the bowls of flowers.

The bar was on his left, closed down, the leather armchairs empty, but his father's favourite corner, opposite the bar and facing the door, so that he could see who was coming and going, was exactly as Martin had last seen it. Even the painting of the tall-masted ships at anchor still hung on the wall above.

As he passed the bar and glanced into it, he wondered if his father had ever returned to it after his retirement. Probably not. Pride would have prevented him from encountering his former clients once the business had been sold and had passed into others' hands.

"I'm on the first floor," Hurst was explaining, leading the way up the stairs.

His room was at the back of the hotel, overlooking a small courtyard garden. Inside, there was evidence of Hurst's literary occupation. A portable typewriter stood on a table under the window, a pile of typescript and a notebook beside it. A map of the area was spread out on the bed.

"Make yourself at home," Hurst said, waving a hand towards the armchair. "I'll get the drinks."

The room was equipped with a small refrigerator built in under the shelf which continued along the wall as the top for a dressing-table and chest of drawers. Taking out a bottle of whisky, Hurst broke the seal and poured two drinks.

"Ice and water?" he asked.

"Yes," Martin said quickly. He was anxious to get these social preliminaries over with as soon as possible. Once the glass was in his hand, he added, "Tell me how you found out about Voyte."

Hurst carried his drink over to the table, where he sat down on the straight-backed chair.

"I first heard of him in the States. A friend of mine lent me his copy of Voyte's little volume of poems which he'd picked up over here one summer in a second-hand bookshop. I read them and I guess I got hooked. Since then, it's been a dream of mine to research into Voyte's background and write a literary appreciation of his work. Although I'm a free-lance writer, it's not my usual line, but I felt I owed it to Voyte to make his name more widely recognised; a kind of thank-you, I guess, for the pleasure he's given me. Anyway, I contacted some of his family and friends and we've been in correspondence about him. Then I made up my mind to come to England this summer and complete the research; make the pilgrimage, if you like." Leaning forward, his face serious, he added, "Look, I'm sorry about this morning. I had no idea you'd be visiting your father, otherwise I'd've suggested I call at another time. And, believe me, I knew nothing about the letters. It was the manuscript poems I'd come to look at."

The frankness of his apology and his obvious embarrassment prompted Martin to reply, "It wasn't your fault. I'm afraid my father and I don't agree about a lot of things. Seeing those letters from Voyte to my mother angered me perhaps more than it should have done. I still think of them as her private property, you understand?" To change the subject and save Hurst further embarrassment, he added, "Who else have you seen?"

Hurst himself seemed relieved that they had passed on to another aspect of the topic.

"Oh, quite a few," he said eagerly. "I've managed to trace a couple of his air-force buddies, including one who was in Voyte's squadron and saw him shot down. And I've got several more interviews lined up for this week, one with David Mallinson, who was with Voyte at Oxford.

He and his sister, Ann, were close friends of his. Then there's another I've arranged with Voyte's mother."

"She's still alive?" Martin asked incredulously. It seemed impossible that this woman about whom his own mother had spoken with so much bitterness and whom he associated with an old passion long since dead should exist at all. It was like learning that the Wicked Queen or Medusa had not only actually lived but were still surviving.

"Oh yes," Hurst was saying. "We've only corresponded so far, but she's agreed to see me on Friday. By a piece of good luck, she's still living in the same house in Suffolk, so I'll not only be able to talk to her about her son, but actually see the place where he was born and brought up."

"Really?" Martin put down his glass. Hurst's words had moved him more than he thought possible. The romance which had formed such a deep impression on him as a child and which he regarded as distanced from any experience in which he himself could participate, as if the events had taken place in another country and at another time, now suddenly moved forward into his own time-scale. Everything was still there, he realised, even though Voyte and his mother were now dead— the house, the fields they had walked across, the lake where they had met.

He said, trying to hide his eagerness, "Could you let me have her address?"

"Sure." To Martin's relief, Hurst seemed to accept the request as quite natural. Stretching back towards the table, he wrote something down on the note-pad, tore off the page and handed it to Martin.

Looking at it quickly before folding it and putting it into his pocket, Martin read, "Mrs. Gilbert Voyte, Gable End, Hatton, Suffolk." A telephone number had been added at the bottom.

"You're thinking of contacting her yourself?" Hurst asked.

His curiosity seemed more acceptable than Trimmer's. It was based, Martin realised, not on mere prurience but on a genuine scholarly interest in anything connected with Voyte and, feeling that he owed Hurst some explanation, he said, "I might do. You see, my mother was in love with Edward Voyte before she married my father. She often spoke about him." He hesitated before adding, "I never knew Voyte, of course. He was killed long before I was born but I've always felt I knew him, almost as if—" He broke off, reluctant to explain that he had the feeling, only half-realised and never raised to full consciousness, that Voyte was closer to him than his natural father, as if some of the passion of that idyllic affair had continued to course, like a hidden stream, to surface again in his own blood. It was a ridiculous notion, of course, but rationality played little part in it. He could only describe it to himself as a fragrance locked away in a drawer which was released years later, still scented, to permeate the air.

"—as if I had actually met him," he concluded lamely.

Hurst, who had been watching Martin's expression closely as he spoke, as if following not only the words but the significance behind them, said, "I know exactly what you mean. I feel the same myself. It's as if he might appear at any moment; as if he's still there."

"Yes," Martin agreed quickly. Hurst had put into the words the feeling which he had never voiced even to himself—a sense of continuing presence. So the lovers were not really dead, after all, but were still there, walking hand in hand under the summer-vaulted sky.

He finished his whisky and rose to his feet, holding out his hand.

"I ought to go. Thanks for the drink." After a pause, he added, "About the letters—if you really want to use them and my father gives his permission, I wouldn't raise any objections."

Hurst's solemn face broke into a wide smile.

"That's really most generous of you, Mr. Holt. I shall be here for the next few days. Perhaps I could call you?"

"My phone's out of order but it should be fixed soon. I'll leave the number and my address," Martin replied.

He wrote them down on Hurst's pad and then left, cutting short Hurst's expressions of gratitude. He was already beginning to regret the offer and, as he crossed the car-park, he felt a sense of betrayal which lingered for several hours afterwards, making him restless and uneasy although his promise to Hurst wasn't entirely to blame.

On returning from any visit to Barnsfield Hall, he always found it difficult to settle. In comparison, his own house seemed cramped and mean and now, turning into the forecourt, he was particularly struck by the ugliness of the little brick-and-slate house with its dilapidated greenhouses and outbuildings which were only kept usable by constant repair; conscious, too, that his roots were not yet established in the place.

Parking in front of the large greenhouse, he was reminded again of the broken-down heating system.

If only he had been able to ask his father for a loan, that worry, at least, would have been off his shoulders.

But perhaps that was too easy a way out, after all. He had bought the place against his father's advice and without his blessing. It was up to him to accept the responsibility even if it meant financial ruin although, if the worst came to the worst, he could always take out another mortgage or sell off some of the land; not that there was much to spare except a small field which he had intended as a trial ground for roses.

Leaving the car, he walked behind the greenhouses to the open land behind. Tucked in to the side of the two fields where he grew strawberries was a triangular paddock, only part of which was cultivated and which was planted with a row of root-stock on which the rose seedling buds he had raised had been grafted. As he walked along it, inspecting each bush individually, he thought that he'd been a fool to imagine it would work.

To grow roses you needed time and money. He couldn't afford to invest either in a project that would take seven years before he could produce a few perfect specimens, even though he had already created them in his imagination, even named them: Elizabeth Holt, a white-scented rose, and Biddy, dark red with a flush of gold in the centre.

Sentimental? Perhaps. But not entirely. He was aware enough of his own capabilities to know he had the patience and the enthusiasm to make a success of it. He was learning the skill. In ten years, it might have been a paying proposition.

All he lacked was the capital.

In the meantime, he had to make a living and, returning to the house, he got out his account books and went over the figures to see if there were any expenses that he could cut down or any extra profit that might be squeezed out of the small margin of return on which he worked.

The answer was none; or, at least, not enough to amount to two thousand pounds.

So that was that.

It would mean mortgaging the property or selling off the rose field.

Either choice was painful. He had struggled for eleven years to get where he was now and to sell even part of the property or put it in the hands of a mortgage company was like being sent tumbling back down a cliff up which he had inched his way from one narrow, dangerous ledge to the next.

Well, it couldn't be helped and he closed the ledger with a slam, reminded, as he did so, of his father's action in shutting the drawer on the Voyte papers. He could now appreciate his father's feelings. It signified the end of an episode which, though distressing, was finished and done with. It was time to move on.

Charlie Webber cycled home from the Swan at closing-time, feeling pleasurably mellow after two or three pints of beer and a few games of dominoes.

On the corner where the telephone kiosk stood, he turned left into Meadow Road towards the smallholding where he worked and which was placed directly opposite the row of council houses where he lived.

He was a small, spry man in his mid-sixties; recently retired from a lifetime as a farm-labourer and the work on Martin Holt's place seemed easy compared to hedging and ditching or ploughing. In fact, he half-despised the stuff Holt grew on the smallholding. Tomatoes and straw-berries! You couldn't call those proper crops, not like barley or sugar-beet.

As he cycled nearer, he noticed lights were on in the larger of the two greenhouses, although the front of Holt's house was in darkness.

He's working late tonight, Charlie thought. Probably catching up on the picking for the following morning when the lorry from Needham's would call to collect the boxes of tomatoes.

He knew Martin had gone to his father's place for dinner—lunch, as he called it. He had mentioned it the previous day; or, rather, Charlie had wheedled the information out of him.

Martin had taken time off to drive down to the village to get his car filled up with petrol, the garage being shut on a Wednesday.

"Going out somewhere?" Charlie had asked and Martin had said, "Only over to my father's for lunch. I can't really spare the time but I suppose I ought to go."

If I'd got the sort of money his father has, Charlie thought, getting off his bike and standing in the road to contemplate the greenhouse, I wouldn't be working at a quarter to eleven at night. No bloody fear! I'd be in front of the telly with my feet up.

Martin never said much about his father; not that he needed to. The name of Holt was so well known, Charlie could draw his own conclusions. The firm's lorries, now taken over by Dalby's, could be seen all over the county and there was hardly a building site or a housing development where their heavy equipment wasn't used.

And to think with all that wealth behind him, Martin Holt still had to go flogging himself half to death trying to work a few acres.

Well, more fool him! Charlie thought, looking across the road with the pleasurable feeling of a man watching someone else at work and knowing that, in the next few minutes, he'd be home and comfortably in bed.

The panes of glass in the greenhouse shone with a subdued brightness, the leaves of the tomato plants obscuring much of the light behind which he could see a figure stooping down.

Picking! Charlie hawked and spat into the road. It did your bloody back in by the end of the day.

He wondered how long Martin could make a go of it; not that he wasn't prepared to work hard; Charlie was willing to give him that. But anyone with half an eye could see that the place needed money spending on it and there were times, he knew, when Martin had to scratch round for the cash to pay the bills. The people who had owned the place before, the Harrisons, had had to sell up because they couldn't make a decent living out of it.

I'll give him two more years, Charlie decided.

Pushing his bike up the steps to the front gate, he turned round for a last look back and, as he did so, the lights in the greenhouse suddenly went out, leaving the place in darkness.

CHAPTER FIVE

The telephone rang and rang.

It woke Bea, who was in the act of throwing back the bedclothes when she heard Hester's bedroom door open and her daughter run down the stairs. Seconds later, the shrill sound was cut off in mid-peal. In the half-empty house in which some of the carpets had not yet been laid nor the curtains hung, the sounds seemed louder than usual and oddly ominous and as Bea came onto the landing, still putting on her dressing-gown, she had a sense of foreboding even before Hester turned to look up the stairs to where her mother was standing.

"That was Rex's gardener," she said, putting down the receiver.

"Mr. Drewett? What on earth is he phoning for at this time in the morning?" Bea demanded, coming down the stairs, and then, catching sight of her daughter's expression, she added, "It's Rex! What's happened?"

Hester said quietly, "There's been an accident, Mother. Mrs. Drewett found him this morning. Rex is dead."

Conscious of her daughter's eyes on her, Bea felt absurdly uncertain how to react. At first, the words had no real meaning for her anyway. Rex dead? It was ridiculous. She had seen him only the previous evening and she could still picture him quite clearly, standing by the desk, writing out the cheque for Martin, his stick propped up beside him and his shoulders hunched forward. It was too vivid to be an image of the dead.

It was followed a moment later by a sense of loss which was so overwhelming that it was like a dark pain and she put both hands against her heart, trying to hold it down.

Hester was saying, "I'll make some tea."

Sitting on the bottom stair, still cradling her grief, Bea was hardly conscious of her daughter's departure.

Rex dead?

"It can't be true!" she cried out loud.

"Drink this."

It was Hester beside her, holding a cup from which Bea drank obediently, swallowing down some of the hot, sweet liquid. Half-way through, she thrust the cup away.

"I must go to him," she said.

"There's nothing you can do, Mother," Hester replied. Something in her voice and expression, that gentle and rational kindness of a person who merely regards bereavement from the outside, released in Bea an anger which she thought she could never feel towards anyone she loved as much as Hester.

"I want to go to him!" she shouted.

The tears came afterwards, flooding out of her, and as Hester held her close, rocking her gently to and fro, she knew without any doubt that Rex was dead.

Later, the storm of weeping over, she felt empty and curiously calm, with the serenity of exhaustion.

Hester had taken her into the sitting-room and had led her to the sofa, where she sat among the unpacked crates of books and china.

"I'm sorry I was angry with you," she said. "But I meant what I said. I want to go to him."

As she spoke, she watched Hester's face, searching it for approval.

How attractive she is! she thought. She felt as if she was seeing her objectively for the first time in years; not as a daughter but as a woman in whom she might be able to confide; a younger, stronger self. Dark-haired and with similar clear features, Hester possessed an edge of brightness about her, a diamond-hard clarity which, unlike her own, had not yet worn down.

Aware of this, she said simply, "I loved him, you see."

It was the first time she had ever confessed as much to her daughter. Hester replied with the same simple directness.

"I know. I saw it whenever you were together." After a pause, she added, "I'll take you to the house whenever you're ready."

It was only when they were in the car that Bea thought to ask, "How did it happen?"

"I'm not sure. Drewett wasn't very explicit. It seems his wife found him in the garden. He'd fallen down the terrace steps. Drewett tried to phone his son first but couldn't get through, so he rang your number."

"Oh God, Martin!" Bea said.

"Are you all right?" Hester asked, slowing down and turning to look at her.

"Yes. Go on. Don't stop," Bea told her. They were entering the drive and she knew that if she faltered now she would not find the courage to continue. But as the shrubbery closed round the car, she felt she was entering a dark tunnel of relationships and loyalties, as tangled and as complex as the branches themselves.

The letter was lying on the doormat as Martin returned from unlocking the greenhouses in readiness for the day's work. Recognising his father's handwriting on the envelope, Martin carried it into the kitchen, where he put the percolator on for coffee before opening it, guessing what the contents were. He had received letters before following a quarrel with his father which contained nothing more than a reiteration of his father's point of view, ending tersely with the hope that he, Martin, would make an effort to appreciate it. As there was never any attempt on his father's part to understand his, Martin usually ignored them. Weeks of silence would then follow until one of them gave in and telephoned the other; more often than not Martin.

When the coffee was ready and poured, Martin tore open the envelope, pulling out the sheet of paper impatiently. Another piece, folded inside the other, fluttered to the floor—a cheque, as Martin discovered as he stooped to pick it up. The words "Five thousand pounds," written in his father's scrawled handwriting, didn't register at first, but the figures stood out clearly enough.

His first reaction was one of enormous relief. He could get the damned heating fixed in the large greenhouse and have money over for other improvements he had in mind: frost-proofing the storage shed and more root-stock for his trial roses.

It was followed by a more sober reaction. His father rarely did anything without some ulterior motive and, laying down the cheque, Martin picked up the letter, expecting to find he had stipulated certain conditions with which he was expected to comply.

In that case, Martin thought, I'll simply post the bloody cheque straight back to him.

The letter surprised him.

"Dear Martin," it read. "I'm sorry the lunch-party ended so abruptly. I had hoped you might stay on longer and get to know Bea a little better. However, I realise you are busy and was pleased you managed to find the time to make the visit. I'm enclosing a cheque which Bea and I feel you might be able to put to good use in the smallholding. Perhaps we can all meet again in the very near future. I hope so." It was signed, as all his letters were since the time when Martin had been away from home at boarding school, "Your affct. Father."

Reading it a second time, however, Martin was aware that, under the unexpectedly reasonable tone of the contents, his father had nevertheless managed to include, more subtly than his usual blunt approach, several points which Martin had no doubt were deliberately intended. The fact that the decision to send the cheque was a joint one between his father and Bea, together with the hope that they would meet again soon, suggested that Rex Holt intended that his son should accept his mistress without reservations. It also implied Bea's concern in his own affairs and her influence over his father, which Martin was not sure he was willing to countenance.

On the other hand, to return the cheque would mean that he intended rejecting her out of hand and that was too positive a reaction. Martin did not want to deny either her or her relationship with his father. The memory of the two of them seated on the terrace under the sun umbrella, Bea's hand on his father's, still moved him with its glimpsed intimacy and the sense of belonging which it had suggested.

So what the hell should he do?

He was still considering the problem when Charlie arrived to begin the day's picking and, stuffing both letter and cheque into his pocket, he went out to the greenhouses.

Half-way through the task, he made up his mind.

He'd accept the cheque. Not only that but he'd telephone his father and thank him personally. He might even make some reference to Bea;

perhaps express the hope that she'd settled into the house. In that way, a step towards reconciliation could be made. After that, the next move was his father's responsibility. But at least he could not make the accusation that his son had rejected him out of hand.

"I'm going down to the village," he told Charlie. "There's a call I have to make and my phone's out of order."

"And I know why," Charlie said with that knowing air of his which Martin sometimes found exasperating. "There's a great old branch been chucked across the wires. Kids, I expect."

The telephone rang for several moments before anyone answered it and then it was Drewett who spoke, not Mrs. Drewett or Rex Holt, which would have been more usual.

As soon as Martin had identified himself, Drewett broke in, his voice sounding too loud and close to the receiver.

"Oh, Mr. Holt, I'm glad you've rung. We've been trying to get in touch with you. I'm afraid I've got some bad news." He hesitated but not long enough to allow Martin to speak. "It's your father. Mrs. Drewett found him dead this morning."

It was a brutal way in which to receive such information and for several seconds Martin stood in silence trying to absorb it. He could hear Drewett's voice repeating, "Are you still there? Can you hear me?"

Pulling himself together, Martin said, "Yes, I heard you. I'll come over immediately." Almost as an afterthought he added, "How did it happen? Was it another stroke?"

"I don't know. The doctor's already arrived and the police have been sent for. Mrs. Chilton's here as well. I'll tell her you're on your way, shall I?"

"Yes, please do."

But Drewett had already hung up and all Martin could hear was the dialling tone. He replaced his own receiver slowly, still trying to come to terms with his father's death.

Its suddenness shocked him; more so, he realised, because he had seen him only the previous day. The transition from life to death seemed too rapid and perfunctory, without sufficient preparation for either of them and he was reminded of an occasion when he had seen a large oak tree being felled. One moment upright, the next it had fallen in a great crashing climax of descent, its impact making the ground tremble.

Driving back in the car, he had time to consider the details of the brief conversation with Drewett. The fact that Bea was at the house didn't surprise him. As his own telephone was out of order, the Drewetts would have naturally contacted her. He tried to imagine her reactions and found it impossible to evoke any mental picture of them, except in the form of the more obvious symbols of grief and bereavement; probably greater than his own. As far as he himself was concerned, he felt more a sense of waste than anything else and an awareness of an abrupt ending not just to his father's life but to a whole episode of his own. But overwhelmingly he was aware of regret; for not having understood him better, for past quarrels, for yesterday's disagreement, for the telephone conversation which he could no longer have.

Drewett's comment that the police had been sent for was more surprising, but he supposed in any case of sudden death their presence would be obligatory.

It was Charlie who put the idea of his inheritance into his mind. As Martin explained what had happened, Charlie commented, after a conventional expression of regret at Rex Holt's death, "So you'll be all right then?"

All right?

For a moment, Martin did not understand the implication behind the remark. But the look on Charlie's face, shrewd, knowing, with an almost crude peasant's evaluation of the importance of property, pulled him up short.

It was impossible to be angry. He had entrusted Charlie with a little information about his own background, enough for the man to have made certain assumptions about his father's wealth and his own lack of it. Besides, the name Holt was too well known across the county for Charlie not to be aware of the fact that Martin stood to inherit a large amount of money on his father's death.

It struck a sour note and, as Martin hurriedly changed into clothes more suitable for the occasion, he considered this aspect for the first time with a sense of shame and self-disgust that it should occupy his thoughts so soon after his father's death.

If only money wasn't so bloody important! he thought. But it was and nothing could change it. It was one of the facts of life he had learned from his father.

The reality of his father's death came more clearly home to him as he turned the car onto the gravelled forecourt in front of the house. Other cars were already there—Bea's Renault and two others which he did not recognise and which belonged presumably to the doctor and perhaps the police. The front door was set open as if these comings and goings were anticipated and, as he approached the steps, Drewett came down the hall towards him. He was a tall, laconic man whom Martin did not know as well as his wife, Grace Drewett.

Meeting Martin at the front door, he seemed relieved, as if the arrival of the son had shifted some of the unwelcome responsibility from his own shoulders.

"So you're here, Mr. Holt!" he said. "I'm glad to see you. It's a bad do."

It was a strange way in which to describe sudden death but the man's obvious embarrassment showed that he was unused to dealing with tragedy and Martin replied, "How did it happen?"

"Like I told you on the phone, the wife found him. She took him his morning cup of tea at the usual time, eight o'clock, only to find the bed empty and the French windows open. Your father was lying at the bottom of the steps leading down to the rose garden. She fetched me and I had a look at him. I could see straight away that he was dead. When I got back to the house, I found the wife taken bad with the shock of it all—in fact, she's not over it yet—so it was me who phoned the doctor. I tried ringing you, only I couldn't get no answer. So I called Mrs. Chilton, who came almost straight away. The doctor's still with him and a police inspector from Welham. The inspector arrived only a few minutes before you."

It was a long speech for Drewett, normally a man of few words, to make and, at the end of it, he looked at Martin as much as to say: There you are! You know as much as I do now. He seemed about to walk away and Martin put out a hand to detain him.

"Where's Mrs. Chilton?" he asked.

"She's sitting on the small lawn round by the dining-room," Drewett replied. "Her daughter's with her. She got me to take some chairs out there and a table; said her mother would be better off waiting in the shade than hanging about in the house."

"Yes, of course," Martin agreed. He was aware of a note of resentment in Drewett's voice, as if the man considered he had been put out by these arrangements although they seemed sensible enough to Martin. The day was hot and the air inside the house, despite the open windows, felt oppressive. As the terrace overlooked the rose garden, where presumably the doctor and the inspector were completing their examination of Rex Holt's body, the choice of the side lawn was an obvious one.

He thought he understood the reason for Drewett's unspoken resentment shortly afterwards when, walking round to the side of the house, he approached the lawn where the two women were sitting. It was a small, formal garden, walled in with high, clipped yew hedges. Not much bigger than an average-sized room, it was furnished like an interior setting with garden statues and stone benches, although more comfortable folding canvas chairs had been drawn up round a rosewood serving-table which normally stood in the dining-room.

No wonder Drewett had regarded its acquisition as an imposition, Martin thought. Especially from the young woman who, seated at Bea's side, watched his progress towards them across the grass.

Even though it was years since he had seen her, he recognised her immediately as Bea's daughter, Hester. Like Bea, she had short, dark hair and small, neat features, wide at the brow and pointed at the chin but the general impression was sharper and more clipped. There was the same fierce, challenging look about her which he remembered disliking on their first meeting and he saw no reason to change that original opinion.

Ignoring her, he took Bea's hand, shocked by her appearance. In the few hours since their last meeting the day before she had grown suddenly old.

"I'm so sorry, Martin," she said, before he could speak, although he had intended offering the same condolence to her. After all, she had been closer to his father than he had ever been.

Knowing this, he could think of nothing to say in reply except the awkwardly conventional remark, "It's been a shock for all of us."

"You've met my daughter before," Bea continued, introducing Hester, who was sitting on the far side of her and who made no attempt to shake hands, merely nodding at him to acknowledge the acquaintanceship before getting to her feet and announcing, "I'll ask Mrs. Drewett to make coffee."

Her assumption of responsibility over the household angered Martin, who replied, "I believe Mrs. Drewett is still suffering from shock."

She looked him over coolly before replying, "In that case, I'll make it myself."

They watched her walk away in silence. Then Bea said, "I'm afraid Hester is too used to organising other people to be able to sit back and do nothing."

Unsure quite how to reply to what amounted to an apology and an explanation of her daughter's high-handedness, Martin merely said, "Coffee would be welcome."

He wondered how much Bea had told her daughter of yesterday's lunch party. No doubt they had discussed him, which could account for Hester's obvious hostility towards him. Well, he didn't care for her either. She was too hard, too damned sure of herself.

He was glad when, returning with the tray of coffee, Hester announced that she didn't want any.

"I'm going for a walk," she told her mother, ignoring Martin.

He waited until she had crossed the lawn towards the far side of the garden before he spoke to Bea, making the offer which he had hesitated to do in front of her daughter and which he intended quite sincerely.

"If there's anything I can do, Bea, you've only got to ask."

She looked up from pouring the coffee. He couldn't see her eyes. She had put on a pair of sun-glasses to hide, he assumed, the signs of grief from him but he was aware her mouth was trembling.

"Thank you, Martin. That's kind of you. I don't think there's much anyone can do. Hester's with me for the week, helping me to move into the house. Having her with me has been an enormous comfort."

He wasn't quite sure how to make the next offer, uncertain what financial arrangements had been made between her and his father.

"If it's a question of money, I could easily let you have some, since my father sent me a cheque which arrived this morning. I think you probably know about it."

He realised how awkward the words sounded. Neither he nor his father had possessed the art of giving gracefully. He was too tentative. His father had been too brusque.

Bea said quickly, "Oh no, Martin. I couldn't! I mean, there's no need."

She spoke rapidly as if to cover up some deep embarrassment. Then, turning aside, she began to search in her handbag. "There's something I must give to you. Your father made me take it last night. It's the key to the bureau upstairs where he keeps all his personal papers. He wanted me to have it, as if . . ."

She broke off, unwilling to continue.

As she spoke, Martin studied the key she had handed to him. It was made of brass with a decorative top to it. Martin recognised it immediately as the key to his mother's bureau, which his father must have appropriated for his own use. Yesterday he might have been angry. Now, sitting next to Bea, who was close to tears, he felt merely a dull ache for a loss which he could not define.

Bea was saying shakily in the same rapid voice which he realised was her way of controlling her emotions, "—as if he knew he was going to die. It was so strange, Martin. That's why he wanted me to have the key for safe keeping. He asked me to put some letters in the bureau, you see, and when I came downstairs, he told me to keep it although I think he wanted you to have it if anything happened to him. He had a spare one for his own use. I don't know what papers are up there. I didn't look, of course, apart from opening the bureau to put the letters away."

Martin heard her out in silence, aware of a great deal more than the mere words conveyed and wondering if Bea herself was conscious of their implication. He suspected she was. Her obvious embarrassment over the episode and her anxiety to explain suggested that she realised its full significance and its possible effects on himself. It was hardly open to misinterpretation. The fact was that his father had entrusted Bea with the key to the bureau, not himself, a measure of the confidence he placed in her. Martin suspected also that, in doing so, his father had attempted to ensure some kind of continuing contact between himself and Bea, a desire which had been implicit in the letter from him which Martin had received only that morning.

As for the letters which Bea had referred to, he had no doubt that they were the Voyte papers which his father had wanted returned to the bureau where they were usually kept.

It was partly his wish to retrieve them as well as to show willingness to co-operate with her which made him say, "Look, Bea, will you come with me? We could look through the bureau together."

"Should we?" She seemed uncertain.

"The letters he asked you to put away belonged to my mother. I'd like to take them. The rest will have to be turned over to his solicitor."

The idea seemed to distress her.

"Will they? All of them? You see, my letters to Rex are in the bureau."

"Then we'll take those as well," he assured her.

The house was silent although, as they mounted the stairs, Drewett crossed the hall on his way to the kitchen.

The bedroom, thank God, was not his mother's but a spare room overlooking the same small formal garden where they had been sitting.

The bureau, the only piece of furniture in the room not covered with dust-sheets, stood between the windows and, as Martin unlocked it and let down the flap, he noticed the interior compartments were now occupied by his father's papers.

The first few were full of bank statements and old cheque-books, the next two contained photocopies of deeds to property, the originals of which were probably held at the solicitor's. With Bea standing beside him, he did not like to examine them in detail although, as he replaced them, he saw that there were about eight of them and the holdings appeared to be scattered. The top two related to land in Barnsfield, rented out to a local farmer, and a row of cottages, also let out to tenants, in Welham. He was surprised by the number of the documents, not realising that his father had invested in so much real estate.

The last compartments contained his father's more personal papers, including his will in a long brown sealed envelope. As he took it out, Bea said quickly, "I don't know what's in it, Martin. He never discussed it with me. But he told me yesterday that he had made financial arrangements which I'd benefit from if anything happened to him."

She spoke defensively and, to cover up his own awkwardness, he merely replied, "I think these must be yours," as he handed her a packet of letters which were lying next to the will.

"Thank you," Bea said quietly, taking them and putting them in her handbag. Without meeting his eyes, she added, "I'll leave you to go through the rest of Rex's papers on your own."

Before he could protest, she had walked away, closing the door quietly behind her.

"Oh, Christ!" Martin said out loud. Without meaning to he had bungled the whole affair. By ignoring her remark about the will, he had meant to convey that it didn't matter to him if she did benefit from his father's estate; that it was only to be expected. After all, it was perfectly just. In many ways, she had been closer to his father than even he had been. Instead, by his silence, he had implied not his willing acceptance, but disapproval.

Well it was too late now. As he stood by the bureau in front of the windows, he saw her cross the lawn towards the chairs set out under the trees, where Hester, returned from her walk, was already waiting.

What followed had all the poignancy and significance of a dumb show. He saw Hester jump up and run forward to meet her mother, whose bent head and dragging walk suggested she was weeping. They spoke to one another although he couldn't hear what was said. He could only guess at the content by the manner in which Hester raised her head to look defiantly up at the bedroom windows where he stood out of sight behind the curtains.

The next moment, Hester was leading her mother away towards the front of the house. Shortly afterwards, he heard the sound of a car starting up and caught a glimpse of the Renault heading down the drive towards the gates.

So that was that.

He would have to find some opportunity of explaining himself to Bea. But of one thing he was quite certain. He had no intention of excusing himself or apologising in front of her daughter if he could help it and with that resolution firmly fixed in his mind, he turned his attention back to the bureau.

Replacing the will where he had found it, he noticed a smaller packet of letters lying in the compartment next to it, held together by an elastic band and, curious to know what it contained, he slipped the band off and went through the contents quickly. Three of the letters were from Reggie Trimmer, thanking his father for loans of money, full of effusive thanks and promises to repay as soon as possible. The fourth, still in its original envelope, which had been forwarded from the firm in Welham and which bore a South African stamp, was addressed in a different and unfamiliar handwriting. Taking out the sheet of paper, in which was enclosed a photograph, Martin scanned the contents. It read, under a Johannesburg address and the date of March 11 four years before: "Dear Uncle Rex, I am sorry to tell you that my father died a few days ago after a short illness. He often spoke of you and the old days in England when you were boys together. He will be buried out here. I found the photograph among his papers and I'm sending it on to you as I thought you might like to have it as a memento. Yours, Jean Browning."

Underneath the signature was a terse note in his father's handwriting: "Send acknowledgement and cheque for £500."

The photograph, folded inside the sheet of paper, was an old snapshot of two boys aged, Martin estimated, eight and ten years old, standing with their arms a little self-consciously around each other's shoulders. Even after all those years, the older one was immediately recognisable as Rex Holt. The stance and set of the head were familiar. The younger boy was slighter in build and finer-featured. Tipping the snapshot towards the light, Martin examined the face more closely. It was the first time he had ever seen a photograph of his father's brother,

Arthur, although he knew a little about him; not from his father; Rex Holt had rarely spoken of him. It was his mother who had supplied the few details of his background, which, Martin realised, mirrored his own to an extent which had not occurred to him before. Arthur Holt, after a quarrel with his own father, had emigrated to South Africa at the age of twenty-one and, apart from infrequent letters to his own mother in her lifetime, had not been in touch with the family for years.

He must have married, Martin thought, and had at least one child, Jean Browning, whose change of surname suggested that she, too, had married.

So he was now dead. It seemed to him extraordinary that his father had never spoken of him, not even to mention his death. The terse note at the bottom of the letter suggested that he had not even replied to it personally but had delegated that duty to someone else, although the reference to the cheque for five hundred pounds implied guilt on his father's part. It smacked to Martin of conscience money, the payment of an old debt of affection, or perhaps a family obligation, which Rex Holt had not known how to settle in any other way.

It was the same, Martin thought wryly, with all his close relationships. None had lasted, except that between his father and Bea. Only _she_ seemed to have maintained any lasting contact with him, which had survived as long as some marriages.

The thought surprised him. He hadn't considered their relationship in that light before. But it was true. They had been like a married couple and he now regretted the misunderstanding over the will, which had clearly distressed her.

Well, he'd put it right by apologising, he decided. He wasn't going to repeat the mistake which his father, and presumably his grandfather before him, had made, of allowing old quarrels to go on festering out of stubbornness and pride.

He was picking up the Voyte papers and putting them into his pocket when Mrs. Drewett knocked and entered, still looking pale and shaken.

"The police inspector'd like to speak to you, Mr. Holt. He's downstairs in the hall."

"Tell him I'll be down straight away," Martin replied, closing the flap of the bureau and locking it.

His intention of sorting through the papers would have to be postponed, he thought, although he supposed he'd have to telephone his father's solicitor and inform him of his father's death. Biddy, too, would have to be told. As for the smallholding, well, Charlie would have to cope until his return.

The inspector was a tall, narrow-faced man, clearly ill at ease.

"I'm sorry about your father, Mr. Holt," he said, his features pulled down into a conventional expression of condolence. Martin was about to make some formal reply of his own but the man hurried on, "I'm afraid there'll have to be a further examination. Dr. Saville's not satisfied about the cause of death."

"I don't understand," Martin said flatly. "Are you trying to tell me it wasn't an accident? That he didn't fall?"

"I couldn't say, sir. I'm not a doctor, so it's not my place to comment. All I can tell you is Dr. Saville wants a second medical opinion and, in view of that, I feel it's my duty to inform CID. I'd like your permission to use the telephone."

"Of course. There's this one," Martin replied, indicating the receiver standing on the hall table. "Or there's an extension in my father's room if you prefer to use that."

"I'll phone from here, sir, and I'd be grateful if no one entered your father's room in the meantime," the inspector replied. "We may need to make a detailed examination of it and I'd rather it remained undisturbed."

"But it's absurd—" Martin began.

The inspector's voice rose above his.

"I'd also be grateful if you didn't leave the premises. The inspector they'll be sending over from headquarters in Chelmsford will want to speak to you when he arrives. Now, if you wouldn't mind, sir . . ."

His hand was on the telephone receiver and, dismissed, Martin walked out of the front door.

Outside, he stood in the bright sunlight, attempting to collect his thoughts.

What the hell had the inspector been implying? Murder?

"But it's absurd!" he repeated out loud.

The doctor must have made a mistake or, at worst, his father had been attacked by an intruder. There seemed no other possible explanation.

Standing there on the forecourt, looking across at Fair Mile Hill, he suddenly made up his mind.

He was damned if he was going to wait about, perhaps for an hour, before the CID turned up. In that time, he could see Biddy, who must now be told before gossip started spreading in the village.

Reentering the hall, which was empty, the inspector having presumably finished his call and returned to the terrace, he sought out Mrs. Drewett in the kitchen.

"I'm going to the village to see Miss Moxon," he told her. "If anyone asks for me, I shan't be long."

"Will you want lunch, sir?" Mrs. Drewett asked.

"Lunch?" It was another absurdity to be thinking of food at such a time but, seeing by her anxious expression that she wanted this domestic detail settled, he added wryly, "Yes, Mrs. Drewett, I'll be back for lunch."

CHAPTER SIX

It was an unsuitable setting for death, Detective Chief Inspector Rudd thought. Lovers should have occupied it, not a corpse. The sunken garden was humming with heat and fragrance, the one striking back from the paving stones of the paths between the formal flower-beds, the other rising with as much power from the roses and the clipped borders of lavender which surrounded them. In the centre, a fountain in the shape of a dolphin sent up jets of mingled light and water, adding its own glitter and cool, bright, liquid sound to the hot, sweet air.

In the middle of all this bright colour and dazzle, Rex Holt's body looked too inert and solid as it lay huddled at the bottom of the flight of steps which led down from the terrace, the dark red dressing-gown it was wearing matching the pool of dried blood which had spread out round the head to stain the paving.

Over it, like little boys examining a new and fascinating toy, squatted the two figures of the doctors: Pardoe, his own police surgeon, small, dapper and sandy, and Saville, tall, rumpled and grey, the dead man's physician, who had been called first to the scene.

Watching them, Rudd thought of Marion Greave. On the last case involving sudden death which he had investigated, she had acted as locum while Pardoe was on leave. It had been a new and disturbing experience for him to work on equal terms with a woman, not just professionally although that had been difficult enough to adjust to. What he had not bargained for had been his emotional response to her. He had never married and, now middle-aged, had grown accustomed to his comfortable bachelor existence with his widowed sister, Dorothy, who kept house for him.

The idea of falling in love had not crossed his mind for years. Indeed, the very image of himself as a lover was faintly ridiculous. With his stocky frame and bluff, open features, the face of a farmer rather than a policeman, he was hardly, as he himself would have admitted, the stuff of which romance was made.

And yet Marion Greave, with her dark hair and cool, amused assurance, had managed to send little ripples of animation across the usually placid surface of his life.

But was it love? Absurdly, he wasn't sure. Although they had met several times since that last occasion when they had worked together, he was still not able to define his feelings with any certainty. He enjoyed her company; he admired her intelligence; he found her attractive although by any objective standard she was not a pretty woman, only the liveliness of her expression and the little humorous puckers under her eyes giving her any claim to physical charm.

The fountain reminded him of her—a ridiculous image really and he found himself half-smiling at the comparison. Yet there was a validity about it all the same. She, too, possessed the same radiance and fresh astringency of the fine water-drops which were flung like a benison into the hot, still air.

Pardoe gave a small exclamation of annoyance, drawing Rudd's attention back to the scene at the bottom of the steps. He himself had only cursorily examined the body, long enough to take note of its general disposition and the clothing it was wearing before moving away to allow the two doctors to take over.

Rex Holt lay on his left side, his left arm thrown out as if, in falling, he had tried to clutch at something to save himself. A walking-stick, presumably his, lay a little to the right of the body. Beneath the dressing-gown protruded legs and feet clad in pale blue pyjamas and brown leather slippers, rather worn and scuffed for a man who owned not only the rose garden and the surrounding grounds but Barnsfield Hall itself, the rear façade of which rose, solid and handsome, above the terrace.

He looked, Rudd thought, like a man who, having got out of a bath, was ready for bed.

It was odd, certainly, that he had been found dead at the bottom of the terrace steps. But did it amount to murder?

There was no way of knowing until the two doctors had finished their examination.

Meanwhile, there was nothing any of them could do except wait. Rudd glanced round at the men quickly. McCullum, the police photographer, was lounging negligently, his camera at his feet; Marsh and several others were sitting along the coping of the low terrace wall while Kyle, the young, fresh-faced DC, was contemplating the fountain like a tripper on a day's outing. Boyce, Rudd's burly, broad-shouldered detective sergeant, very red in the face and, Rudd guessed, simmering not only with the heat but with impatience at the delay, was prowling up and down the terrace, looking all the world like a park attendant keeping a watchful eye on visitors to a public garden.

Rudd himself stood with his hands behind his back, his expression bland, giving a good impression of a farmer at a cattle market, not letting on to any of those around him whether he was interested in the bidding or not.

Without any warning, the two doctors rose to their feet together, conferred briefly for a moment over the dead man's outstretched legs and then turned towards the chief inspector.

Things were evidently happening at last and a ripple of movement passed outwards from their epicentre. Men stood up; Kyle, still gazing at the fountain, was nudged into awareness by Wylie. Boyce hurried across to Rudd's side.

"Thank God," he muttered under his breath. "I thought they'd never make up their minds."

"There's no guarantee they have now," Rudd murmured back as Pardoe and Saville approached.

It was Pardoe who spoke. For some reason, perhaps to maintain professional standards, he was wearing, despite the heat, a suit as well as a collar and tie and looked, in consequence, more short-tempered than usual. In contrast, Saville appeared too loose and informal, a disadvantage he was aware of himself, his first remark to Rudd having been an apology for his appearance.

"Murder," Pardoe announced snappily, as if it were all Rudd's fault. "You're sure?"

It was an unwise remark to make. Pardoe bristled up at once.

"Of course I'm sure! The man was killed by a blow to the side of the head but it wasn't caused, although that's what we're supposed to think, by the edge of the bottom step. That came later. If you want my opinion, and you can rest assured the pathologist will agree with me, he was killed before he fell. The head was then banged down against the step and the body arranged, as you see it now, to look like an accident. And Saville agrees with me."

Dr. Saville nodded unhappily.

"There are two distinct wounds which I noticed when I first examined him, Chief Inspector," he said. "The first is a large, circular injury which has bled considerably. Overlying it is a second, much longer, narrower wound. That's the reason why I told Inspector Branch from Welham that I wasn't satisfied it was accidental death."

Pardoe, who had been swaying backwards and forwards impatiently on the balls of his feet during this account, broke in, "Quite right! Quite right! You can examine the injuries yourself if you don't believe us."

"I'll take your word for it," Rudd replied.

"As for the time of death," Pardoe continued, "the man's watch has stopped as eight minutes past ten. What you make of that is up to you. I simply give it to you as a fact. Whether or not the post-mortem will confirm it is another matter entirely."

"He was wearing a watch?" Rudd asked. He hadn't noticed it when he had made his own brief examination of the body, the left cuff of the dressing-gown having hidden the wrist. That, too, like the setting, seemed another incongruity.

"He was," Pardoe retorted, as if Rudd was calling even that point into question. He took a last look back at the body. "He's all yours now, Chief Inspector. I've done everything I can for the present. You can move him when you're ready. Well, I'm going," he announced to Saville before walking briskly away.

Saville lingered for a few more moments, waiting until the trim, upright, little figure of the police surgeon had disappeared along the terrace. With Pardoe's departure, he seemed more relaxed.

"The question of the time was another factor which made me uneasy," he said to Rudd. "Rex Holt was my patient, not that he consulted me frequently. On the whole, he was in reasonably good health and he wasn't the type of man to make a fuss about himself. But he suffered a minor stroke last year which left him with a limp and I know that he got very tired towards the end of the day. Even a short walk in the evening was too much for him. He told me so himself. That's what made me think it was unlikely that he'd gone out onto the terrace alone at that time of night."

"I see. Thank you," Rudd replied, keeping to himself the comment that, on a warm summer evening, even Rex Holt might have been tempted to stroll as far as the top of the terrace steps. But now that murder had been established, the whole question of Rex Holt's movements before he met his death was open to an entirely new interpretation.

He examined the watch himself, folding back the cuff and turning the wrist so that he could see its face. The glass was still in place but had been starred across with a series of tiny cracks radiating out from the central point of impact, under which the hands were just visible, pointing, as Pardoe had said, to eight minutes past ten.

Had it broken as he fell? he wondered. The position of the wrist, with the back of it against the paving stones and the grazed skin across the knuckles, would suggest that it had. Or had the murderer altered the time before smashing the watch deliberately in order to give himself an alibi?

He looked at the wounds next, making no attempt to touch them. Although he was no expert, he could see what Saville had meant. The first blow had been made with some weapon roughly circular in shape which had smashed the temple and extended down towards the cheekbone. The second wound ran towards the eye and back into the hairline, a long, narrow injury, not as deep as the first but cutting nevertheless into the already broken tissue. Blood and hair on the edge of the bottom step suggested that it was against this that the second wound had been made.

As he explained to Boyce as the sergeant joined him, it would be easy enough, once the man had fallen, to make the second blow, simply by smashing the side of his head against the stone edge.

"But why?" he asked in conclusion.

Boyce shrugged.

"Perhaps he thought he wasn't dead, so the murderer decided to have a second go."

"What I meant was, why not hit him again with the same weapon?"

"Panic?" suggested Boyce. "Or perhaps he'd already chucked the weapon away and couldn't find it in the dark."

"Possible," Rudd agreed. "In that case it should still be lying about."

Getting to his feet, he called Stapleton, the tall, slow-moving inspector, to join them.

"I want a thorough search made of the whole area, including the terrace," Rudd told him. "You're looking in particular for a weapon, something hard and round, like a large stone or a rock." As Stapleton moved off to collect up the uniformed men, Rudd turned to his own group of experts, Marsh, Wylie and the others. "McCullum, take some close-ups of the head injuries and the watch as well as a few more general shots. Kyle, I know you've made a scene-of-crime search already but go over the immediate vicinity again, will you? Marsh—"

"Fingerprints from the corpse?" Marsh suggested. Like Boyce he was suffering from the heat, his heavy face glistening with sweat.

"If anyone wants me," Rudd continued, "I'll be in Rex Holt's room. Tom, you come with me."

It was pleasant to escape from the direct sun into the house, although the heat pursued them there through the open French windows.

"I'll start with Mrs. Drewett," Rudd said as they entered. "She found the body."

"You want to interview her in here?" Boyce asked.

"Yes. There are one or two points I want to clear up with her regarding Holt's movements last night. She'll probably know his habits better than anyone else."

"Right you are," Boyce said and left the room.

While he was gone, Rudd took the opportunity to look in more detail about him, having only glanced inside the room earlier on his way to the rose garden. He had already noted that there was no sign of either a break-in or disturbance, which seemed to rule out the possibility that robbery had been the motive.

The room was large and had evidently been used as a drawing-room before Rex Holt had turned it into a bed-sitting-room, for his own convenience, Rudd assumed. A divan was placed against the wall, facing the windows, the covers turned back but the bed unslept in. Beside it, on a table, stood a lamp and a cold cup of tea. At the foot was a trolley with a television set standing on it, presumably to allow Holt to watch it from his bed, an assumption which was borne out by the remote control box on the bedside table.

The rest of the room was furnished as a sitting-room with armchairs, a pair of low tables, a plain oak desk with a telephone on it and a swivel chair drawn up in front of it. Another table was placed against the far wall, on which stood a silver tray with a number of bottles on it and half a dozen cut crystal glasses.

Beside it was a door, which Rudd opened. It led into a smaller room, equipped partly as a bathroom and partly as a dressing-room.

A towel hung over the edge of the bath and clothes had been laid on a chair under a window with frosted glass panels. Talcum powder was scattered over the carpet.

Stepping into the room, Rudd ran his hand over the towel. It had been thrown down carelessly and the inner folds were still damp. As he rubbed his fingers thoughtfully across the fabric, there came the sound of voices from the hall outside and he returned to Holt's bedroom just as Boyce and Mrs. Drewett entered by the other door.

He had been warned of Mrs. Drewett's state of shock by her husband, who had met them on their arrival, and her wan face with its anxious expression prompted him to take her gently through the first part of the interview.

What she had to tell them was straightforward enough. She had knocked and entered the room at eight o'clock that morning, the usual time, with Mr. Holt's cup of tea, the same one which still stood on the bedside table, its surface gathering a wrinkled brown skin. The lights were on and the French windows were open, the curtains undrawn. Finding the bed empty, she had gone out on to the terrace and had seen Mr. Holt lying at the foot of the steps which led down to the rose garden.

She had run back into the house to call her husband, who, on examining Mr. Holt's body, had told her he was dead. She had been too shocked herself to do anything and it was Drewett who had telephoned the doctor. He had also tried to get in touch with Martin, Mr. Holt's son, but the line seemed to be out of order, so he had rung Mrs. Chilton.

"Mrs. Chilton?" Rudd asked.

Mrs. Drewett looked uncomfortable.

"She's an old family friend of Mr. Holt's he's known for years; leastways, that's the way he introduced her when she came here a few days ago to look round the house. She's moved down here recently from London. Mr. Holt told me she might be staying here as a guest. As a matter of fact, she was here only yesterday for lunch. There was a little party, just a few guests with champagne and cold salmon—"

"A celebration?" Rudd suggested, cutting short what was evidently going to be a full account of the menu. "Who else was there?"

"His son, Mr. Martin Holt, and Mr. Trimmer. He lives in the village and he often calls on Mr. Holt. He's another old friend."

"So Martin Holt was here yesterday?"

"Yes. Not that he stayed long. He left about half past three and gave Mr. Trimmer a lift back into the village. I thought they were going to stay on longer. At least, Mr. Holt told me to expect four for tea but there was only the two of them, Mr. Holt himself and Mrs. Chilton."

Rudd made no comment himself on her remark regarding Martin Holt's early departure, merely asking, "What time did Mrs. Chilton leave?"

"I'm not sure, sir. Drewett and I always go off duty at seven. We don't live in, you see. We sleep at the gatehouse. When we left, Mrs. Chilton was still here. Unless there's a dinner party, in which case I stay on longer, Mr. Holt usually has a light supper in his room, which I leave ready for him in the kitchen. He ordered supper for two last night, so I put some of the game pie left over from lunch out ready for them and half a bottle of claret."

"Just a minute," Rudd said, interrupting these domestic details, "there's a couple of points I'd like cleared up. Firstly, am I correct in thinking Mr. Holt is alone in the house at night?"

"That's right, sir. It's his idea, not ours. Drewett and I would willingly live in but Mr. Holt prefers we didn't. Mind you, there's burglar alarms on all the doors and windows and, since he had his stroke last year, he's had a bell put in by his bed which he can ring if he needs us in the night. It's connected to the gatehouse so we'd hear it when we're off duty."

She nodded towards the bed, where a white bell-push had been inserted into the wall.

"What about security?" Boyce put in. "Who sees to that?"

"Drewett usually does. He makes sure everything's locked up and the alarm system's switched on before we go off duty. But since we've had this warm weather, Mr. Holt's told him to leave the French windows open. He closes them himself before he goes to bed."

"And what's his routine after you've left?" Rudd asked. "Have you any idea?"

"As far as I know, he goes to bed fairly early, between ten and half past, unless he has guests. But he's not done so much entertaining since his stroke. I know he watches television. He likes to see the ten o'clock news."

"And does he usually have a bath before going to bed?"

"Oh yes; or a shower. I tidy up the bathroom while he has his cup of tea first thing in the morning and put out fresh clothes for him."

Rudd went towards the door leading into the bathroom.

"He'd use this room?"

"Yes. It used to be what was known as the housekeeper's room. He had it converted and the connecting door put in after he had his stroke. He can't manage the stairs so well these days."

"The other point I wanted clearing up is this." Rudd continued. "If Mr. Martin Holt's telephone was out of order when your husband tried to call him this morning, how did you let him know of his father's death?"

"Oh, he rang himself about half past nine from a call-box. My husband answered."

"Do you know why he rang? Was it to thank his father for the lunch yesterday?"

"I couldn't say. I don't think so. He's never done it before. Mr. Drewett told him about his father and young Mr. Holt said he'd come over straight away. Is that all, sir? Only there's lunch to prepare . . ."

"I shan't keep you much longer," Rudd assured her. "Before you go, I'd like you to look round the room and tell me if anything's missing."

Mrs. Drewett glanced carefully about her, even going over to the desk to check the objects standing on it before replying.

"No, sir. There's nothing missing."

"What about the desk itself? Do you know what's kept in the drawers?"

"Only papers as far as I know. I couldn't say if they're all there."

She looked suddenly flustered, her face turning an unbecoming red.

"Yes, Mrs. Drewett?" Rudd prompted.

"I don't know if it's my place to mention it, but this morning, before you arrived, the other inspector, the one from Welham, wanted to speak to young Mr. Holt. Drewett said he'd seen him going upstairs, so I went up to find him. He was in one of the spare bedrooms where his father keeps—kept, I mean—a bureau. He was just locking it up as I went in and I saw him put some papers in his pocket."

"I see," Rudd said, giving nothing away either in his voice or expression. "Do you have a key to the bureau yourself?"

"No, but Mr. Holt kept one on his key-ring."

"Thank you, Mrs. Drewett. That's all," Rudd told her. "Could you tell Mrs. Chilton I'd like to see her?"

"Mrs. Chilton's gone, sir," she replied. "She wasn't feeling very well and her daughter's taken her home."

"I see." Rudd's face was bland. "I'll speak to young Mr. Holt in that case."

"He's gone, too, sir."

"Gone!" Rudd's reaction was more positive this time. "I thought everyone was told they should stay in case I needed to speak to them."

Mrs. Drewett looked unhappy, as if the blame was entirely hers.

"I don't know about that, sir. Mrs. Chilton and her daughter simply left. Young Mr. Holt said he'd be back for lunch. He's gone to see someone in the village—Miss Moxon. She used to be housekeeper here and Mr. Holt's known her since he was a little boy." Still looking anxious, she added, "I suppose I ought to have told you about the other gentleman who came yesterday. He didn't stay to lunch and as you only asked about the guests at the party . . ."

"That's all right, Mrs. Drewett," Rudd said more gently, aware of her anxiety. "Who was he?"

"He was an American gentleman, a Mr. Hurst. I don't quite know why he was here except he had an appointment with Mr. Holt for ten o'clock. He was still here when young Mr. Holt arrived but, like I said, Mr. Hurst left before lunch."

"Do you know where he's staying?"

"I'm sorry, sir, I don't."

"Thank you," Rudd repeated.

She seemed relieved to go.

When the door closed behind her, Rudd turned to Boyce.

"See if you can find the key to that bureau upstairs. Try the desk but for God's sake don't get your dabs on it. Wylie hasn't gone over the room yet for prints."

Boyce crossed to the desk and began sliding open the drawers with the point of a penknife.

"Nothing much in here," he remarked, "only account books, bank statements, a cheque-book . . ."

Rudd peered over his shoulder.

"That looks like a current cheque-book," he pointed out. "Let's have a look at it."

Flicking over the stubs, he stopped at the most recent one.

"Look at this!" he said to Boyce. "That's interesting. Rex Holt evidently wrote out a cheque for five thousand pounds only yesterday for his son. At least, it's got 'Martin' written across the counterfoil."

"It's a lot of money," Boyce commented.

"Rex Holt must be worth a hell of a lot more than five thousand," Rudd replied.

"Motive?" Boyce suggested succinctly.

"It's possible but it's too early to start thinking of that yet. It certainly wasn't robbery unless the thief took something that Mrs. Drewett hasn't missed."

"Like papers? The son certainly didn't waste much time helping himself to some of those this morning."

Rudd felt mildly exasperated.

"You're still jumping to conclusions, Tom. If you're suggesting Martin Holt killed his father—and for all we know he may have a cast-iron alibi for last night—why didn't he help himself to what he wanted there and then? Why wait until this morning to take it and in front of Mrs. Drewett, too? It doesn't make sense. Have you found that key yet?"

"No," Boyce said.

Much to Boyce's chagrin, they found the key-ring on the bedside table, behind the cold cup of tea.

"You said 'look in the desk,' " he muttered as he followed Rudd out of the room.

The upper floor of Barnsfield Hall seemed to be unused. Rudd walked along the long L-shaped gallery landing, trying doors, each one of which with only one exception opened into an unoccupied bedroom, the windows closed, the furniture sheeted.

"What a waste!" he commented, half to himself, as he closed the fifth.

All those beds and curtains and mirrors! Valuable stuff, too, by the look of it. Enough to fill several antique shops and all of it shut away out of sight.

The next bedroom, the sixth, and they were only half-way down the middle landing, contained the bureau, unsheeted, the figured veneer of the flap showing clear signs of fingerprints on its polished surface.

"Get Wylie and McCullum up here," Rudd told Boyce.

When the two experts had finished fingerprinting and photographing the front of the bureau, Rudd unlocked it and let down the flap, Boyce helping him to search through the inner compartments.

"Put aside anything you think might be important," he told the sergeant. "We'll go over it again in more detail another time."

It was Boyce who found the IOU's.

"Interesting," he commented, handing them over to the chief inspector.

Reading quickly through the letters, which were signed merely 'Reggie,' Rudd noticed that the address was a local one, and he sent Boyce off to find out from Mrs. Drewett who Reggie might be although he had already guessed it was probably Trimmer.

In Boyce's absence, he came across several photocopies of deeds, which he glanced at very briefly, and Rex Holt's will in its unopened envelope. He was making a note of the name of the solicitor printed on the outside when Boyce returned.

"It's Trimmer," he announced. "Mrs. Drewett's quite sure. She's often heard Holt address him as 'Reggie.' "

"So he owed Holt money," Rudd commented.

"Over a thousand quid," Boyce pointed out.

"And I wonder if he benefits from the will," Rudd continued, brandishing the long envelope. "I've got another job for you, Tom. See if you can get hold of Holt's solicitor, Walter Gilham. Use the phone in Holt's room but make sure you get the place examined and printed first. I'd like to know who else has been in there beside Holt himself and Mrs. Drewett. While that's being done, I'm going to have a chat with Drewett about the phone call he took from Martin Holt this morning."

He found the Drewetts in the kitchen, a large room which was used by the housekeeper and the gardener as their general living-room, judging by the table occupying the centre, at which Drewett was sitting eating a ham sandwich while his wife laid a tray with plates and cutlery, for Martin Holt's lunch, Rudd assumed.

Drewett had little to add to what Mrs. Drewett had already told the chief inspector about Martin Holt's telephone call.

"No, I don't know what he was ringing about," he said. "He just asked to speak to his father and when I told him what had happened, he said he'd be over as soon as he could. That's all."

"It was a bit odd him ringing up, wasn't it, George?' Mrs. Drewett put in, "although thank God he did, otherwise I don't know how we'd've got in touch with him."

"Local police station," Drewett said dismissively, as if that much were obvious, at which Mrs. Drewett looked abashed.

"I hadn't thought of that," she admitted.

"Odd?" Rudd picked up the word.

"Well, he didn't phone his father all that often, did he?" Mrs. Drewett appealed to her husband, who indicated with one raised shoulder that he didn't know and didn't much care either.

"Not on friendly terms, were they?" Rudd suggested.

Mrs. Drewett glanced again at her husband but he refused to be drawn.

"Not really," she admitted at last. "Mind you, I don't know the ins and outs of it, but I gather young Mr. Holt should have taken over the family business only there was a row. He doesn't come over here all that often and, when he does, there's usually some unpleasantness."

"Quarrels, you mean?" Rudd asked.

Mrs. Drewett looked unhappy at having to explain the euphemism.

"Not exactly quarrels; more disagreements. I've heard them arguing together more than once. And Mr. Holt's always that short-tempered after his son's left; like a bear with a sore head. I've said many times, haven't I, George, that I dread him coming?"

This time Drewett went so far as to nod his head to show agreement.

"And what with Mrs. Chilton coming to live in the village *and* turning up for lunch yesterday, I knew there'd be trouble. I said to you, didn't I, 'You mark my words, the son's not going to like it.'?"

"It's not our business," Drewett said flatly.

She flared up immediately, stung by his lack of responsiveness.

"It's all very well for you! You're outside most of the time! You don't have to put up with his bad temper. If it wasn't for the money, I'd give my notice in tomorrow."

She spoke as if Holt was still alive, Rudd thought. The resentment she expressed was evidently of long standing, not that Drewett seemed moved by it.

"We could do worse" was his only comment.

"*You* might think that," she retorted, "but what about me?"

Interested though Rudd was by this exchange between husband and wife, which told him a great deal, not only about their own relationship but about Mrs. Drewett's with her dead employer, there was another which intrigued him more.

"About Mrs. Chilton," he put in. "How close was she to Mr. Holt? Just an old friend, or something more?"

But the outburst was over and Mrs. Drewett subsided into the more sullen mood of the servant who, while knowing her place, still resents it.

"I couldn't say, sir. You'd better ask her. All I know is Mr. Holt said she might be staying the night sometimes and would I see a bedroom was made ready for her." She stopped short, frightened that she had said too much.

"I see," Rudd said easily. He had heard enough and, getting to his feet, he went in search of Boyce, whom he found in Rex Holt's room, supervising the plain-clothes men who were busy fingerprinting and examining it.

As he entered, Boyce said, "I got hold of Mr. Gilham, Holt's solicitor. He's willing to see you any time you like. I said you'd ring back."

"I'll do that later," Rudd replied. "I want to get the body moved first. You've finished with it?" he added, addressing Wylie.

"Yes, sir," Wylie replied.

"Then get it organised, Tom."

When Boyce left to carry out his orders, Rudd lingered at the open French windows, gathering up his impressions before joining the others outside.

Despite his warning to Boyce not to jump to conclusions, he felt there were a few assumptions he could make with some degree of certainty. Firstly, Rex Holt had been ready for bed, an impression he had received when he had first examined the body. Not only that, but he had taken a bath as well, which, in conjunction with Mrs. Drewett's statement regarding Holt's nightly routine, led the chief inspector to assume that the murder had taken place between ten and half past the previous night. On the basis of that evidence, the time shown on the watch, eight minutes past ten, could be taken therefore as a guide to the timing of the murder although Rudd was prepared to keep an open mind on this particular point. It seemed odd to him that Holt should be wearing it. Wouldn't he have taken it off before he had his bath? And, that being the case, why had he put it on again? Or had the murderer replaced it on his wrist before deliberately smashing it?

Secondly, it seemed more than likely, as robbery did not appear to be a motive and there was no sign of a struggle inside the room, that Rex Holt had willingly accompanied his murderer out onto the terrace, where he had then been struck down.

And if that assumption were correct, it narrowed the field of suspects down to those within Holt's personal acquaintanceship whether family, friends or previous employees.

It was a damned nuisance, therefore, that the two people closest to the dead man, his son and the woman whom Rudd guessed was probably his mistress, were unavailable for immediate interview.

As he stood there, Rex Holt's body was carried past him along the terrace, tucked neatly into its bag and zipped shut, like so much dry-cleaning, and was borne away to the front of the house, where the ambulance awaited its arrival.

CHAPTER SEVEN

Biddy took the news well, although Martin saw her mouth tremble. He made her sit down on one of the low armchairs, watching her face and thinking that in all the years he had known her he had never seen her cry, not even when his mother died. She sat obediently, hands clasped in her lap, as if she were a guest in someone else's house.

"I'll make some tea," Martin said, guessing she would probably prefer to be alone.

When he returned to the little sitting-room, Biddy was on her feet in front of the sideboard, in the act, it seemed, of shutting the lid of a small box which stood on top of it and which, as a child, he had always referred to as her treasure chest. It was made of sandalwood and had given off, he remembered, a spicy scent whenever it was opened.

As he entered, she turned back to her chair and sat down again.

"Were you looking for something?" he asked, setting the tea-tray down on the brass table.

"It'll wait till later," she told him. Her expression was inscrutable but Martin had the same impression he had felt the previous day that there was something on her mind.

Whatever it was, she did not refer to it. Instead, she told him, as he lifted the jug, "Not too much milk for me."

"I can't stay long, Biddy," Martin explained, handing her the cup. "The police will want to talk to me; not that I can tell them much. But I'll try to call back as soon as I can to let you know what's happening."

"Don't you worry yourself about me, my lad," Biddy replied. "You've got enough to worry about. I'll be all right." She paused to sip her tea before adding, "I shall miss him."

She meant his father, Martin realised, and he asked, "Did he come to see you often?"

"Once a week generally. He'd get that man of his, Drewett, to stop by when he was driving into Welham."

The news surprised Martin. He knew his father visited Biddy but had not guessed it was on so regular a basis.

Her next remark was more in keeping with his accustomed image.

"Never stayed long, mind you. Always in a hurry. Had to get to the bank or the solicitor's although, since his stroke, he used to stay on a bit longer. He seemed to want to talk about the time we were living in Welham before he moved out here. You were only a little boy then. I don't know if you remember."

"Yes, I do," Martin replied.

It was years since he had thought about those days and the recollections of them were scattered. He could recall only dimly the tall, narrow house, demolished years ago to enlarge the business premises, which had stood near the gates leading into the yard, of being lifted up by his father to look down on the parked lorries, each blazoned with the name HOLT; of a walled garden and an upstairs room, with a rocking-horse in it, where he used to play.

Biddy set down her cup with a purposeful air, as if coming to a decision.

"I think I ought to tell you," she announced, "that your father paid for this cottage when I retired. He made me promise I'd say nothing, but now he's dead, I don't feel I'm bound any more to hold my tongue. So now you know."

She was sitting very upright, looking straight into his eyes.

It was the second time that morning that someone had made a similar statement regarding their obligation to Rex Holt and his money; first Bea, and now Biddy. This time Martin managed the situation better. Taking one of her hands in his, he said, "I'm glad. I would have done the same in his place."

"Thank you," she said simply. "I know you would."

He patted her hand and then rose to his feet.

"I ought to go. They may be looking for me."

Biddy went with him to the door.

"You'll come and tell me yourself if they find out anything?" she asked. "I'd rather hear it from you."

"Of course," he assured her quickly. "But, as I told you, I think there's been a dreadful mistake. He must have fallen. There's no other explanation."

"Don't be too sure of that," Biddy warned him.

She would say nothing more. Martin could tell that by the set of her lips and, as he bent down to kiss her cheek, he found himself wondering at her conviction. The simple statement seemed to express a knowledge of human nature which summed up a lifetime's experience.

He had intended going straight back to the Hall but a reluctance to return there and a desire to put things right with Bea made him change his mind and he drove instead into the village.

Mill Lane was a narrow turning, only wide enough to take a single car, so he parked in front of the mill itself, drawing off the road onto the broad cobbled forecourt, where once the grain-carts had waited to be unloaded. The hoist was still there, its wooden beam jutting out of the brick-and-flint façade above the pair of doors which opened into the granary itself.

He remembered being taken there as a boy when it was still a working mill and tramping behind his father up flights of wooden steps, the air dusty with flying grains of flour and loud with the sound of heavy machinery and the great, slow-turning millstones.

After the death of Langley, the miller, the place had been run as a pottery for many years. But, eighteen months before, that, too, had closed down and the building was now empty, the door padlocked and the windows covered with great crosses of wood.

Glancing up at it as he locked the car door, he thought what a pity it was no one had tried to resurrect the place. It had a simple beauty which he liked. In a few years it would be a ruin.

Bea's house was at the bottom of the lane where it ended with a stile, beyond which a grassy track led down through the water-meadows towards the river, long familiar to him. As a boy, he had come this way to go fishing along the bank.

It was a small, detached house, its prim and rather formal façade softened by a wisteria whose large, decorative leaves hung down over the brickwork. Bea's Renault, together with Hester's Metro, were parked in the driveway that ran alongside the house, suggesting both women were at home.

As he walked up the path to the front door, Martin hoped Bea would answer it. He had no wish to encounter the daughter for a second time. But it was Hester who opened it, wearing jeans and a striped T-shirt, her hair tied back in a red-spotted scarf. Seeing it was he on the doorstep, she said unsmilingly, "What do you want?"

"I'd like to speak to Bea if I may," he replied with the same curtness.

Beyond her, he could see a long hall, littered with rolls of carpet and pictures propped up against the walls.

"You can't," she retorted. "I've given her a tranquillizer and she's lying down."

It was quite clear that she blamed him entirely for her mother's indisposition and he mumbled awkwardly, "I'm sorry about that."

He was about to add that he would call again later and then thought,

Why the hell should I? He had no intention of explaining himself to Bea's daughter.

Before he had time even to turn away, she had slammed the door shut on him.

Upstairs, Bea heard the voices and the front door bang and called out to Hester.

"Who was it?" she asked as her daughter entered the bedroom.

"Martin Holt," Hester replied.

"What did he want?"

"I don't know," Hester sounded dismissive. "Anyway, he's gone now."

Bea was lying propped up on pillows on the bed. The windows were open and the curtains drawn to keep out the sun but even so the room was stiflingly hot.

The unaccustomed heat and the disorder in the room—her clothes hanging on a temporary rail, a box of bedding still not unpacked—added to the dream-like confusion which the tranquillizer had induced in her.

Any moment, she would wake up, she thought, and find none of it was real. Even Rex's death.

In the meantime, she lay there, so heavy she felt she must sink like a stone into the mattress, her arms and legs as huge and as inert as tree-trunks.

"I wish . . ." she began.

She meant to say that she wished she could sleep and then wake to find it was all over, Rex still alive, the day's events wiped clean away. But it seemed too foolish. She was not sure either how Hester would respond. At times, she was intimidated by her daughter's independence. She seemed to need nothing from her any more.

Instead, she said, "I wish now I hadn't said anything to you about him."

"Why?" Hester asked.

"I don't know," Bea moved her head restlessly on the pillows, unable to concentrate properly even on her thoughts.

When she had returned to the garden, after having been upstairs with Martin searching through the bureau, and had broken down in front of Hester, it hadn't only been his silence over her remark regarding Rex's will which had distressed her although she had used it as the reason for explaining her sudden tears. God knows why. It had been the simplest to put into words perhaps.

The rest—her letters to him, which she had put away in her handbag and which symbolised for her more than anything else that everything was over, that he was gone and she was now alone—had been too close to her heart to find an adequate expression.

What she hadn't expected was the force of Hester's reaction.

Looking up at the windows, she had said furiously, "Damn him! Why shouldn't Rex leave you some of his money, for God's sake! You'd put up with him for all those years."

Bea hadn't known what to say in reply.

Put up with him?

The phrase, spoken in anger, had told her too much about Hester's real feelings both towards Rex and to her own relationship with him.

She had given way to real grief then, a descent into an abyss of emotion which was close to madness. Shaking, incoherent, the tears washing out of her, she had allowed Hester to take her home.

Some of the shame she had felt at the time still lingered and she turned her head away, feeling tears gathering again behind her lids although there was no more grief to express, only an overwhelming exhaustion.

Hester said, "I'm going to give you another tranquillizer, Mother. You must sleep."

"I don't want any more," she replied.

All the same, she took the tablet obediently, not meeting her daughter's eyes.

And it was better, she thought, when Hester had left the room and she felt the heavy drowsiness begin to spread through her body, to accept the oblivion in which loneliness and grief and regret had no more power to hurt her.

Rudd was squatting down, hands on knees to keep his balance, inspecting a stone which one of his men, escorting the body to the ambulance, had drawn his attention to, when a uniformed PC brought him the information that Martin Holt had returned.

The chief inspector merely grunted in reply.

None of the small semicircle of men surrounding him showed much interest either, their attention, like Rudd's, being centred on the stone, or rather the flint, which nestled a little coyly and incongruously in the centre of the clump of hypericum growing along the edge of the path.

The flint was of a size to fit naturally into the palm of a hand and was of an irregular but rounded shape, pitted with tiny clusters of crystals which winked and glittered in the strong sunlight. And with something else as well.

It might have been some important archaeological find for the attention it was receiving; a Stone Age implement, which indeed, as Rudd realised, it could very well have been. As a weapon, it was eminently handy for cracking a marrow-bone. Or a man's skull, for that matter.

In contrast to it, the yellow flowers of the hypericum seemed fragilly beautiful, the cups of petals shining as if they had been freshly lacquered.

At the same time, Rudd was aware, more infuriatingly, of the sun on the back of his neck and the shoes of the men who awaited his conclusion, shifting a little impatiently on the gravel just within his line of vision.

He bent lower, his nose almost touching the flowers, eyes intent on one facet of the flint on which the shining blobs and filaments were clustered.

Blood, human hair and something else which could be flesh, although he preferred not to make too precise an identification, came into closer focus.

Standing up and hearing his knees crack as he did so, he said, "I think we've found it. Boyce, I want some of the men searching the rose garden to go over the whole of this path down as far as the terrace."

While McCullum photographed the stone *in situ* and Wylie and Kyle measured the distance from its position to the chalked outline on the York paving stones, which was all that remained to indicate where Rex Holt's body had been lying, Rudd made his own calculations.

The sunken garden was roughly thirty yards away from the point where the stone lay on the edge of the gravelled path which led from the terrace round the side of the house to join the main drive.

If he were right and he had found the murder weapon, he could therefore plot the route the murderer had taken. Having killed Rex Holt, he, or she, had walked to the front of the house, dropping the stone on route.

It therefore knocked on the head—an unfortunate phrase to use, Rudd realised, considering the circumstances—Boyce's theory that the murderer had finished off his victim by cracking the side of his head down on the bottom of the terrace steps because he had thrown away the murder weapon.

He couldn't have done so. The angle was too acute. No one, not even a Test cricketer, could have lobbed a stone from the terrace round the corner of the house to its resting place beside the path.

And that opened up a whole new field of speculation through which, he realised, he would have to pick his way carefully.

Why drop it there? Why not simply chuck it away at the scene of the crime? A good, hefty throw would have landed it anywhere in the rose garden or even beyond it in the surrounding shrubbery. Or, if hiding it was his motive, why hadn't he taken it away with him? He could have dropped it miles from the scene of the murder.

It was a series of questions he put to Boyce, who merely shrugged.

"God knows. I sometimes think I'll never understand what goes on in the mind of a murderer. By the way, don't forget Martin Holt's here. Are you going to interview him?"

The juxtaposition of the two remarks could have been fortuitous but, as Rudd returned to the house, accompanied by Boyce, he could not help feeling that the sergeant's mental processes were only too easy to follow.

They found Martin Holt walking aimlessly about the garden in the front of the house. Noticing the chairs and table set out on the shady side on a small lawn, Rudd suggested it as the place to hold the interview, a setting which had its own incongruity, he decided, as the three of them sat down on canvas chairs round an inlaid rosewood table, placed on the grass against the background of high yew hedges and garden statuary.

It might, he thought, be a scene from Alice in Wonderland or from the Swedish film to which he had accompanied Marion Greave the week before at the film club of which she was a member, and in which the characters had acted out some bewildering symbolic drama in a similar setting.

He began with his own piece of ritual, expressing regret at the death of Martin Holt's father, for which Holt thanked him briefly.

There was a watchful air about the man even though he had taken up a relaxed position on one of the garden chairs.

Pose, the chief inspector decided, noticing the alert expression in Holt's eyes. He was clearly on his guard and was too intelligent to be easily rattled.

"I'm afraid," Rudd continued, his own expression bland, "that your father's death wasn't an accident. We have reason to believe it was murder."

"So the inspector from Welham informed me," Martin Holt replied. "It seems incredible. How did it happen? Did he surprise someone trying to break into the house?"

For the first time, he showed a positive reaction, leaning forwards in his chair, his eyes on Rudd's face, eager to pick up his response.

"I don't think that's likely," Rudd replied. "Nothing's been stolen and there's no sign of a break-in or a struggle. On the contrary, there seems to be evidence that your father may have known his murderer. For that reason, Mr. Holt, I'm afraid I shall have to interview everyone who was connected with him, such as yourself, if only to eliminate each person from the inquiry—"

"Are you suggesting I might have killed my own father?" Martin Holt interrupted, "It's absurd! You can't be serious!"

Rudd paused deliberately before replying. In his time, he had witnessed the reactions of many suspects, ranging from silence to physical violence. Holt's was interesting. With its overtones of ironic incredulity, it seemed genuine.

"I'm suggesting nothing," he said quietly. "I'm simply here to ask questions."

Martin Holt sat back. The chief inspector's calm, low-key response had a deflationary effect which he suspected was employed in order to eliminate all personality. To the shock at Rudd's comments regarding his father's death and his own possible part in it was added a further mental adjustment to the man himself. At their first encounter, Martin had not been impressed by the stocky, untidy figure of the chief inspector nor the sergeant who accompanied him. With his tall bulk and heavy shoulders, he had seemed nothing more than a hanger-on.

Now, seated opposite the pair of them, he was aware of their professionalism; the sergeant's listening attitude, pen poised over notebook, and, more alarmingly, Rudd's air of quiet authority, and he realised that, although he had been on his guard as soon as the interview began, for quite what reason even he himself wasn't sure except it had become a habit never to relax whenever he was at his father's house, he had been totally unprepared for the confrontation and it took him several moments to absorb what Rudd was saying.

". . . go over yesterday's events," the chief inspector concluded.

Martin Holt made an effort to rouse himself.

"Yesterday?"

"I believe you were here on a visit?"

"Yes, I was. My father had asked me to lunch."

"To meet Mrs. Chilton?" Rudd suggested amiably.

Martin hesitated. He had no intention of explaining in detail the cross-currents of emotion which had run below the surface and he merely replied, "Yes, that's correct."

Aware of Holt's reticence, Rudd asked, "How well do you know her?"

"Hardly at all. I had met her only once before, years ago."

"I believe she was an old friend of your father?"

Again there was a slight hesitation before Martin Holt said simply, "Yes."

"And that was all?"

"I think you'd better ask Mrs. Chilton that question," Martin Holt replied.

"Indeed I will," Rudd said cheerfully. "About the lunch party yesterday, I believe you left early?"

It would be useless trying to deny it, Martin thought. Rudd had already got hold of the information, probably from Mrs. Drewett. He also felt an inexplicable urge to tell the truth. His father was dead—murdered by someone who had intended his death—and the time for pretence was over. He felt he owed him that much.

"Yes, I left early," he replied. "There was a disagreement, as there usually was whenever my father and I met. That was why I rarely visited him. The dispute yesterday was about my business. I run a smallholding about twenty miles away. My father made some comment about the limited capital behind it, which I thought had nothing to do with him, so I left."

"You're financially independent of him?" Rudd asked.

"I've never asked him for a penny nor taken one," Martin Holt replied. There was a proud lift to his head as he spoke.

"But I believe," Rudd said, watching his face closely, "that your father gave you five thousand pounds. At least, we've found a cheque stub made out to you for that amount, dated yesterday."

Martin was silent. In the turmoil of the day's events, he had forgotten about the cheque. Now, taking it from his pocket, he laid it on the table in front of the chief inspector.

"It arrived this morning by post. The letter that came with it is at home if you want to read it. You'll see that my father wrote the cheque without any prompting from me. It was partly Bea's idea that he send it."

"Bea?"

"Mrs. Chilton."

"She suggested your father send the money?"

"So it would seem."

Boyce raised his head from his notebook.

"Did you intend keeping the money, Mr. Holt?"

"Yes." Martin answered without any hesitation. "I felt my father was trying to apologise for what happened yesterday and I didn't want to turn it down for that reason. If I had, it would have also meant refusing to accept his friendship with Mrs. Chilton."

"That was explicit in the letter?" Rudd asked, noticing the faint ironic emphasis on the word "friendship."

"Not in so many words," Holt replied. "But it was implied. Lastly, I needed the money. So I decided that, if my father was in a reasonable mood when I rang this morning, I'd thank him and accept the cheque."

"That's why you telephoned him?" Rudd seemed pleased to have this small point cleared up.

"Yes. Instead I spoke to Drewett, who told me my father was dead."

"You said you needed the money," Rudd continued, picking up the remark Martin Holt had made earlier. Head cocked, he waited for Holt's reply.

"Yes," he said simply. "In fact, I'd considered asking my father for a loan yesterday, but we quarrelled before I could do so. The cheque was therefore very welcome. I wanted the money for some urgent repairs."

"You're very frank, Mr. Holt." Rudd remarked. He made the comment deliberately in order to see what response it provoked in Martin Holt, who replied with the same ironic expression, "I thought that was the purpose of this interview—to get at the truth."

Rudd nodded, as if acknowledging the validity of the remark before deciding to press home the point.

If Holt was so intent on frankness, he thought, let's see what he makes of this next question.

"You would inherit quite a large sum of money under your father's will, I assume?"

So it had come at last, Martin thought. He had been expecting it. Indeed, the question of his inheritance had run like a dark theme not only through today's events but yesterday's as well. Biddy had spoken of it. So had Bea. Even Charlie had referred to it.

"Yes, I suppose I would," he replied.

"Do you know how much?"

"If you mean, do I know the contents of my father's will, no, I don't. I should imagine it's a large amount. After all, he was a rich man."

There was a note of bitterness in his voice as he spoke which the chief inspector found surprising, as if Holt resented his father's wealth, or rather disdained it. He decided to leave it there. The question of Holt's inheritance was a subject he intended returning to at a later date after he had seen Rex Holt's solicitor and had established just how much the son stood to gain by his father's death.

Now, nodding briefly to Boyce to take up the questioning, he sat back, intent on observing Martin Holt's reactions as the sergeant took him through an account of his movements the previous evening.

The same frankness which Martin Holt had shown over the question of the cheque and his father's will was also evident in his answers to Boyce's questions.

How far it was the candour of an innocent man, however, was debatable. Holt did not possess that kind of artlessness, Rudd concluded. He had a much more complex personality, quite capable of using the truth for his own hidden reasons.

Was he trying to divert suspicion from himself? He was too intelligent not to realise he must be one of the chief suspects in the case. The apparent truthfulness could be nothing more than an attempt to disarm that suspicion. Rudd wasn't sure.

Holt had motive, as he himself had implied. He was in need of money and stood to inherit a fortune at his father's death.

And, moreover, he had no alibi, as the account he was giving to Boyce established.

He made no attempt to hide this fact. Listening to it, Rudd could tell by Holt's expression that the man realised this also. There was an almost defiant air about him. He had returned home, done his accounts and then made a start on picking the tomato crop for the following day, finishing at about a quarter to eleven. He had then had a late supper and gone to bed.

"No," he replied to Boyce's question, "there were no witnesses. I was alone for the whole evening."

Rudd felt obliged to put in a question of his own, if only to help the man out.

"Did you make any phone calls or receive any?"

Holt's upper lip lifted in amusement.

"My phone was out of order, chief inspector. I reported it yesterday after I arrived here. The line was still dead this morning. That's why I had to call the house from a phone box. Charlie, the man who helps me at the smallholding, said there was a branch across the line."

"I see," Rudd replied, his face expressionless.

It was Martin Holt who remarked, with the same ironic expression, "So it would seem I had the opportunity to kill my father, wouldn't it? I suppose it's a waste of time stating that I didn't murder him? We often quarrelled but at no point have I ever wished him dead."

His tone of voice and expression had taken on the same disdainful air which he had assumed when speaking of his father's will and Rudd realised that Holt was a proud man for whom any attempt to explain or excuse himself would not come easily.

In view of this, Rudd was reluctant to ask the question he had been saving until last with the intention of rounding off the interview with a body blow. But it had to be raised.

"I believe you removed some papers this morning from your father's bureau?" he said.

Holt showed no sign of being shaken, but rather seemed to accept the question as inevitable. Putting his hand into his jacket pocket, which he had hung on the back of his chair, he took out a small bundle of papers and laid them on the table.

"I took these. They're nothing to do with my father. They belonged to my mother. They're letters written to her by a man called Edward Voyte, a poet, who was shot down in the Battle of Britain. My mother was in love with him before she married my father. You'll find a photograph of Voyte in with them and a volume of his poems."

For the second time during the interview, Martin Holt showed some sign of reaction.

"My father had taken it on himself to show the letters to an American, Lawrence Hurst, who photocopied the poems they contained and was going to use them in a book he's writing about Edward Voyte. I was very angry about this. They were private and shouldn't have been seen by anyone outside the family. That was why I took them. They have nothing to do with my father's estate and I didn't see why they should be handed over to the solicitor along with all his other papers."

"Lawrence Hurst was the visitor who called yesterday?" Rudd asked.

"That's right. He was here when I arrived. I gather he's over in England researching for his book on Voyte."

"Do you happen to know where he's staying?"

"Yes, as a matter of fact, I do. He's putting up at the Red Lion in Welham. I was held up in the traffic going home yesterday when he came up to me in the car and invited me to have a drink with him, which I did. He wanted to apologise for what had happened. He had no idea Voyte's letters would start off a family row."

Rudd said, "I'm afraid I'm going to have to take them, Mr. Holt, even though they are private. I'll return them to you as soon as I can."

As he spoke, he saw Kyle approach and stand expectantly at the edge of the lawn as if trying to attract his attention. Rising to his feet and pocketing the papers, he added, "I have no further questions for the moment. You can leave when you like but make you sure you give your address and the key of the bureau to my sergeant before you do."

He walked away without a backward glance towards the DC, who said excitedly, "We've found something, sir, that I think you ought to look at."

The something turned out to be a few dark green woollen threads, caught on the branch of a climbing rose which grew at the corner of the house close to the path where the stone had been discovered. They hung between the leaves at the height of a man's arm, Rudd estimated, and could have been plucked from a jacket sleeve as someone brushed against it on his way along the terrace from the rose garden.

"Get those packed up," he told Wylie. "I want forensic to examine them."

He should have felt pleased at the discovery of this evidence but, as he watched Wylie picking them off carefully with a pair of tweezers and transferring them to a plastic bag, he had the uneasy feeling that they had turned up just a little too conveniently in the hunt for the identity of Rex Holt's murderer.

CHAPTER EIGHT

Boyce said, "If we can prove those threads came from one of Holt's jackets, then we've got an open-and-shut case against him. You haven't asked him yet if he owns a dark green coat, have you?"

"No," said Rudd, "and I don't intend to. That can wait until we interview him again and next time we'll make it on his own ground. I want to see what sort of a set-up he has. Besides, even if we can prove the threads came from a jacket belonging to him, it doesn't necessarily follow he murdered his father. He could have caught his sleeve on that bush yesterday afternoon when he was here having lunch."

They were in the car, heading down the drive of Barnsfield Hall on their way to interview Trimmer and Mrs. Chilton.

Rudd would have preferred to be silent. The case disturbed him. The discovery—first of the murder weapon, lying so snugly at the side of the path, and now the threads caught on the rose at the corner of the house—still caused him disquiet, quite why he wasn't sure and, until he had rationalised the feeling, he would rather not have discussed the case with Boyce.

Trimmer lived in a small, modern bungalow, squatting at the end of a long expanse of open lawn, and called, quite inappropriately, Woodlands. The pretentiousness of the name was further compounded by the enormous stone urns filled with geraniums which flanked the tiny porch and the quantity of white-painted wrought iron about the place in the shape of double drive-gates and an ornamental screen at the side of the house with an arched entrance through which Reggie Trimmer emerged before the chief inspector even had time to ring the front doorbell.

"I thought I heard a car," he remarked. "What can I do for you?"

"I'm Detective Chief Inspector Rudd," Rudd replied, producing his official ID. "And this is my detective sergeant, Boyce."

"Police?" Trimmer seemed curious rather than alarmed, his protuberant pale eyes glancing inquisitively at the pair of them.

"I'm making inquiries into a sudden death at Barnsfield Hall," Rudd continued, keeping the information deliberately vague.

Trimmer's reaction was interesting.

"Good God! Not Rex?" he said immediately.

Now why should he jump to that conclusion? Rudd thought.

"I'm afraid so," he replied.

"God, how awful. I can't believe it! Look, come round to the patio, Chief Inspector. I need a drink."

He preceded them through the archway to the back of the house, where a table and chairs had been set out on a narrow paved area overlooking a garden of lawn and rose-beds; a scaled-down version of the grounds of Barnsfield Hall, Rudd decided, noticing the tubs of flowers and the tiny pond from the centre of which a single jet of water shot straight up into the air.

Still expressing his horror and disbelief, Reggie Trimmer helped himself liberally to a bottle of whisky which stood on the table.

"It seems impossible! Rex dead? How absolutely appalling!"

It was a good effort on Trimmer's part although not entirely convincing. The protestations were just a little too glib to be entirely sincere. Rudd let him run on as he waited for the inevitable question.

"How did it happen?"

"He fell down the terrace steps last night," Rudd replied, shaking his head as Trimmer, having downed one large whisky, held up the bottle in the chief inspector's direction before refilling his own glass. "The circumstances of his death are not entirely clear, which is why we're interested in establishing what Mr. Holt was doing earlier in the day."

Anyone with a modicum of intelligence would have seen the dubiousness of this explanation. But Trimmer was more anxious about the effect he was making on Rudd and the sergeant than the speciousness of the chief inspector's remarks.

"Of course! Of course! Anything I can do to help," he said expansively, seating himself, glass in one hand, and waving them towards the chairs with the other.

"I believe you had lunch with him yesterday," Rudd continued as he and Boyce sat down.

"That's correct."

"At which Martin Holt and Mrs. Chilton were also present?"

"On the button again, Chief Inspector." The expressions of shock had been replaced by a waggish air, as if Trimmer saw the interview as an opportunity for a witty exchange between the pair of them. Leaning forwards confidentially, he continued, "It was intended as a little celebration to mark Bea's arrival in the village—Mrs. Chilton, that is."

With some witnesses like Trimmer, there was almost no need for the chief inspector to ask any direct questions. An interested look, an encouraging nod of the head was enough to set them going, in the same way that a mechanical toy, once wound up, can be kept in motion by the occasional nudge.

Rudd raised his eyebrows inquiringly.

"Old friend of Rex's," Trimmer explained. "Known her for years. Used to visit her in London. Enough said?" He lifted his glass to drink, looking knowingly at Rudd over the rim. "Not that it's any of my business," he continued, setting down the glass, "but I could tell which way the wind was blowing yesterday. Only took half an eye." He pulled a face, shaking his head at the same time. "Uncomfortable atmosphere. But what could you expect? Martin wasn't going to take too kindly to her. Rex should have realised that. Did my best to keep the chat going. Social responsibility, you know. But it was hard work. Then this argument broke out. Damned unpleasant."

"What about?" Rudd asked. He had caught the main drift of Trimmer's inconsequential remarks but this point needed clarifying.

"About Martin's business. You know he quarrelled with his father and set up on his own? Years ago, mind you. Not that Rex had forgiven him. Shouldn't speak ill of the dead, I know, but there you are. Rex could be a hard man at times. Stubborn. Didn't like to be crossed. Made for ill feeling all round. Not the first time either. I've heard them arguing on more than one occasion. Usually about business, Rex giving advice and Martin not wanting to hear it. Like that yesterday. So we left."

"What time was this?" Boyce put in.

Trimmer looked across at him, aware for the first time of the notebook open on the table in front of the sergeant. His expression immediately became wary.

"About half past three. We'd sat on after lunch was finished. Martin got up to leave and Rex suggested he gave me a lift home. Bloody rude, I thought. I'd expected to stay longer."

"Did you call back at the Hall later that day?" Rudd asked casually.

"No I damned well didn't! It was up to Rex to get in touch with me. Bloody rude!" Trimmer repeated. Evidently, the sudden dismissal still rankled. "Besides," he continued with another look and a wink, "I thought it better to leave the love-birds on their own. Didn't like to intrude."

"So what did you do yesterday evening?"

For the first time, Trimmer seemed aware of the significance of the questioning.

"Me? What have I got to do with it? I thought you were asking what Rex had got up to."

"If you would just answer the question, Mr. Trimmer," Rudd persisted, his voice bland and rather bored.

"I object, Chief Inspector. I have my rights."

Even though angry, Trimmer still looked ridiculous, his little moustache rigid with indignation.

"Of course," Rudd agreed, "although in any serious investigation we like to feel we have the full co-operation of any potential witnesses. It helps if we're not obstructed in our inquiries."

As he had intended, the veiled threat behind the remark and the deliberate use of pompous officialese deflated Trimmer like the elderly windbag he was.

"I didn't mean to be obstructive," he protested. "I simply didn't see the point."

Boyce added his own weight, pen poised, expression lugubrious.

"Your movements yesterday evening, Mr. Trimmer," he insisted.

Rudd sat back, letting the sergeant take over the questioning, amused at the faint air of controlled menace Boyce was able to exude on such occasions.

"I was here," Trimmer replied, looking flustered.

"Alone?"

"Yes. I sat in the garden reading the newspaper, then I made myself a bite to eat, had a few drinks and watched television."

"No witnesses?"

"Witnesses!"

Trimmer rolled his eyes in Rudd's direction, seeking help, but the chief inspector merely repeated the sergeant's words. "Yes, Mr. Trimmer. Witnesses. Any phone calls, visitors, that sort of thing."

Trimmer refilled his glass, the neck of the bottle rattling against the rim.

"No, I was quite alone," he replied, avoiding their eyes.

Rudd waited until he had put down the glass before producing his final thrust. Taking the IOU's from his pocket, he laid them down on the table.

"I believe these are yours," he remarked.

Trimmer made no attempt to touch them although, from his expression, Rudd could tell that the man recognised them.

"A thousand pounds?" the chief inspector continued, his tone full of gentle inquiry.

"It was just a loan," Trimmer said quickly, eager to explain although, by now fairly drunk, he had difficulty in enunciating all the words. "I intended paying Rex back. Got into a spot of difficulty, you see, backing the fillies. Damned fool, but there you are. Learned my lesson. Rex helped me out. Good friend, Rex. One of the best. God, I shall miss him! Dreadful shock!"

They had come full circle and Rudd rose to leave. As they walked away, they could hear Trimmer's voice still raised in tipsy protestation behind them.

"Place won't be the same without him. Damned shame! Poor old Rex!"

"What do you think?" Rudd asked as they got into the car.

"Me?"

Boyce seemed as surprised as Trimmer.

"A potential murderer?" Rudd hinted, wondering how far Boyce could be tempted.

The sergeant looked wary.

"Could be," he agreed dubiously. "No alibi."

"And he has a motive," the chief inspector pointed out wickedly. "A thousand pounds would be a lot of money to a man like Trimmer. Supposing Rex Holt was insisting he paid it back?"

Boyce looked at him sideways, scenting a trap.

"All right," he conceded. "I agree Trimmer can't be left off the list, but my money's still on the son."

"You shouldn't bet," Rudd admonished him. "Look what problems it got Trimmer into. Besides, we haven't seen all the runners yet. There's Mrs. Chilton still to come. Always inspect the field first before parting with your money."

The door was opened to them by a young woman, Mrs. Chilton's daughter, Hester, as she explained, leading the way into a room at the back of the house.

Seeing her, Rudd felt a familiar lurch to his heart. She reminded him of Marion Greave. She was younger, of course, but had the same dark hair and positive, challenging air about her, which in Hester Chilton's case was more forceful and intimidating.

She certainly had no hesitation about making her feelings quite apparent.

"If you must interview my mother," she said, addressing Rudd, "then I insist on being present. She's not yet recovered from the shock. I also insist on reserving the right to break off the interview if I consider she's getting overtired or too distressed."

The clipped tone of her voice and the direct manner in which she faced the chief inspector, head held high, hands thrust deep into the pockets of her jeans, suggested that she was used to authority and was not at all impressed either by the presence of the two policemen or by Rudd's rank.

"Very well," Rudd agreed, thinking that whatever man took her on would have his hands full.

Boyce's reaction was more succinct.

"Crikey!" he remarked under his breath as the door closed behind her.

Rudd was aware of a gentler and more feminine side to her nature as she escorted her mother into the room, perching herself on the arm of her mother's chair and taking her hand in hers.

Rudd could understand her solicitude. Mrs. Chilton looked exhausted, the pallor of her face accentuating the large, dark eyes, which looked at him without expression and seemed to dominate her features.

Rudd began quietly, taking her through the events of the previous day step by step, demanding nothing from her except a factual account, first of the lunch party, about which he already had statements from Martin Holt and Trimmer.

"I believe it ended at half past three when Martin Holt left?" he asked.

"Yes," Mrs. Chilton agreed and said nothing more.

Rudd decided to leave the subject there for the time being.

"And afterwards?" he prompted.

"We walked in the garden for a short time," Mrs. Chilton continued. "Then we went into the house. Rex wanted to send a cheque to Martin. He wrote it out together with a letter which he gave to Drewett to post in Welham. We then had tea on the terrace and sat out there talking. Later we had supper, which Mrs. Drewett had left in the kitchen as she and her husband had gone off duty. I returned the tray to the kitchen at about nine o'clock and left shortly afterwards."

The account was recited in a flat, dull voice, as if she were talking of events which had happened a long time ago and to another person.

"You can verify the time, Miss Chilton?" Rudd asked, turning to the daughter. Before she could speak, Mrs. Chilton interrupted. "No, she can't, Chief Inspector. Hester didn't arrive until soon after eleven o'clock. I left Rex's early in order to have a meal ready for her when she came."

"So you were alone in the house between, let's say, ten past nine and just after eleven?" Rudd asked. He had to have this point verified.

"Yes," she replied simply.

"Did you receive any visitors or phone calls?"

Hester Chilton broke in, her voice sharp.

"Why are you checking up on my mother? Do you suppose she had anything to do with Rex's death?"

"I have to ask these questions, Miss Chilton," Rudd began with an apologetic air, intended more for Mrs. Chilton's sake than her daughter's.

It was Mrs. Chilton who calmed down the situation.

"Please, Hester," she protested quietly. "The chief inspector's right.

He has to find out how Rex died." Turning to Rudd, she continued, "No, I didn't have any visitors or phone calls. I was quite alone until Hester arrived."

"What about Mr. Holt? Did he say whether he was expecting anyone to visit him yesterday evening?"

"No. Before I left, he said he would get ready for bed and watch the ten o'clock news on television. He was sitting in the chair by the French windows, which he told me to leave open." Her mouth trembled as she spoke, as if this last image she had of him in her mind remained too clear and poignant.

Across the room, Boyce came to the end of a page in his notebook and turned to the next. The sharp rustle of paper seemed to express what he and Rudd were both thinking: no alibi.

"To return to the lunch party," Rudd continued. "I understand the son, Martin Holt, left early?"

"Yes, he did," Mrs. Chilton replied. "He was anxious to get home. I believe he had a lot to do on the smallholding."

"Wasn't there some disagreement with his father?" Rudd persisted, noticing her attempt to cover up the real reason for Martin Holt's sudden departure and wondering what this signified regarding her attitude to Rex Holt's son.

Bea hesitated. The first part of the interview was over, she realised, and they were now approaching the more difficult area of relationships. She felt too exhausted to find the words to explain them. She was not even sure that she understood them herself properly. Although she was certain of her love for Rex, her feelings towards Martin were too complex and ambiguous. As for the relationship between Rex and his son, how could she attempt to describe in a few sentences that combination of affection, pride, exasperation and guilt which made up the strange, mutual bond between them?

"There was no obvious quarrel," she replied. "Martin and his father were very similar in many ways and this caused tension between them. Rex liked giving advice. Martin wasn't in the mood to take it. That was all."

The explanation in no way approximated the atmosphere which had surrounded the lunch party. It was more complex than that; much subtler, with more left unsaid than had been spoken aloud. But she could think of no other way in which to describe it.

"Tension?" Rudd picked up the word. "I'm sorry to have to ask this, Mrs. Chilton, but I need to understand Martin Holt's reaction to your presence at the lunch party yesterday. Was that any cause of the dispute between Rex Holt and his son?"

Bea threw back her head in a challenging gesture which was very like her daughter's.

"If you mean, did Martin disapprove of my relationship with Rex, then I suggest you ask Martin himself. I'm not competent to judge his feelings."

As Bea was speaking, Hester Chilton got to her feet.

"I think we can close the interview at this point, Chief Inspector," she said. "I don't see that this has any bearing on the case."

Rudd came close to losing his temper although his expression remained bland. Only Boyce, glancing up from his notebook, noticed the tightening of muscles high up along the jawline and realised that the chief inspector was very angry indeed.

"Miss Chilton," Rudd replied, keeping his voice quiet and even, "I'm investigating a case of murder. I'm not interested in your mother's private life. But certain questions have to be asked. If you consider your mother is too unwell to continue this interview, then I'll postpone it to a later date. But it will only be a postponement. I have no intention of cutting my inquiry short because you consider my line of questioning is irrelevant. That's for me to decide."

She had the grace to blush, the colour spreading up her face and making her look much younger and more vulnerable.

"I'm sorry," she said.

The apology was direct and unequivocal. Rudd accepted it with a small inclination of the head, feeling himself warm to her. The girl certainly had courage and the kind of honesty which, however reluctantly, he was forced to admire.

Bea said quickly, anxious to relieve the situation, "Hester, would you like to make tea for us? I'm sure the chief inspector and his sergeant would like something to drink." As soon as her daughter had left the room, she continued, "I'm sorry about that. I'm afraid both Hester and I are overtired and Rex's death has been a great shock. You wanted to know about my relationship with him? It's quite simply explained, Chief Inspector. Rex and I had been lovers for many years. His own marriage wasn't very happy. As for myself, I was widowed a long time ago. We kept the affair secret for as long as possible. I'm not sure, in fact, how much Martin or his mother, when she was alive, knew about it although I met Martin once years ago in London when he was a boy and I think he guessed the truth then."

"But you'd moved recently to the village?" Rudd asked.

"Yes; only a few days ago, as a matter of fact. I'd retired from my job and Rex wanted me to be nearer to him."

"Was marriage ever discussed between you?"

She looked him directly in the eyes, raising her voice a little.

"Yes, it was. But I'd refused. As I explained to Rex, I've been independent for too long to want to give up my freedom."

It was the same reason, Rudd thought wryly, which Marion Greave might give if ever he decided to ask her to marry him. Listening to Mrs. Chilton's reply, he wondered if he wouldn't be a fool to try a similar proposal.

"Besides," she was continuing, "there was another reason. Although I loved Rex, I don't think I could have shared a house with him. He wasn't an easy man to live with."

She was still speaking in the raised voice and Rudd wondered why. Was it for the daughter's benefit? It seemed a possibility. Although Hester Chilton had left the room, a serving hatch, which was in the wall behind Mrs. Chilton's chair and from behind which came the subdued rattle of china, led directly into the kitchen. If the remark was intended to be overheard by Hester Chilton, it raised the entirely new question of the relationship between Bea's daughter and Rex Holt.

As she finished speaking, the hatch was slid aside and Hester Chilton pushed a tray into the opening, which Boyce, with an alactrity which Rudd rarely knew him to demonstrate, collected and carried over to the small coffee-table.

He was rewarded with a smile from Hester Chilton as she entered the room; a brief smile, it was true, but none the less genuine, which transformed her face, making her look suddenly much prettier.

Rudd postponed the rest of the interview until the tea was finished. Only a few questions remained anyway and they were soon disposed of.

"I believe you gave Martin Holt a key to his father's bureau?" he asked, setting down his cup.

"Yes," Mrs. Chilton replied.

"How did it come into your possession?"

"Rex gave it to me yesterday evening. He wanted me to have it."

"Do you know why?"

"Not exactly. He spoke several times during the afternoon about getting older, as if he realised he couldn't live much longer. I think the stroke he had last year had put the idea into his mind. He wanted to make sure someone knew where his personal papers were kept."

The next question had to be asked.

"Wouldn't it have been more natural to give the key to his son?"

"Yes," Bea agreed, "but I happened to be there when the idea came to him. Rex sometimes acted on impulse like that. I think he wanted me to pass it on to Martin when I saw him, which I did this morning."

It was only an approximation of the truth but she felt incapable of explaining the intricacies of motive behind Rex's decision to give the key to her rather than Martin or her own feelings about his action.

"Were you present when Martin opened the bureau?"

"Yes."

Bea waited for the next question, which she assumed would relate to her own removal of her letters to Rex, but all Rudd asked was "I believe he took some papers from it?"

"I wasn't there at the time but I understood he wanted to collect some private letters belonging to his mother."

So Martin hadn't mentioned her action after all and she thanked him silently for his loyalty.

"Hadn't there been some disagreement with his father over showing the letters to an American researcher?" Rudd continued.

"I believe so. Rex spoke of it but it happened before I arrived."

"Is that all, Chief Inspector? I can see my mother is getting very tired." Hester Chilton broke into the conversation again, more pleasantly this time and with better reason. Mrs. Chilton was indeed looking exhausted.

"Just one more question," Rudd replied. "Rex Holt's will was kept in that bureau. Do you happen to know its contents?"

"No, I don't, Chief Inspector."

"He had never discussed them with you?"

She hesitated briefly before replying, "No. Rex was a business man. He kept his own counsel where his financial affairs were concerned. I doubt if he even discussed them with his son."

"But my bet is she guessed she'd benefit," Rudd remarked a few minutes later, getting into the car beside Boyce.

"You think so?" Boyce sounded distracted, his attention on backing and turning the car in the narrow lane.

"She'd been his mistress for many years. It stands to reason he'd leave her something, probably a substantial amount."

"And that would give her a motive." Boyce picked up the point.

"Exactly. We'll check with Holt's solicitor exactly what the will contained when we see him. I've rung him back, by the way, and arranged to call on him later at his house." Almost as an afterthought, he added, "There's also the daughter to keep in mind."

"Come off it!" Boyce protested. "What reason could she have for murdering Rex Holt?"

"To prevent her mother from marrying him?" Rudd made the suggestion lightly, as if he didn't consider it very seriously himself.

Boyce looked interested all the same.

"Jealousy?"

"Or a deep antipathy towards Rex Holt. Even Mrs. Chilton agreed he wasn't a very easy man to get on with. And if Mrs. Chilton had no alibi for last night, neither has the daughter. She could have stopped off at Barnsfield Hall on her way to her mother's house, confronted Holt and killed him in a quarrel, setting it up afterwards to look like an accident."

Even as he said it, Rudd was aware once again of the uneasiness which this aspect of the case aroused in him.

Boyce seemed unconcerned by such considerations.

"She'd have the nerve all right," he agreed. "More so than the mother. I wouldn't put it past her to wallop anyone if she lost her temper."

He spoke with a reluctant admiration. Evidently Hester Chilton had impressed him more than he was willing to admit.

"A murder made to look like an accident," Rudd said musingly, half to himself. "Or was it the other way round?"

"You mean an accident made to look like a murder?" Boyce asked, his voice incredulous.

Rudd roused himself, trying to gather up his thoughts.

"No, not exactly, Tom. I meant a murder made to look like a murder."

Boyce shot him a sideways look.

"That doesn't make sense."

"No, it doesn't," Rudd agreed equably and settled back in the passenger seat in silence.

It would be pointless, he thought, trying to explain the theory further for Boyce's benefit, whose literal-mindedness could at times be infuriating. But as the car headed towards Welham along the country roads, he gazed out of the window, oblivious of the passing scenery.

A murder made to look like a murder.

The idea appealed to him.

One thing was certain, though. He'd have to be more sure of his ground before he tried it out on Boyce because, if he were right, it could let Martin Holt off the hook and he couldn't see the sergeant taking very willingly to that suggestion.

"So you refused to marry him?" Hester asked her mother.

They were seated in the garden, Bea having declined to return to the bedroom to lie down. Instead, Hester had carried out two cane reclining chairs which she had placed on a patch of shaggy lawn under an apple tree which was hung with small, bright red fruit. Like a Christmas tree, Bea thought vaguely, looking up into its loaded branches.

By a tacit agreement, neither of them had referred to the interview which had just ended but had instead been discussing the garden.

"It all needs reorganising," Hester had remarked.

"Yes, darling," Bea had agreed. "But we mustn't cut down the trees. They're so pretty."

A silence had followed, the sort of uneasy silence which told Bea Hester was waiting to say something which was on her mind.

It was then the question came.

"So you refused to marry him?"

"Yes," Bea replied, her eyes still intent on the branches of the tree. "Why?"

Bea closed her eyes.

"For the same reason I gave the chief inspector. I valued my freedom too much."

"And you wouldn't have changed your mind?"

"No," Bea said, still keeping her eyes closed.

How easy it is to lie! she thought. For Rudd, the deception had been free of any sense of guilt. She had lied because it had been simpler than trying to explain the truth and because, ultimately, it was none of his business. In her daughter's case, the latter reason was certainly not applicable. Indeed, it was because of Hester's close involvement that Bea felt the need to deceive her. After all, what would be the point in confusing this involvement further by admitting that Rex might have eventually persuaded her to change her mind? He was dead. The question was no longer valid and her own uncertainty over the issue concerned no one but herself.

There was a question of her own which she in turn had to ask and, opening her eyes, she looked at her daughter.

"Would you have minded very much if I had?"

"Do you want me to tell you the truth?" Hester replied.

"Please, darling."

"Then the answer would be yes, although I suppose I should have got used to the idea in the end."

As she spoke, she turned her face away, presenting only her profile for scrutiny. Bea studied it. There was a fastidiousness about the set of her lips which was familiar. How many times had she seen that expression before? Too many. And too often she had discounted it. But not any more. All her loyalty now must be with the living and not with the dead.

"You didn't like him."

She presented it as a fact, not a question.

Hester turned to her quickly, her face distressed.

"Oh please, Mother, not now!"

"I must talk about it."

If we don't now, Bea thought, we never shall.

"Rex is dead," Hester said.

"And it's because he's dead that we can discuss him. Can't you see that? Whatever you say will make no difference to the way I feel about him. I loved him. But you didn't. It's as simple as that."

"Is it?" Hester demanded. The colour had run up into her face as it used to do when she was a child fighting back tears.

Bea took both her hands in hers, as she had done on those occasions, speaking softly but, underneath the gentleness, willing the pride to break and the tears to flow.

"I loved him for his courage and his tenacity, which wouldn't let him admit to any weakness. I used to feel he was like a great tree I could lean against. So safe! Nothing could shake it. Did you see nothing of this, Hester? Was all you noticed about him his stubbornness and his insensitivity?"

"You saw it, too?" Hester asked. The tears had gathered under her lids but still refused to fall.

"Of course. There were times when I almost disliked him. But that didn't stop me from loving him."

"Oh, Christ!" Hester pulled her hands free and ran her fingers under her eyes. "He was so bloody false!"

"False?" It was the last word Bea had imagined could ever be applied to Rex.

"Yes, false! Coming to see you, loaded down with presents for me! Buying me off! You remember them? The doll? The pretty dresses I never wanted to wear. And that joviality of his! Oh God, Mother, how

I used to hate it! Because none of it was genuine. He never gave anything that really mattered, even to you. He only took."

"Yes, I can see that," Bea replied more calmly than she felt, for part of her wanted to cry out that it wasn't true. Rex wasn't like that! And yet, there was a terrible validity in what Hester was saying. His generosity had almost always been on a material level because that was the only way in which he knew how to express it. Look at the cheque he had sent Martin! How could Rex have ever imagined that five thousand pounds would convey his pride in his son, his concern for his future, his regret for the misunderstanding between them? The pity of it was, Rex knew of no other way. Or, if he did, he was afraid to use it.

"But he didn't only take," she continued, anxious to set the record straight. "He gave me more than I could ever repay him for."

"Such as what?" Hester demanded.

The tears had dried and there was a defiant lift to her chin.

Bea hesitated, uncertain how Hester would react.

"A sense of being loved and needed."

Hester's response confirmed her fears.

"Needed? For God's sake, Mother, is that all you wanted? To be *needed!*"

It was futile to go on, Bea decided. They were talking from opposite sides of a chasm, mouthing words at each other which had no meaning, as if they were speaking different languages.

"You've never been in love" was all she could find to say.

"No, thank God," Hester retorted with genuine feeling.

And that was that. Nothing was left that could be safely said; certainly not to voice the guilt Bea felt for the distorted image of love which she and Rex had unwittingly held up to Hester's scrutiny and which it was too late now to change or attempt to justify.

CHAPTER NINE

On their way through Welham, they passed the Red Lion hotel and, remembering the American, Lawrence Hurst, was staying there, Rudd told Boyce to stop.

"Why?" Boyce asked. "I thought we were going to see Holt's solicitor. Hurst isn't going to be able to tell us much."

"Probably not," Rudd replied, "but it'll be interesting to hear his version of what happened between Rex Holt and his son over the Voyte letters. Martin Holt admits there was a disagreement."

"Rex Holt is dead?" Hurst was shocked by the news. He stood facing Rudd and Boyce in his bedroom, the manager having conducted them personally upstairs on learning the chief inspector's identity. "But I only saw him yesterday."

"It's about your visit that I came to see you," Rudd said, picking up his comment. "I believe Martin Holt was present and there was a family argument over some papers."

He left the remark deliberately vague to encourage Hurst to fill out the details.

Still shocked, Hurst waved to them to sit down with a distracted air, Rudd taking the only armchair, which left Boyce to perch himself on the bed.

As they sat down, Hurst on the straight-backed chair drawn up to the table under the window, which he turned to face them, Rudd gave the room and its occupant a rapid appraisal. Hurst was in his shirt-sleeves, a tall, loose-limbed man in his late thirties, with pleasant, craggy features. He had evidently been interrupted in the middle of working, for a portable typewriter stood on the table, a sheet of paper in its roller. The room was L-shaped, a small bathroom having been partitioned off on the left just inside the door, and was furnished in the style of most second-class, country hotels with comfortable but nondescript furniture.

Hurst was saying, "Yes; Martin Holt arrived when I was still interviewing his father. If I'd known he was going to visit, I'd've suggested another day for the appointment. It was rather embarrassing, Chief Inspector."

He seemed ready to leave it there and Rudd cocked his head encouragingly.

"He quite clearly objected to his father showing me the Voyte papers," Hurst continued, "although I've spoken to Martin Holt since and we've settled the matter amicably. In fact, he may allow me to use the letters for the book I'm writing on Voyte. You know about him? Voyte, I mean."

"Martin Holt gave me a brief account," Rudd said quickly. He was anxious to get Hurst back to the subject of the dispute between Martin Holt and his father. "What exactly happened between them during the interview?"

"Nothing much *happened*," Hurst replied, his eager expression fading. He seemed reluctant to be diverted from the subject of Voyte, evidently his chief interest. "There was a lot of tension in the air, that's all. Voyte and Martin's mother had some boy-and-girl romance and he felt that the letters in particular were private property. I didn't get to read them although I copied the manuscript poems and Voyte's photograph."

Rudd did not feel it necessary to explain that he himself was now in possession not only of the same photograph and poems but also the letters. It was up to Martin Holt to decide whether or not he made them available to Hurst once they were back in his possession. But before that happened, Rudd intended reading them himself. Although he could not see what possible bearing they could have on Rex Holt's murder, he was nevertheless interested in them if only because of the disagreement they had caused between the father and son.

"Were you introduced to Mr. Holt's other guest, Mrs. Chilton?" he asked, hoping that Hurst might have witnessed the meeting between Martin Holt and his father's mistress.

To his disappointment, Hurst shook his head.

"No. I was there when the housekeeper announced she'd arrived. Mr. Holt sent his son to meet her. I left shortly afterwards without seeing her."

There seemed nothing much else to ask, except to make the routine request to check Hurst's passport, which the American complied with readily enough, producing it from the inside pocket of his jacket, which hung on the back of his chair.

Rudd opened it briefly before passing it on to Boyce to note down the details. It seemed in order. The one entry stamp it contained was dated ten days earlier, July 18.

To fill in the time while Boyce was busy with the passport, Rudd continued, "You said you made an appointment to see Mr. Holt about the Voyte papers. When exactly did you contact him?"

"A couple of months ago. You can see a copy of the letter if you like. I brought all the correspondence with me just in case there were any queries."

Before Rudd could protest, Hurst had leaned across to the bedside table and extracted a manila folder from beneath a pile of books and typescript which he passed to Rudd. On opening it, the chief inspector saw that it contained letters and carbon copies of letters, passed between Hurst and his various contacts in England. They seemed innocuous enough.

Rudd read them through quickly, making a mental note of Hurst's New York address: 240 Kane Street, Brooklyn, New York.

Boyce, meanwhile, had finished with the passport. It was time to go.

As he rose to his feet, Finch added, "How long do you intend staying, Mr. Hurst?"

"In the hotel, you mean? Or in England?"

"Both."

"I'm booked in here until Saturday, as I have another appointment with Voyte's mother tomorrow; the last one, in fact. She lives in Suffolk, which I see from the map isn't too far to drive to from here."

"You've hired a car?"

"That's right."

"And then?"

"Oh, I intend spending a few days in London just being a tourist, seeing some of the places I've only read about, Westminster Abbey, the Tower. I fly back to the States next Friday."

"Well, you've got good weather for it," Rudd remarked pleasantly, nodding towards the window. "Have a good trip."

The Americanism seemed to please Hurst, who smiled broadly at them before shaking hands and showing them out of the room.

Downstairs, they encountered the manager, a small, plump, smartly dressed man, who was waiting for them at the reception desk, anxious and also a little curious about the reason for their visit.

"Everything's all right, Chief Inspector?" he asked, hurrying forward as Rudd and Boyce reached the foot of the stairs.

"Perfectly," Rudd replied.

"Only I wouldn't like to think there were any problems concerning one of our guests."

The remark was not entirely superfluous. Rudd guessed the man was eager to be on good terms with the police if only as an insurance against possible future contingencies.

On an impulse, he replied, "Just one small point. Did Mr. Hurst dine here yesterday evening?"

The manager answered without any hesitation.

"Yes, he did. At eight o'clock. I happened to notice him myself."

"And did he leave the hotel at any time after that?"

"No, he didn't."

The man seemed so positive that Rudd was prompted to ask, "How do you know?"

"He rang down to reception—at what time was it, Carol? About five to ten?" He turned in appeal to the pretty receptionist, who nodded to confirm the time. "He asked for a bottle of whisky to be sent up to his room. The waiters and the bar staff were very busy—we were catering for a twenty-first-birthday party with nearly fifty guests—so I took Mr. Hurst's order up to his room myself."

"And he was there?"

"Yes, Chief Inspector. He opened the door for me and told me to put the bottle on the table. Which I did."

"Thank you, Mr. Benson. That's all I wanted to know," Rudd said, turning away as the manager seemed about to ask him the reason for his questions.

Outside, Boyce said, "What was all that about? You don't seriously think Hurst had anything to do with Holt's murder?"

"No, but it seemed worth checking up on him while we were there. After all, he'd met Holt and whoever killed him must have been known to him. But there's no possible motive that I can see."

"Or opportunity," Boyce added. "If he was in his room at about five to ten, there's no way he could have got over to Barnsfield Hall by eight minutes past."

"Of course," Rudd agreed although he didn't point out that the time on Rex Holt's watch could have been altered. That was one aspect of the case which would need further investigation and he didn't feel in the mood to argue it through at that stage with Boyce. "Damn Benson!" he continued, "If he hadn't been hanging about waiting for us in the foyer, there was a phone call I wanted to make."

"Something to do with the case?" Boyce asked nosily.

"No, a private matter," Rudd replied and left it there. He had no intention of explaining to the sergeant that the call would have been to Marion Greave. Ever since meeting Hester Chilton, who had reminded him of her, he had been thinking of her and wanting to hear her voice. Absurd, really. If he had phoned her, what on earth would he have found to say?

As far as Boyce was concerned, Marion Greave had passed out of his life months ago when Pardoe had returned from leave to take over again as police surgeon. Their continuing relationship, if so casual a contact could be described in such positive terms, was a personal matter which Rudd guarded scrupulously even from his own sister. But Dorothy was away that week, visiting a friend, and it would have been a good time to arrange to meet her, for dinner perhaps, or another evening at the cinema.

"I could always stop on the way at a phone box," Boyce suggested with a helpful air.

"Thanks, Tom, but we've wasted enough time already. Let's get over to Lanston and see Holt's solicitor. I may make the call later."

But probably not, he decided. With a murder inquiry on his hands, there was little chance anyway that he'd get an evening off.

They saw Walter Gilham in his study, a sombre room full of heavy, dark furniture, a suitable background for the man himself, who, as dry and elderly as the law books shut up behind glass in the cases which lined the walls, faced them with an air of faint disapproval as they seated themselves opposite him.

The news of Rex Holt's murder was passed over almost without a tremor. His only comment was "I'm shocked to hear it." It was said with a grave air which conveyed more feeling than all Reggie Trimmer's protestations. For a moment, the thin lips were pressed together. Then he returned to the business in hand. "I assume you are here to make inquiries regarding Mr. Holt's will?"

"Yes. It's possible that whoever murdered him stood to gain from his death."

"Of course." Mr. Gilham accepted this suggestion as perfectly proper, much to Rudd's relief. He had expected the man would demur on the grounds of professional etiquette. Instead, he continued, "I don't have a copy of Mr. Holt's will here. It's kept at the office. I can, however, give you a brief verbal summary of its contents." The precise voice paused, waiting for Rudd's agreement and as the chief inspector nodded, it resumed. "The chief beneficiary is, of course, the son, Martin Holt. He inherits the house, Barnsfield Hall, and its contents, together with all the land and property held in his father's name."

"Which consists of what exactly?" Rudd asked.

"I can't be precise on the details. The deeds are also at the office although Mr. Holt has copies of them."

Damn! thought Rudd, remembering he had seen them in Holt's bureau. He should have brought them with him although the omission wasn't important. He could always collect them another time.

"He also inherits shares and investments which amount altogether to about three hundred thousand pounds."

Rudd kept his face expressionless although he heard Boyce shift in the chair beside him. Over a quarter of a million! It was a hell of a lot of money.

If Mr. Gilham was aware of the sergeant's reaction, he showed no sign. The dry voice continued, "The next main beneficiary is Mrs. Beatrice Chilton. Mr. Holt took out a life insurance policy on which she would claim one hundred fifty thousand pounds on his death."

This time Boyce sat perfectly still, only his pen making slight scratching noises as it formed the series of noughts in his notebook.

"The other beneficiaries will inherit smaller amounts. I don't know if you wish to have those details?" Mr. Gilham inquired.

"Please," Rudd replied.

Mr. Gilham ran through them quickly with an abstracted air as if they were mere trivialities.

"Miss Moxon, twenty-five thousand pounds and the deeds of her cottage, the freehold of which will pass to her and her heirs; Miss Hester Chilton, Mrs. Chilton's daughter, twenty thousand pounds; Mr. Reginald Trimmer, fifteen thousand pounds; Mr. and Mrs. Drewett, ten thousand pounds; Mr. Henry Barnard, also ten thousand pounds; and the same amount to Mrs. Jean Browning, including any residue."

"Mr. Barnard and Mrs. Browning?" Rudd asked. Neither name was familiar to him.

"Mr. Barnard was Mr. Holt's former manager at his firm, before they both retired. Mrs. Browning is Mr. Holt's niece."

"Niece?" Rudd repeated. "I didn't know he had any other relatives apart from his son."

Mr. Gilham paused to reflect, as if debating with himself how much the chief inspector needed to know about his dead client's private affairs.

After a moment, he replied, "Mrs. Browning is the daughter of Rex Holt's younger brother, Arthur Holt. I gather there was some family disagreement and he emigrated to South Africa many years ago, where he has since died. There was no contact between Mr. Holt and his brother although I understand Mrs. Browning informed Mr. Holt of her father's death."

"So she's still living in South Africa?"

"No," Mr. Gilham corrected him. "She is now living in London. About two years ago, Mr. Holt brought me a card which she had sent him, informing him of her new address. He asked me to file it with his other documents."

"What is her address?"

Mr. Gilham looked pained.

"I really cannot remember it, Chief Inspector. I could ask my clerk to telephone you tomorrow with the details. I have had no reason, you

understand, to correspond with Mrs. Browning, apart from acknowledging the receipt of her address. Mr. Holt asked specifically that she
should not be informed of the terms of his will."

"Did he say why?" Rudd asked, intrigued by Rex Holt's motives and
scenting a possible family scandal.

"None of the beneficiaries were informed. Mr. Holt made a point of
keeping his financial affairs very much to himself. I understand that not
even his son knew the exact details of his father's estate."

"But he must have been aware that his father was a very rich man,"
Rudd pointed out.

Mr. Gilham declined to comment although, by a slight inclination of
the head, he indicated that this was indeed very probably the case. At
the same time, he half-rose from his desk, suggesting there was nothing
more he could add. The interview was over.

Before he left, Rudd handed him his card.

"My telephone number," he said before shaking hands and leaving
the room, accompanied by Boyce, who hardly waited until the front
door was closed behind them before making the comment which was
clearly uppermost in his thoughts, as it was in the chief inspector's.

"More than quarter of a million quid! That's a hell of a lot of
money!"

It was almost exactly a word-for-word repetition of the silent comment which had passed through Rudd's mind when the solicitor had
first given them the information.

He got into the car, slamming the door. For some reason which he
couldn't quite rationalise, he felt in a sour mood.

Boyce climbed in behind the wheel.

"And that's not taking into account the house and its contents," he
continued. "Not to mention any other property Holt owned. What do
you reckon Barnsfield Hall is worth? Another quarter of a million?"

"Possibly," Rudd said sharply. He wished to God Boyce would shut
up.

"So he could probably end up a bloody millionaire!"

"There'd be capital transfer tax to pay," Rudd pointed out.

"All the same . . ." Boyce didn't even bother to finish the sentence.
They both knew what he meant. Even when that had been paid, Martin Holt would still be a rich man by anyone's standards.

Yes, a hell of a lot of money, as Boyce had said. And a hell of a lot of
motive for murder.

Murder made to look like murder? The theory which had excited him only a short time ago no longer seemed valid. It was only an idea after all. But he still couldn't get it out of his head. Nor the mental image of all that sheeted furniture in the upstairs rooms in Barnsfield Hall, which had somehow become confused with another recollection of Rex Holt's body being carried along the terrace to the waiting ambulance.

"There's a phone box," Boyce said, slowing down. "Do you want to make that call?"

"No." Rudd came to a sudden decision. He was in no frame of mind to speak to Marion Greave. "Drive on."

"Where to?" Boyce asked. "Back to the office?"

The car was idling in bottom gear along the side of the verge.

"No, to Martin Holt's place," Rudd snapped, as though Boyce was a fool not to have realised this for himself. "I think it's time we confronted him on his own ground."

It was half past five. Time to knock off for the day. Charlie indicated as much by saying, "Well, I reckon that's the lot!" as he returned from stacking the last box of tomatoes in the shed. He added with elaborate offhandedness, "I don't know about you, but I'm parched."

Martin took the hint.

"If you'll lock up the greenhouses, Charlie," he told him, "I'll put the kettle on."

Although Charlie lived only across the road, he always liked to stay on for an after-work cup of tea, regarding it perhaps as a bonus or a free perk in addition to his wages.

They drank it sitting in the kitchen with the door open, facing the yard with its surrounding outbuildings and greenhouses, the glass of which still caught the sun, reflecting it back in sheets of brightness.

"Yes," Charlie added, as if continuing a conversation which had only recently been interrupted, "I reckon you're going to have your work cut out, sorting out your father's affairs."

"The solicitor will handle that," Martin replied.

During the day, he had managed to steer the conversation away from the subject of his father's death and his inheritance. Both of them had been too busy to maintain any subject for long and, as soon as Charlie had broached the topic, Martin had been able to find an excuse to cut it short.

Now, comfortably installed in the kitchen, his elbows on the table, Charlie seemed in no hurry to leave.

"Oh ah, a solicitor," he replied, investing the word with a country-man's contempt for smart-alec townies. "My father didn't bother with nothing like that; told each of us what we was to have when he died. 'Elsie,' he said, that's my sister, 'you take the bedroom furniture and the clock from the front room.'"

Martin nodded, only half-listening. He had heard the story before in another guise: a long complaint from Charlie regarding the same sister who had helped herself to more than her due after the old man's death fifteen years before. They were still not on speaking terms.

"Though in your case," Charlie went on. "It'll be more than a few sticks of furniture."

There was a slight interrogative lift to the end of the sentence, inviting Martin's confidence.

Martin said, "I don't know what he left, Charlie. I've never seen his will."

Charlie was silent, pausing as he thought out his next remark. Martin could see him ruminating over it, running the tip of his tongue into the corner of his mouth.

He was in no mood for it. He felt physically tired by the day's work and mentally exhausted with the effort of trying to come to terms with his father's death. Throughout the day, his mind had been filled with recollections from his early childhood, brief scraps of recalled images which were nevertheless disturbingly vivid: his father throwing a ball for him across the lawn at Barnsfield Hall; of holding him up at the office window to look down on the lorries in the yard; of the expression on his face the first time he had showed Martin how to hold a fishing-rod.

He concentrated on those earlier memories in order to keep at bay more recent and painful recollections—his father sitting on the terrace, his chin lowered to his chest, Bea's hand on his; his own anger when the drawer was slammed shut and his own deliberate act of turning away.

The letters troubled him also. He wished he had not handed them over to Rudd although at the time he had had no choice in the matter. He had intended reading them again himself in order to come to a better understanding of his mother. Now, he felt that they might bring him closer to both his parents and, in a strange way, to Bea also. The three of them seemed linked together in a cross-web of relationships, the first threads of which, spun all those years ago in the love affair between his mother and Edward Voyte, reached out to touch him, too.

He felt he had been searching for something all his life. But for what? A lost perfume? A reflected image?

He was incapable of thinking about it too precisely. He lacked the words because the concepts themselves were too undefined.

Hurst, with the clearer perception of the outsider and the scholar, had referred to it as a pilgrimage. It was a better description than Martin himself could have devised.

Charlie was saying, "I know what I'd do if I came into money. I'd pack up work tomorrow. Not that I ain't enjoyed working for you," he was quick to add, "and the wage's useful. But I'd start taking life easy for a change; have a lie in in the mornings. What'll you do? Retire, eh? Go on a world cruise?"

The question was asked in a jocular manner, designed to disarm any accusation of inquisitiveness, and Martin smiled as he said in the same half-humorous fashion, "No, not a world cruise, Charlie. I might get caught up in one of those shipboard romances and come back married." Coming to a sudden decision, he set down his empty cup. "If you've finished, I'd like to lock up and push off."

"Going over to Barnsfield Hall, are you?" Charlie asked. "I hope there ain't any more trouble over there."

"No, not to Barnsfield. To Suffolk. It's a personal matter."

Fetching his jacket from the back of the door, he stood waiting on the threshold with it over his arm, dangling the house-keys in his hand so that Charlie could see them.

Charlie finished his cup of tea and, wiping the back of his hand across his mouth, followed him outside, where Martin locked the door.

"See you tomorrow morning!" he called out, crossing the yard to his car.

On the outskirts of the village, he drew off the road onto the verge and, reaching into the glove compartment, got out the road-map.

Hatton was off the A134, in a tangle of minor roads some of which were unnumbered.

Tracing out a route through Braintree and Halstead, he realised he had not considered what he would do when he got there. At the time, he had come to the decision for no clearer a motive than it seemed better to be on the move, to take some positive action rather than to remain static, parrying Charlie's questions or, what was worse, reflecting alone on his own thoughts.

God knows what he'd discover there either. He hadn't even thought about that. An image focused more sharply, perhaps? The past brought a little closer to the present?

There'd be a lake. He knew that much. And for the moment, it was sufficient. He would drive to Hatton and look at the lake and, the reason for the journey now established, he started the car and drove off.

CHAPTER TEN

Hatton was smaller than he had imagined; more of an overgrown village than a town. The narrow by-road which led to it opened into a miniature market square. Round the square, and straggling into two side-streets, were a collection of shops, including a baker's with a single shop window and a step up to the door. It had changed hands since the time his mother had stayed there as a girl with her uncle and aunt, for the name above it was unfamiliar to him. Instead, he couldn't even be sure that it was the same building although he glanced up curiously at the sash-windows above the fascia, assuming that she had known the rooms behind the net curtains. After all, the place could not have altered all that much. There was an ageless quality about it, as if it had been stranded in some backwater at the turn of the century, which neither the television aerials on the roofs nor the modern cars parked in the road could dispel.

It was curiously silent and empty also, which added to this impression. No one was about; not even in the pub, the Cricketers, where Martin went for a drink and to ask directions to the lake. Apart from one old man seated in a corner and the publican polishing glasses behind the bar with the air of a man finding something to do to keep himself looking busy, the place was empty.

"The lake?" the landlord repeated. "If you mean the mere, you want to take the footpath behind the church and then cut across the fields. But it's private property."

Martin thanked him and drank his beer quickly. He was anxious to be gone before his resolution failed him. The quest—the pilgrimage, if you like—which he had entered into so impulsively now seemed slightly foolish.

Once he had turned down the footpath, his mood lifted although some of the melancholy of Hatton still lingered. It was a still, silent evening, the air warm, the leaves on the hedges which lined the path hanging motionless. In front of him, the whole western sky was gilded by the setting sun, which flooded the countryside with a golden light, touching everything, the trees, the bushes, the grass, with a rich splendour.

He wondered if Edward Voyte and his mother had seen such a sunset themselves and had witnessed a similar transfiguration of the fields. He found it strange that he could not summon them up as he had expected he would. There was no sense of their presence although from time to time he made a deliberate effort to associate his mother with his surroundings, telling himself that she must have known this tree, the same one perhaps where Edward Voyte had left the letters and poems for her to find, or this distant view of woodland glimpsed through a gap in the hedge where she might have paused.

He could not even recall her face as it appeared in the photograph in Biddy's sitting-room; only an impression of her apprehension and that look of startled innocence.

The path sloped downwards. At the bottom, where it levelled off, a gate led off to the right with a notice announcing PRIVATE PROPERTY nailed to the crossbar.

Climbing over it, Martin set off across flat meadowland, following a faint track in the grass towards a distant line of trees. The sun had sunk lower and was hidden below the horizon although it still cast up its brightness, which was now barred with narrow, horizontal bands of cloud, lit from the underside and burning dark orange.

Emerging from the belt of trees, he found himself on top of a slight incline leading down towards a field of coarse marsh grass, deeply pitted and rutted with mud holes, caked and dried out in the sun. Beyond lay the lake; or rather the mere. The landlord's word for it was a better description.

Martin had no clear idea of what he had been expecting. Some great expanse of shining water perhaps, overshadowed by trees which hung low to touch the surface with their branches, a flash of brilliant blue as a kingfisher darted along the bank.

What he saw was a shallow depression in the ground which merged only gradually to open water through the ranks of tall reeds which surrounded it and which, even in the still air, kept up a constant, sibilant whisper.

And yet he was not disappointed. The place had a desolate beauty of its own. The water lay motionless, reflecting back the barred splendour of the sunset in the double image which Edward Voyte had described and, as Martin walked through the reeds onto a narrow jetty of warped planking to stand at its edge, he could see his own figure stretching before him on the surface as if in a mirror of green glass.

There on the jetty, he felt for the first time close to the dead lovers. It was the only point at which it was possible to approach the open water and, glancing back, he saw how private the place was. The reed banks clustered close, shutting it off from observation. If one sat or lay down, one would disappear from sight.

So it must have been here, as she knelt down to look into the water, that Edward Voyte had caught the image of her face looking back at him.

He knelt himself, feeling the rough planks with their hard knots pressing into his knees and smelling the faint, sweet smell of rotting vegetation and wood rise from the water. Behind him, the reeds kept up their low susurration like human voices, reminding him of the lines in one of Voyte's published poems:

> They criticise
> But cannot enter
> Our silent, solitary kingdom
> Of water, light and sky
> Which we inhabit,
> Where their voices
> Fall dying through the air.

He had seen it before only as a poignant omen of Voyte's death. Now, kneeling and peering down through his own reflection to the green depths where water-weed, as fine as hair, clustered in long, slowly drifting layers, he was aware that he, too, had entered their silent kingdom and felt strangely at peace.

Boyce drew up on the narrow gravelled forecourt which fronted Martin Holt's smallholding and cast an inquiring glance at the chief inspector who sat beside him in the front of the car. But Rudd seemed in no hurry to get out. Still seated, he contemplated the house and its outbuildings with a speculative eye, like a prospective buyer, noting the cramped, ugly dimensions of the house itself and the two greenhouses, one small and relatively modern, in the door of which a CLOSED notice was hanging; the other a larger, wooden construction which, despite the new paint, looked old and out of date. The range of outbuildings

which ran alongside them had the same out-worn but carefully maintained appearance.

There was an air of improvisation about the smallholding which
suggested that money was short, a fact which Holt himself had not
attempted to hide. If five thousand pounds would be welcome, what
sort of difference would the whole of Rex Holt's estate make to his
son's standard of living?

One hell of a lot, Rudd decided, climbing out of the passenger seat
and walking across the forecourt to the rear of the house. No one
answered his knock and when he cupped his hands round his face to
peer through the window beside the back door, he could see little
except a table on which stood two cups and a teapot. The place seemed
to be empty.

Boyce had no more luck at the greenhouses, announcing, as Rudd
joined him, that both were locked.

"So it looks as if Holt's out," Rudd said. "I wonder where the hell
he's gone?"

He felt exasperated at the wasted journey although Holt's absence
gave him the chance to inspect the place more freely and, nodding to
Boyce to follow, he walked towards the outbuildings. The first two were
firmly padlocked but the third, a small shed of creosoted planking,
leaning as if tired against the second, looked less secure, the hasp holding the door closed having come loose from the jamb.

It contained, as they discovered once they had prised the door open,
nothing of value except lumber, neatly stacked in one corner, and a pile
of old fertilizer bags folded in half, which was probably why Holt had
not bothered fixing the hasp.

And the jacket.

It was hanging on a nail just inside the door. Rudd brushed against it
as he entered, feeling its rough texture against the side of his face.

Carrying it outside to examine it more carefully in the daylight, he
saw that it was old and well worn, the cuffs frayed and the lining torn.
But the tweed, of a green and brown mixture, was still good; certainly
good enough to wear for working in.

He said nothing, waiting for Boyce to make the obvious comment as
the sergeant rubbed his fingers across the cloth.

"I bet you ten quid that's where those threads came from!"

"No takers," Rudd said sourly.

He found it impossible to match Boyce's jubilant mood. The discovery of the jacket roused in him nothing more than the same sense of

uneasiness which he had felt about the finding of the stone and the threads. It was all a little too damned convenient.

Boyce, a little downcast by the chief inspector's lack of response, asked, "I suppose you'll want forensic to compare the coat with the threads?"

"Of course," Rudd agreed, pulling a few fibres from the frayed edge of a cuff and tucking them away inside his wallet. "Put the coat back where we found it, Tom. We can pick it up next time we see Holt."

As Boyce hung the jacket up on the nail inside the outhouse and walked across the yard towards the car, Rudd shut the shed before strolling more slowly after him, pausing at the door of the larger greenhouse to peer inside at the close-packed rows of tomato plants, each one strung up to a wire, the big dark green leaves and great swags of ripening fruit hanging with an almost tropical lushness.

As he did so, the sound of footsteps on the gravel behind him caught his attention and, turning round, he saw a small, elderly, bright-eyed man standing at the edge of the forecourt, regarding them suspiciously.

"The place is shut," he told them. "What do you want nosing about here for?"

"Police," Rudd announced, approaching him and showing his ID. "We wanted to speak to Mr. Holt."

"He's out," the man replied, not at all impressed by their identity but continuing to look them over with the same wary yet amused curiosity, as if it would give him the greatest pleasure to thwart any inquiries they were thinking of making.

On the principle that attack is the best form of defence, Rudd retaliated sharply.

"And who are you?" he demanded.

Even then the man took his time before answering, pondering the question infuriatingly, as if unsure himself of his own identity.

"Charlie Webber," he said at last. "I help Mr. Holt round the small-holding and I like to keep an eye on the place when he ain't here." Jerking his head backwards towards the row of houses opposite, he added in further explanation, "I live just over there. I saw the car and came across to see what's up."

"Nothing's up," Rudd said. "I was simply looking for Mr. Holt. Do you know where he's gone or what time he'll be back?"

Webber considered that query also before replying, "Couldn't say. All he told me was he was off to Suffolk to see someone. He locked up and left when we knocked off at half past five." The little bright eyes regarded Rudd with interest. "Anything I can do to help?"

Well, why not, Rudd thought, seeing the man was there? But aware of his curiosity, he made the question sound casual.

"You don't happen to know if Mr. Holt was at home yesterday evening, do you?"

On the basis of Martin Holt's own statement regarding his movements on the night his father was murdered, Rudd expected Webber's answer would be a negative. He was surprised, therefore, when Webber said promptly, "Yes, I do. He was here."

The answer clearly shook Boyce as well, who broke in abruptly with a question of his own.

"What time was this?"

"About quarter to eleven," Webber replied. He looked from one to the other of them, aware of their surprise and pleased at having provoked it. "I was on my way home from the pub. He was working in that greenhouse over there." He jerked his head this time in the direction of the larger of the two greenhouses. "Probably catching up on the picking for today, seeing as how he'd been over at his father's place most of yesterday."

Boyce was quick with his objection.

"But it was dark by then."

Webber smiled knowingly.

"Maybe it was but that didn't stop me from seeing him. There's electricity laid on in both them houses. The lights was on in the big'un, that's why I noticed him. I thought at the time, He's working late. But the summer's one of our busiest times, what with the tomato crop—"

"So you actually saw him?" Rudd interrupted.

"How many more times do I have to tell you?" Webber demanded indignantly. "There ain't nothing wrong with my eyesight, mister. I tell you he was working in that greenhouse. And if that ain't enough for you, I saw the lights go out just as I turned in at my front gate."

"And you'd be willing to sign a statement to that effect?" Rudd persisted.

Webber paused but this time to give himself a few moments to gather together his forces. When he spoke, his voice had the laconic drawl of the countryman who, sure of his ground, sees no point in forfeiting the advantage by losing his temper.

"You bring anyone you like, mister—the vicar, the chief constable, the Archbishop of Canterbury hisself if you want, and I'll sign on my Bible oath in front of the whole bloody lot of them."

With that, he turned and walked away, moving unhurriedly and not without a certain dignity, the set of his shoulders expressing satisfaction at having had the last word.

"He's lying," Boyce said as soon as he was out of earshot.

"I don't think so," Rudd replied.

"But if Martin Holt has an alibi—"

"It puts him out of the running as a suspect."

The chief inspector completed the sentence for him, feeling a perverse satisfaction himself at the sergeant's discomfiture as well as at the unexpected turn of events which had upset the seemingly straightforward nature of the case. It seemed to vindicate his own uneasy feeling that the evidence against Martin Holt had been just a little too pat and he climbed into the passenger seat in a mood of cheerful jauntiness that the inquiry had hit a major snag, a reaction which Boyce, judging by his gloomy profile as he started up the car, had the good sense not to share.

It was growing dusk as Martin returned to the village. The lights were on in the Cricketers and voices, coming through the open windows into the warm, still air, gave the tiny market centre a sense of animation. With the onset of evening, the place had come to life.

He had intended driving straight home but the lights and the sound of laughter made him change his mind. His own place would be empty and silent and he wanted suddenly to extend the contact he had had with the past into the present.

The pilgrimage on behalf of the dead was over but Mrs. Voyte was still alive.

Should he try to see her?

Having come so far, it seemed absurd not to. After all, he risked nothing except her refusal and the possibility of appearing a fool, which he was prepared to take. Besides, the visit to the lake had aroused his curiosity as well as his sense of the past, neither of which would be entirely satisfied until he had spoken to Mrs. Voyte.

All the same, he made a bargain with himself. If he didn't find the house within five minutes and without asking for directions, he would return home and write to her instead, asking formally for an appointment to see her, he thought, turning down one of the narrow sidestreets which led out of the village square.

The house was facing him at the far end, its name, GABLE END, written in white letters on an oval plaque fixed to a tall iron gate which shut off the front garden from the street.

It was smaller and more ordinary than he had imagined, which was a disappointment although he could imagine his mother, as a girl, being impressed by its solid, Victorian, red brick façade and its double gables, from which no doubt it took its name. Set between the smaller cottages which adjoined it, it gave the impression of being more imposing than it actually was.

A light was shining through the glass panels in the front door, so someone was at home.

The woman who answered the door wasn't Mrs. Voyte. She was too young. A housekeeper, perhaps? The blue nylon overall she was wearing suggested a domestic role.

As he was explaining that he had called in the hope of being able to speak to Mrs. Voyte concerning a family connection, a door at the far end of the long, dimly lit hall opened and a woman appeared in the dazzle of light from the room beyond.

Outlined in the doorway, the figure in the wheelchair took on a dramatic and sinister appearance which startled Martin for a moment and roused in him a long-forgotten and, he thought, conquered feeling of mixed fear, pity and repulsion which, as a child, he had always felt for the crippled or the maimed.

"Who is it?" Mrs. Voyte demanded. The voice was peremptory. "What does he want?"

"My name's Martin Holt," Martin repeated, raising his voice to carry the length of the hall and wishing to God he hadn't come. "My mother used to know your son. I hoped I might—"

"Tell him to come in," Mrs. Voyte interrupted, addressing the housekeeper. "Bring him into the drawing-room."

The housekeeper went ahead to help manoeuvre the wheelchair through the doorway, Martin following behind more slowly. By the time he entered the room, Mrs. Voyte was already established by the side of the fireplace under the brilliant light of a standard lamp, very much centre-stage, where she sat regarding him with a bright-eyed, alert attention.

There was no need, he realised, to waste either pity or fear on her. Mrs. Voyte might be physically disabled but mentally she was any-body's match. The face was long, fine-boned and fastidious, as if the features, through careful breeding over the generations, had been pared down to a purity and spareseness of line to eliminate all coarse, excess flesh. Although she in no way conformed to the picture of the dark-haired, red-robed queen, flashing with gold, which he had carried in his mind's eyes for all those years, he was not disappointed. Edward Voyte's mother was still a proud and domineering woman who liked to have her own way.

"Well?" Mrs. Voyte was asking, fixing him with a bright, hard stare.

"I was in the area," Martin began a little awkwardly, running through the explanation he had already rehearsed in his mind, "and I called in the hope you might see me. I recently met an American, Lawrence Hurst, who is researching a book about your son. As I have some of his letters among the family papers which Hurst was interested in, I was curious myself to find out a little more about the background—"

"You have some of my son's correspondence?" Mrs. Voyte broke in sharply.

"And several of his unpublished poems," Martin replied.

"How did you come by them?"

"Your son sent them to my mother when she was a girl. Lawrence Hurst must have heard about them and—"

"I know all about Mr. Hurst," Mrs. Voyte said impatiently, as if this were a trivial matter of no great concern to her. "He has written to me and I have agreed to meet him tomorrow to discuss my son's literary career. You spoke of your mother. Who was she? What exactly was her relationship with Edward?"

"Her maiden name was Elizabeth Renfrew. She met your son when she was a girl here in Hatton in the summer of '39."

Mrs. Voyte frowned.

"Elizabeth Renfrew? I don't recall anyone of that name."

It had been a mistake to come, Martin decided. God knows how he had imagined the interview with Mrs. Voyte would proceed but he hadn't been prepared for her inability to remember anything about the romance.

"She was only sixteen," he continued. "Your son wrote to her and sent her some of his poems, which she kept . . ."

To his relief, recollection returned although not in the way he had expected.

"Oh, Elizabeth Renfrew!" Mrs. Voyte said dismissively. "Not a local girl, if I remember correctly. Wasn't she staying in the village with an uncle? Yes, I do recall her now. Rather a pretty, quiet, little thing. I believe Edward was quite fond of her."

"They were in love with one another," Martin corrected her. He spoke quietly in order to hide his anger. He could see now where her power lay: in her ability to destroy by a mere phrase or gesture of contempt. It was clever but cruel. Even he felt touched by it. He could only imagine what effect it must have had on a naive sixteen-year-old girl.

"In love, Mr. Holt?" Mrs. Voyte repeated the words in a tone of disbelief. "I can't think how you came by such an idea. There may have been some boy-and-girl flirtation between them but I can assure you it wasn't serious, certainly not on Edward's part."

"But the letters and poems he sent her!" he protested.

Mrs. Voyte smiled, the corners of her lips pressing upwards although there was no change in the expression in her eyes, which continued to hold his with the same hard, direct stare.

"I am sure you would wish me to be perfectly frank with you, Mr. Holt. Although I have no idea what those poems and letters contain, I know from what my son told me at the time that he didn't regard the affair at all seriously. It was one of the reasons why I disapproved of it."

As Martin opened his mouth to protest again, she raised her voice, cutting him short.

"In the end, Edward himself was embarrassed by the relationship. I am sorry to have to tell you that, after he returned to Oxford, your mother sent him several hysterical letters, pleading with him to marry her. Finally, he had to write to her, cutting off any further correspondence between them. You see, Mr. Holt, that summer when he met your mother, he was already committed to another girl, the sister of one of his Oxford friends. They were to become engaged on her twenty-first birthday. Unfortunately, he was killed before it could take place."

"Is her name Ann Mallinson?" Martin asked, remembering Hurst had referred to someone of that name, the sister of one of Voyte's fellow students.

"Yes, although she has since married and is now, I believe, a Mrs. Quenton."

Martin rose to his feet. He had no doubt that she was speaking the truth. The account made too much sense for her to be lying. The gaps and inconsequentialities of his mother's version of the story, especially that part of it concerned with Voyte's return to Oxford, were now explained. Edward Voyte had wanted to break off the relationship. It was she who had refused to face the truth, spinning out of the strands of that brief affair, lasting no more than a few summer weeks, the substance of a grand passion which she had continued to cling to for a lifetime.

As for himself, he felt only relief. It was as if Mrs. Voyte's words had released him from a bondage to the past which had held him spellbound by the same insubstantial filaments.

Mrs. Voyte was saying, "I assume my son sent that letter. I know he consulted me about the contents. I advised him to tell her the truth and explain that he was in love with someone else."

"I'm sure he did," Martin agreed lightly. "I expect my mother burned it."

It seemed the most likely explanation. She would hardly have kept such evidence of her own negation or of the romantic fiction she had woven round the brief affair.

He held out his hand.

"I'm grateful that you allowed me to speak to you. I've wanted for a long time to know the truth."

She took his hand with a gracious, almost queenly gesture.

"My son was very charming, Mr. Holt. But a dreamer; not very practical or particularly wise."

It was intended, Martin realised, as an apology and also as an explanation, the nearest she would probably ever bring herself to make, and he accepted it as such although, as he left the room, the word which came most strongly to his mind, the same adjective which had occurred to him when he had seen Edward Voyte's photograph caught in the bright light of the flash bulb from Hurst's camera, was weak.

At the time, he had dismissed the impression as too derogatory. Now he saw no reason for changing that original opinion. Oddly enough, the realisation strengthened his own resolve and he walked briskly back to the car, aware of a new lightness and sense of purpose.

Rudd, too, had intended to go straight home after his return from Martin Holt's. Having dropped Boyce off at his house, he drove on to the headquarters to leave the threads from the jacket for forensic examination and then, remembering the Voyte papers were still in his pocket, he climbed the stairs to his office.

It was growing dusk and, turning on the lights, he sat down at his desk, spreading the papers out on the desk.

There were not many of them: three white envelopes, unstamped and unaddressed except for the name Elizabeth written across the front, a small book of poems and a postcard-size photograph of a man's head and shoulders.

He glanced at the photograph first before laying it to one side. Young, good-looking but something unsatisfactory about the face, he thought, summing up the features briefly, It was a little too self-conscious, as if Voyte has assumed the pensive, romantic expression of the young poet—a Shelley, perhaps, or a Keats—for the benefit of the camera.

It was an impression which seemed borne out by the letters. Like the envelopes, they carried no address and were undated except for the day of the week written across the top. The sheets of paper looked worn and well handled, the folds so deeply creased that in places the paper was perforated, making them difficult to handle.

He spread them out carefully on the desk, setting aside for the moment the poems, written on separate sheets, which were enclosed in the same envelopes.

It was years since Rudd himself had written a love letter to a girl but he could still remember the conscious searching for words and phrases that would please her and the feeling that what he was writing was not so much a spontaneous expression of his real emotions as a declaration of what she would want to read.

Voyte's letters were better expressed, of course. The language flowed with a more easy grace and yet, behind the apparent spontaneity of the ardour, Rudd thought he could detect the same self-conscious strivings of the lover.

Not that he was entirely cynical. Despite his reservations, the letters roused in him a regret for old, forgotten passions and for the loss of that reckless desire which would have given him the courage to declare his feelings to Marion Greave months ago.

He was too prudent now to express himself as freely as Voyte had done; too circumspect; too afraid of appearing a fool.

And even if he found the confidence, would she welcome such a declaration? He wasn't sure.

All the same, he reread some of the phrases, testing out their expressions of desire. My darling girl. My beloved. My sweet Elizabeth.

My sweet Marion?

It hardly suited, he thought, calling to mind her cool astringency, the amused and slightly mocking lift to the corner of her eyes, as he folded up the letters and replaced them in their envelopes.

As for the poems, he was even less capable of judging their worth, he decided, turning over pages in the book before reading those in manuscript. Even if he had been in the mood, he was not academically equipped to assess them fairly.

But Marion Greave might know.

He remembered her drawing-room with its lamps and flowers, the shelves full of books, and he had a sudden and overwhelming desire to enter it again, to sit facing her, listening to her voice and watching those little puckers of amusement gather underneath her eyes.

It wasn't too late to phone her, he decided, amused himself at his own middle-aged concern for the practicalities as he checked his watch. Voyte would no doubt have considered such a detail as the time quite unimportant.

He even managed to keep his voice steady as he explained, when she picked up the receiver, that he wanted her advice on a case he was working on.

"Advice? Is it a medical matter?"

Her voice was pleasantly friendly, nothing more.

"No, its some poems I'd like your opinion on."

Her laughter restored his own good humour and equanimity.

"You intrigue me. I'd love to see them. Bring them over and you can join me for coffee."

CHAPTER ELEVEN

Her house was in the Springfield area, the last in a short, tree-lined cul-de-sac which, with its plain façade and long sash-windows, had the appearance of a prim country parsonage.

Marion Greave met him at the door, smiling but making no attempt to hold out her hand. Apart from the occasion of their first meeting, when Pardoe had introduced her to Rudd as his locum and they had shaken hands, there had never been any physical contact between them, not even in the most conventional form. At first, Rudd had been grateful for this distance. Uncertain of his own feelings, he had preferred the lack of intimacy which had kept their relationship cordially professional but nothing more.

Now, he found it less desirable. They had met several times since for dinner and the occasional visit to a cinema, both at her invitation as well as his, and an easier friendship had developed in which the distance had narrowed but had not been entirely bridged.

Should he attempt to cross it?

It was a question he had asked himself several times and one which Voyte's love-letters and poems had made him reconsider. But he was no nearer finding the answer, he realised, as he followed her down the hall, into the large drawing-room at the back of the house, where the French windows were open onto the garden, half-hidden in the dusk, and the lamps were already alight.

While she fetched coffee and sandwiches, he sat down, placing the packet of Voyte papers on the low table between their two chairs and glancing about him with pleasure at the room. He always felt absurdly at ease there, as if the bridge were already crossed and he had come home.

Some lines in one of Voyte's poems summed it up for him:

> Then come, my love,
> And take possession
> Of our solitary, sunlit kingdom.
> Give me your hand
> And cross the threshold.
> Here sky and water intermingle
> And our kisses
> Fall softly through the air.

The only trouble was, he thought wryly, that, unlike Voyte, he did not possess the words to express his similar longings. Nor could he be sure that she would welcome him across the threshold.

She returned while he was pondering this dilemma, bending down to place the tray between them, so close that he could have touched her quite easily simply by putting out his hand. For those few seconds, he studied her profile, always more beautiful when seen in close-up than at a distance, the thick, short lashes lying against the upward sweep of her cheeks where the fine-pored skin had caught a bloom of light from the lamps and the dark hair, brushed back, revealing the tip of one ear and the line of her neck.

The next moment, she had sat down in her chair, tucking her feet under the skirt of the long linen kaftan she was wearing and the illusion of beauty had gone. She was pleasantly plain, as Rudd had decided at their first meeting, and not even love, if that's what he felt for her, could disguise that fact.

But all the same, it was an interesting face, far more fascinating to him than one with mere physical attractiveness. He had tried many times to analyse it and had come to the conclusion that it was what it expressed that beguiled him: intelligence, humour and an utter lack of self-consciousness.

Sitting relaxed in the armchair, her cup of coffee held between both her hands, she said, "Tell me about the case."

The directness was typical of her and, as he might have done for any professional colleague, he gave her a straightforward, factual account of Rex Holt's death, leaving out only his own interpretation of it.

"So Pardoe thinks it's murder," she commented as he finished.

"He seems convinced of it. The nature of the wounds suggests it couldn't be accidental."

She frowned slightly as she concentrated.

"And although it was murder, the crime was committed in such a way as to make it appear it was an accident but was so clumsily carried out that murder is the only possible conclusion?"

With that quick reasoning of hers, she had put her finger immediately on the aspect of the case which had troubled him and which he had tried to explain to Boyce.

"Exactly!" he said. "A murder made to appear like a murder."

She saw the point at once.

"But is it significant?" she asked. "How would that theory connect with your chief suspect? I assume you have one?"

"Martin Holt, the dead man's son. He stands to inherit a considerable fortune from his father's will. There are others but Boyce is convinced Holt's guilty. The only trouble with that theory is, he has an alibi."

"What alibi?"

"He was seen by someone."

"A reliable witness?"

"I don't think the man was lying."

"What about the watch the dead man, Rex Holt, was wearing? You said it had been smashed at eight minutes past ten. It is possible it was deliberately broken?"

"So the time on it would give the murderer an alibi?" Rudd asked, thinking it was bright of her to pick up this point. He had merely mentioned the watch but had made no reference to any theory regarding it. "But other evidence suggests Holt must have been killed about that time."

"I was thinking more of the watch being used to confirm an alibi," Marion Greave replied.

Rudd put down his coffee-cup.

"You mean whoever killed him appeared to have an alibi for eight minutes past ten?"

"Exactly. Which would make it seem impossible for him or her to have murdered Rex Holt." The little, smiling crinkles appeared underneath her eyes. "I'm assuming you have a woman among your suspects?"

"Two," Rudd said distractedly. He was running through the suspects in his mind. Of the four he had interviewed, discounting the Drewetts, only Martin Holt had an alibi which covered, or seemed to cover, the relevant time, unless he included Hester Chilton, who had supposedly been driving down to Barnsfield, not arriving at her mother's house until just after eleven o'clock. But if Marion Greave were right, her theory would better fit Martin Holt than Hester Chilton.

He continued out loud, "So the point of smashing the watch was to confirm the time of death, not change it, because the murderer wanted us to know exactly when Rex Holt died because he had a faked alibi to cover that time?"

"That's what I had in mind. We both know how difficult it is to be precise about the timing in a case of sudden death. Certainly, as a doctor, the best I can sometimes do is to approximate it within a couple of hours."

Rudd was ridiculously pleased to hear her refer to them both, almost as if they were a couple, even though it was on a purely professional basis.

The implications, however, behind the rest of the remark were more disturbing and, voicing his thoughts, he said, "I don't know how the hell he could have faked it."

"The son, you mean?"

"Yes. He was *seen.*"

"But otherwise the case against him is a strong one?"

"I don't know." His former uncertainty returned. "There's other evidence which points to him. He was in need of money. He had quarrelled with his father. We found some threads caught on a rosebush near the murder site which almost certainly came from a jacket belonging to him. Forensic will have to confirm it, of course, but—"

"You're not convinced he's guilty." Marion Greave completed the sentence for him. "Why?"

He looked at her and smiled ruefully.

"Instinct. No, don't laugh!" he protested as he saw the corners of her mouth lift in amusement. "I know only women are supposed to work on intuition but it's not just your prerogative, you know. Men can feel it as well. We don't call it by such a fancy name, of course."

"Gut reaction?" she suggested, this time making no attempt to hide her laughter, in which he joined, thinking how much he needed her common sense and even her mockery to counterbalance his own tendency to take his work too seriously at times.

"But I've got no gut reaction about these," he added, picking up the Voyte papers. "The letters seemed a little self-conscious but I'm no judge of the poems. That's why I wanted your opinion."

Aware of their content, he felt a little self-conscious himself as he handed them to her. Voyte's expressions of love seemed to make his own feelings too transparent. All the same, he watched her face carefully as she read them, trying to gauge her thoughts. But it gave nothing away except a studious concentration.

"When were these written?" she asked, laying the sheets in her lap when she had finished.

"Just before the beginning of the last war. Voyte was evidently a student at Oxford at the time. He was killed in the Battle of Britain."

"So he'd be in his early twenties?"

"I suppose so."

"Do they have any bearing on the case?"

"I don't think so. They belonged to Martin Holt's mother. I was curious because Holt seemed very anxious to get hold of them, to the extent of taking them out of his father's bureau the morning after the murder had been discovered. In fact, I suspect he went off to Suffolk earlier today to see Voyte's mother, who's still alive. It seemed a strange thing to do in the middle of a murder inquiry in which he's the chief suspect; or, at least, was until I found out about his alibi this evening."

She gathered up the sheets of paper and glanced over them again, as if confirming an original impression before handing them back to him.

"You're right about the letters. They are self-conscious. I think the poems show the same tendency. They're very much a young man's, more in love with the idea of love than the real girl. She's a symbol of desire, nothing more."

As Rudd refolded the papers and returned them to their envelopes, he felt ridiculously humbled, as if she had rejected him, not just Voyte's letters and poems.

He heard the rustle of her long gown as she got to her feet. The next moment, she had crossed behind his chair and, taking a book from the shelves which lined the wall, had opened it and passed it to him over his shoulder.

As she stood behind him, only her hand and part of her arm visible to him, the embroidered linen cuff falling back to reveal her wrist, he was acutely aware of her physical presence, so close and yet largely unseen.

"If you want a good example of love poetry written at about the same period," she said, "I'd recommend this one by Alun Lewis. Like Voyte, he was killed in the war, only in Burma."

It was entitled "Corfe Castle" and Finch's attention was drawn particularly to three lines:

> . . . Yet, love,
> Before we go be simple as this grass.
> Lie rustling for this last time in my arms.

"Yes," he said quietly, when he had finished reading it, "I see what you mean."

She had remained behind his chair, following the lines in the poem with him and, although there was no actual contact between them, he could feel her aura, like a warm, palpable sensation, spreading out to touch his hair and the back of his neck.

At the same time, he was aware of a tightness in his chest which made speech difficult and, even as the words struggled out, he listened to his own voice as if it were someone else's.

" 'Lie rustling for this last time in my arms.' " And then, after a short silence, "I love you, Marion."

He sat perfectly still after he had said it. She, too, was motionless. In the silence of the room, he could hear the faint lift and stir of the leaves beyond the open windows, as if the garden were gently breathing in and out.

The closer susurration of her skirt seemed part of the same natural exhalation and he closed his eyes briefly, drawing it in.

When he opened them, she was seated again in the chair facing him. "My dear," she said.

He shut the book and placed it with infinite care on the low table. It seemed terribly important that he should line it up exactly with the edge of the tray so that their sides formed a perfect parallel.

Watching his hands as he aligned the book, he continued, "But it's no use."

It was a statement, not a question. The tone of her voice as she spoke those two words had told him he was rejected. It was gentle, tender, compassionate even; hardly the voice of a woman who addresses a lover.

"I'm so sorry, Jack. If I were capable of loving anybody, it would be you."

Her answer genuinely surprised him and he looked directly across at her.

"Capable?"

She lifted a hand as if to express her inability to explain.

"I'm too selfish. Unwilling, anyway, to commit myself."

He understood her perfectly. It had been for exactly the same reason that he himself had hesitated for so long.

It was ironic, he thought. Private people both of them, they would have made a perfect couple and yet it was this very need for independence and solitude which kept them separate. For his part, he would have sacrificed both for love and companionship. Perhaps she, too, felt that lack, for, as he rose, she cried out in quick protest, "Oh, don't go!"

"I think I must," he replied.

She said nothing more but followed him to the door, where she put one hand on his arm. He felt its warmth through the thin fabric of the summer jacket he was wearing.

"But you'll come again?" she said.

He glanced over her shoulder down the hall towards the drawing-room, her solitary, lamp-lit kingdom.

"If I may. As a friend, of course."

He added the last remark to please her, he told himself, although he knew that, had he walked away, closing the door for ever, it would have been he, not she, who was the greater loser.

"And thank you for helping me with the poetry," he added. It was meant as a final remark, one of those awkward, parting conventionalities, which, in the absence of anything else to say, was all he could think of.

She said, "Let me know how the case goes. I really am interested, Jack. I hope your insight's right and the son's alibi wasn't faked so that he can inherit."

At the time, he took the comment to mean merely her interest in his concerns, for which he was grateful. Its full significance didn't occur to him until later.

The house was in darkness and, as he let himself in, turning on the hall light, he was aware of the total silence. Normally, his sister would have been there to welcome him. Tonight, he was grateful for her absence, which saved him from the necessity of lying to her.

He had never discussed Marion Greave with her, partly out of a natural reticence but mainly, as he himself admitted in his more honest moments, out of guilt. She had kept house for him for many years, since the death of her husband, devoting to him that same anxious, loving care which his mother had shown towards him and which, at times, he found exasperating. He preferred Marion Greave's cool independence and self-sufficiency, the sense of space she created round herself, which, to him, was both a challenge and a release. But to choose it in preference to his sister's devotion amounted to nothing less than a betrayal.

And, anyway, he thought wryly, switching on the electric kettle to make himself tea, the question was now entirely academic. Marion Greave had rejected him, so the problem of what to do about Dorothy no longer arose. They would continue, he supposed, their usual pattern and, if ever he saw Marion Greave again—as a friend, of course, he was careful to make that stipulation to himself as he poured the boiling water into the teapot—he would make the old lies and excuses to his sister so that the calm surface of their lives wouldn't be disturbed.

The telephone rang just as he had sat down with his mug of tea. It was Boyce, speaking too close to the mouthpiece as usual, so that Rudd had to hold the receiver some distance from his ear.

"Oh, so you're home. I've been trying to get hold of you for the past hour," Boyce said in an aggrieved voice, as if it were all Rudd's fault that he hadn't been available.

"I was at the office," Rudd replied.

"I tried there, too, only there wasn't any answer."

Rudd merely said, "What do you want, Tom?"

He had no intention of expanding his sphere of obligation by lying to Boyce as well.

"You know my brother-in-law?" the sergeant began after a small silence in which Rudd could feel his curiosity coming across the line in almost palpable waves.

"I've heard you speak of him," Rudd replied, wishing to God Boyce would come to the point.

"Well, he's an electrician. I happened to see him tonight down the Crown and mentioned to him that business of the light going out in Martin Holt's greenhouse. Not in so many words," Boyce was quick to add, as if he knew Rudd had opened his mouth in protest. "I didn't discuss the case with him. I just asked him was it possible to turn lights off without anybody being there. And he said, Yes, you can get time-switches. Well," and here Boyce paused for the maximum effect, "it crossed my mind that Holt might have fixed up something similar."

"But Webber saw him," Rudd began and then stopped. As he spoke the words, he had a clear mental image of the greenhouse as he had seen it only that afternoon with the leaves pressed close up against the glass. He continued rapidly, "You've got a greenhouse, haven't you, Tom?"

"Yes, I have."

The sergeant sounded surprised.

"What do you grow in it?"

"Me? I don't grow anything. It's the wife—" He must have heard Rudd's impatient intake of breath because he added quickly, "Tomatoes. But I don't see—"

"I'm coming over," the chief inspector broke in.

"What, now?"

Rudd rang off without bothering to answer.

It was a bizarre end to the evening. The time was close on midnight when Rudd arrived at Boyce's house, where the sergeant, wearing pyjamas and a dressing-grown, let him in.

"I had a bath earlier," he explained, in the same aggrieved voice he had used on the telephone. "The wife's gone to bed. What's all this about the greenhouse?"

"Just an experiment," Rudd replied. They were speaking in low voices as the sergeant led the way into the kitchen, where he shut the door. "Is there a light in there?"

"No," Boyce sounded bemused.

"Can you fix one up?"

Boyce suddenly grinned, as if he'd seen the point.

"There's a long extension lead in the garage. I could plug that in with a reading-lamp on the other end. Would that do?"

They worked like conspirators in the darkness, Rudd going ahead with a torch while the sergeant unreeled the flex. The garden was small, thank God, a mere suburban plot, like Rudd's, and contained little more than a rectangle of lawn with surrounding flower-beds and a small greenhouse at the far end.

While Boyce returned to the house to collect a reading lamp, Rudd stood in the dark, snuffing up the warm, green odour of the plants.

The rear façade of the row of semi-detached houses was in darkness, their occupants asleep, respectable and snug behind drawn curtains. He wondered if Martin Holt was also in bed, but awake or not, he'd be unaware that two middle-aged policemen, with the suppressed excitement of a couple of schoolboys setting up a prank, were attempting to break his alibi.

Boyce came treading softly back, holding a bedside lamp with a fringed shade.

"It's from our bedroom," he explained in a whisper. "It's all I could find. Woke the wife up getting it, too."

He nodded his head backwards towards the house where one window was now illuminated, staring down out of the pebble-dashed façade like a disapproving eye.

Plugging in the lamp, Boyce began snorting with uncontrollable, suppressed laughter, his shoulders shaking as he bent down to click on the switch.

Pink light flooded the tiny interior, casting rosy shadows on the undersides of the leaves.

"Christ!" Boyce remarked, straightening up and glancing about him. "It looks like a tart's bedroom. Will it do?"

"It'll give me a rough idea," Rudd replied. "If it works, we'll have to check it more carefully, of course. How far away was Webber, do you reckon?"

"About eighty feet—if not more."

"So if I stand by your back door, it should be far enough."

"You're giving him the benefit of the doubt," Boyce replied. "Webber was a good twenty feet further away. What do you want me to do?"

"Just stand there," Rudd told him.

He retreated up the garden, suppressing any curiosity to glance back over his shoulder, only turning round when he reached the door step. The little greenhouse shone pinkly at the end of the lawn, the leaves showing as a dark mass against the glass. Shoulders humped, Rudd surveyed it for a few moments before tramping back to join Boyce.

"Well?" the sergeant asked, his eagerness apparent.

"It's possible," Rudd replied. He felt suddenly in a desolate mood, exhausted and empty, as if every spark of vitality had been quenched in that one instance. Odd, he thought, that Marion Greave's rejection of him should strike him more forcibly now than at the time it had happened.

"But could you see me?" Boyce persisted.

"Only a vague shape behind the leaves," he replied.

"He could have fixed something up," Boyce was quick to point out.

He enlarged on this point a few minutes later when, on their return to the kitchen, he produced a bottle of whisky and a couple of glasses.

So it was to be a celebration, Rudd thought with a black, sardonic humour as he squashed himself, glass in hand, behind the tiny breakfast table.

Boyce was saying, "How do you reckon he did it? A cardboard cut-out? Or some kind of dummy dressed up?"

"I don't know, Tom," Rudd replied, trying to look interested for Boyce's sake. "And don't be too keen. We still have to prove that Holt knew Webber would be passing the smallholding at the right time to establish his alibi."

Even as he said it, he knew what the answer to that particular objection would be. Like many old countrymen, Webber would no doubt have established a routine by which one could almost set one's watch.

The rest of it fitted only too neatly and he remembered Marion Greave's comment about the watch. If she were right and it had been smashed to confirm an alibi, then Martin Holt could not only have motive but opportunity as well.

The same thought must have been passing through the sergeant's mind, for Boyce said, "So he'll be a rich man. It must have been a hell of a temptation, knowing he'd inherit that much money."

The remark reminded Rudd of Marion Greave's passing comment, which, at the time, he had passed over as a mere pleasantry to soften her rejection of him as a lover and to indicate her continuing interest in him as a friend.

But the words were not exactly the same.

Marion had said, "I hope you'll find the son's alibi wasn't faked so that he'll be able to inherit."

"So." That was the important word.

Finch wondered why the hell he hadn't seen it before. It was so damned obvious.

He said, "Wait a minute, Tom. If Holt killed his father, he won't inherit. It's the law. Anyone found guilty of a crime can't benefit from it."

"Well?" Boyce didn't sound all that impressed by the argument. "Holt didn't expect to be found out."

"No!" Rudd was quite positive this time. The former doubts and uncertainties which before he had hesitated to voice aloud to Boyce now took coherent shape. Even his mood of desolation lifted a little in the excitement of the moment. "Holt's no fool. He's an intelligent man. He's also . . ." Here Rudd paused, searching for a word which Marion Greave had used when discussing the case with him, and he momentarily closed his eyes, seeing her again sitting opposite him in the armchair, the lamplight lying in pools in the folds of her skirt.

A murder clumsily contrived.

"But he isn't clumsy," Rudd said out loud, opening his eyes to see Boyce looking at him with a wary but carefully controlled expression, as if he suspected that the chief inspector had suffered some sudden mental aberration and was about to blurt out God knows what across the tiny table.

"I don't get it," he said flatly.

"Listen, Tom," Rudd said. He spoke urgently, keeping his voice low but aware that what he said had to be convincing, not just for Boyce's sake but his own. "Remember that shed where we found Holt's jacket?"

"Yes," Boyce conceded that much.

"What was in it?"

It was important to Rudd that it was Boyce who expressed the idea and he found himself wishing that the sergeant would hurry up and complete the mental processes which would bring him to the same conclusion.

Boyce frowned as he concentrated.

"Not much. Fertilizer sacks. Lumber."

"Go on," Rudd encouraged him. "What about them?"

Boyce looked across at him in odd appeal, as if he were confronted by an idea which he wasn't sure he could articulate, perhaps because it was so damned obvious.

"Well, the sacks were folded in a pile and the lumber was stacked in one corner."

It was said in an offhand manner, almost with a shrug.

Rudd beamed at him.

"Exactly! Folded. Stacked. Neat, in other words. Organised. Certainly not clumsy. And the murder of Rex Holt was botched, Tom. Whoever did it made a balls-up. But not Martin Holt. If Holt had wanted to kill his father, he'd've made a better job of it. He certainly wouldn't have left the murder weapon lying by the side of that path for us to find. He'd've been careful, too, not to catch the sleeve of his jacket on that rose-bush."

Boyce opened his mouth to argue and then, thinking better of it, shut it again but his expression was dubious.

Rudd ploughed on.

"So we're left with the conclusion that Martin Holt isn't guilty."

Boyce did object to that.

"Conclusion?"

"Supposition, then. But let's follow it through by looking at the evidence from the point of view of Holt's innocence, not his guilt. If he didn't do it, who did?"

"Any of the others mentioned in Holt's will, I suppose," Boyce said with the same grudging air. "Mrs. Chilton, Trimmer, the Drewetts . . ."

"Don't forget Bea Chilton's daughter."

"All right, then; her, too. That's the lot, isn't it, apart from Holt's former manager, Barnard or whatever his name was?"

"You forgot the niece," Rudd pointed out.

"Oh, come off it!" Boyce sounded incredulous. "You're not serious?"

"Yes, I am. If Martin Holt is found guilty of murdering his father, he won't inherit a penny of his estate. The lot will go to the next in line. And the only other living relative is the niece, Jean Browning."

"Now, hang on a minute," Boyce broke in. "That's jumping to one hell of a conclusion. You're assuming she murdered Rex Holt and then set it up to look as if Martin Holt was guilty?"

"Yes," Rudd said simply.

"Planted the evidence?" Boyce persisted. "The murder weapon? The threads from Holt's jacket?"

"It'd be easy enough. That shed's unlocked. Anyone could have got in and pulled a few fibres from the sleeve. Don't forget, we didn't have any problem doing exactly that ourselves. There's also the telephone."

"You've lost me," Boyce admitted. "What phone?"

"Martin Holt's. If you remember, it was out of order. He had to ring up his father's house from a call-box. Someone could have damaged the line deliberately."

"But what was the point in doing that?"

"To make sure he couldn't prove an alibi for yesterday evening?" Rudd suggested. "If the line was dead, he couldn't make or receive any calls. She could have watched the house, too, at the same time, checking up on what he does in the evening and if he lives alone."

"But Holt did have an alibi; at least, he seemed to have one until we proved it could have been faked. Webber said he saw him."

"Agreed," Rudd conceded. "But Webber's evidence was something she hadn't bargained for. She had to work on the assumption that Martin Holt would be on his own that evening and couldn't prove where he was or what he was doing at the time his father was murdered." As Boyce was silent, he continued, "Doesn't it make sense, Tom? It does to me."

"But it's only a theory," Boyce replied, still unwilling to be persuaded. "You've no real evidence."

"No. But tomorrow I intend interviewing Jean Browning just as soon as I've got her address from Gilham, Holt's solicitor."

Boyce didn't say that, in his opinion, they'd be wasting their time but, as Rudd finished his whisky and got up from the table, the sergeant's expression indicated as much.

Outside, Rudd paused before getting into his car. The night was still warm and the sky had the deep, soft texture to it of plush, bloomed with a reddish glow cast up by the lights of the city, which extinguished most stars except for the brighter constellations. He could see the Plough and Orion, which seemed suspended just above the suburban roof-tops and which reminded him of a couplet from one of Voyte's poems:

> Orion strides between us
> Yet links us to his stars.

It was a familiar concept—that of the parted lovers united in their observation of the same object. Yet he had the absurd hope that Marion Greave might possibly still be awake and standing at her bedroom window, watching the same brilliant pattern as himself.

CHAPTER TWELVE

Number seventeen, Belmont Road, Streatham, was one of a row of terraced houses built, Rudd guessed, in the 1930s when the vogue for the half-timbered cottage was beginning to wane. All the proportions looked skimped, from the miniature front garden to the tiny porch tacked on over the front door.

Rudd rang the bell.

There was no answer although their arrival had not gone unnoticed in number fifteen, where a net curtain was momentarily twitched to one side.

When a second peal on the bell was unsuccessful, Rudd nodded his head in the direction of the house next door and, with Boyce in tow, tramped round to the neighbouring porch.

An elderly man in shirt-sleeves and slippers opened the door, looking surprised, as if their presence was totally unexpected.

Rudd flourished his ID.

"We're making a few routine inquiries," he announced in his blandest voice. "Mrs. Browning seems to be out."

"She's at work," the man replied. "Cashier at Woodward's round the corner. Won't be home till nearly six."

"In that case," Rudd continued, "you may be able to help us, Mr. . . . ?"

"Me?" The man seemed gratified at the suggestion. "You'd better come inside, then. The name's Barton," he added over his shoulder as he led the way into a tiny hall and from there into a back living-room, where a single door, set into a pair of casement windows, opened onto a patch of garden not much bigger than the room itself.

"I'm retired myself," Mr. Barton said half-apologetically but whether in explanation for his presence at home on a Friday morning or to excuse the cluttered state of the room wasn't clear. He whisked newspapers and clothes off chairs before inviting them to sit down. "Worked on the buses for years. Still." There was a weight of philosophical acceptance in the last word which seemed to sum up a whole working life reduced to pottering about in the small house and garden which now constituted his entire world. "What can I do to help you?"

Rudd said carefully, "There's been a sudden death in Mrs. Browning's family and we wondered if Mrs. Browning has had any contact with her uncle recently. It seemed he had a visitor on Wednesday night. Was she out, do you know?"

"No, she was home."

It was said quite positively and Boyce, picking up Rudd's low-key manner, asked laconically, "You saw her, then?"

"No, but I heard her." To their surprise, he leaned across and tapped on the fireplace wall, which connected with number seventeen immediately next door. "Like cardboard these walls are. You can hear a cat sneeze. Heard the telly, heard doors shutting, heard the telly go off at eleven o'clock. She went up to bed soon after that because I was in bed myself by that time and heard her moving about. Mind you, I'm not complaining. It's not her fault. The people on the other side are worse, playing pop music at all hours, only I don't hear so much of them because the hall's between. That's why I sleep in front—only the one neighbour to worry about."

"She lives alone?" Rudd asked, picking up the last remark.

"There's no husband that I know of. Could be divorced. Or widowed, like me. Pleasant enough to speak to, not that I have much to do with her except to say hello if I see her in the garden."

"Goes out much, does she?" Rudd asked casually.

"Not that I've known her to all the two years she's been here, not even on a Wednesday her half-day. Does her washing and cleaning then. I saw the clothes out on the back line and heard a Hoover going."

"Rather a quiet life for a young woman," Rudd suggested.

"That type," Mr. Barton said, nodding his head in concurrence with this brief assessment.

It was a description which Rudd was inclined to agree with when, shortly afterwards, they drove round to the parade of shops which served the local housing estate. Woodward's was a small supermarket, its double windows plastered with posters advertising special offers and bargains of the week. Peering between them, he saw three check-out desks, the first empty, the central one occupied by a young West Indian woman. So it had to be Jean Browning who was sitting in the third.

She was serving a customer, lifting the goods out of the wire basket and ringing up the prices on the till. Watching her profile, Rudd was struck by her quiet, self-contained air. Although only in her late twenties, she gave the impression of someone older, preoccupied with the task in hand, only glancing up at the customer when she handed over the change. Even her smile was merely dutiful, fading the moment the woman had gathered up her shopping and left.

Joyless.

The word seemed to sum her up.

It was apparent in her physical appearance, as if she took only a minimal interest in herself. She wasn't unattractive, as Rudd saw when, a few minutes later, having spoken to the manager, he watched her enter the office and, at his invitation, take the chair facing him across the desk. The features were good but lacked animation, while the dark hair was drawn back off her face as if she couldn't be bothered with a more elaborate style.

There was a resemblance to Martin Holt both in the hair colouring and in a stubborn look about the mouth and chin. And in another quality, too, which Rudd found less easy to define and which he could only describe as an aloofness. In Martin Holt, it took the form of a sardonic nonchalance, as if he genuinely didn't give a damn for other people's opinion. Hers was much tighter and more buttoned-down.

She said, "You wanted to see me?"

Her voice still retained a trace of South African accent which, with its pinched vowels and flattened intonation, added to the impression of polite indifference as she approached the manager's desk, behind which Rudd had installed himself.

God knows what he had been expecting. Certainly not this nondescript young woman, dressed in the supermarket's blue-and-white checked overall, with her air of unshakable passivity.

He began brusquely, as soon as he had introduced himself and Boyce, hoping to shock her into a reaction.

"I'm afraid I have bad news for you, Mrs. Browning. Your uncle, Rex Holt, has been found dead."

Her eyes, which had been fixed on some neutral point between them, sharpened their focus and she looked directly at him for the first time.

"Uncle Rex. When did this happen?"

"Wednesday evening."

Rudd deliberately left it there, wondering what she would make of the information. So far, she had shown little more than the minimal surprise the death of a distant relative might cause.

After a pause, she asked, "What did he die of?"

"He fell." Rudd offered the next small piece of information and again waited.

It was an interviewing technique he had often used before, inviting communication by his own silence. But in this case, it was a slow if not embarrassing procedure. She seemed to think it was not her place to initiate conversation, only to respond if directly appealed to.

"I see," was all she said and then, after a silence in which she appeared to be searching for some further response, "Had he been ill?"

"You haven't had any contact with him recently?" Rudd asked, sidestepping her question with one of his own. The exact circumstances of Rex Holt's death was a matter which he preferred to save until later.

"No," she replied. "I've written to him twice, but not for a long time."

"So you didn't call to see him on Wednesday?"

"Wednesday?" She seemed bewildered by the question. "On the day he died? No, I didn't."

"What did you do on Wednesday?" Boyce put in. It was part of the interviewing process that, from time to time, the sergeant should interpose a question of his own, adding, as it were, a sniper's cross-fire from the sidelines.

She looked across at him as if seeing him for the first time.

"I was at home in the afternoon. It's my half-day."

"All afternoon?"

"Yes."

"Doing what?"

"I did some housework and the washing."

"And in the evening?"

"I watched television."

"You didn't go out?"

"No."

"Do you own a car, Mrs. Browning?"

"No, I don't." The rapid questioning had some effect on her because she turned in appeal to the chief inspector. "I don't see the point of these questions. What have they got to do with Uncle Rex dying?"

Rudd switched techniques. With Boyce now established as the police heavy, rattling off questions in rapid succession, he could now play the role of the friendly father figure, the policeman who understands.

"I believe you haven't been living very long in this country, Mrs. Browning. You must find it difficult adjusting to a new way of life. What made you decide to come here?"

Her response was still low-keyed but at least he had prompted a more positive reaction in her. With her eyes on his face as if reading his expression for some sign of sympathy or perhaps lack of it, she said, "There was nothing to keep me in South Africa. My father died a few years ago. I suppose I wanted to come back to my roots. He'd often spoken of England as home. I grew up with that idea."

"And your husband?" Rudd prompted.

He'd lost her. She merely replied, "I was divorced about three years ago."

"No children?"

"No."

"So you had no one to keep you in Johannesburg?"

She merely shook her head.

"You said you wrote to your uncle. When was this?"

"When my father died."

"Did he reply?"

"He sent some money."

The impassivity had returned. Even her eyes had shifted focus, no longer looking at him directly but at that midway point between them.

"And that was the only time you contacted him?"

Rudd knew from Gilham what her answer ought to be. It would be interesting to see how far she told the truth.

She said, "I wrote again letting him know my address after I'd arrived in England."

"Did he reply to that?"

"I got a letter from his solicitor, telling me he'd received it."

"Nothing else?"

"No, that was all."

"Were you disappointed he didn't write to you himself?"

She hesitated, glancing across at him as if from the other side of the void.

Void was the right word, Rudd decided. He had rarely met anyone who created so much emptiness about her. But whether it was natural, acquired or perhaps even cultivated, it was impossible to tell. Too little emanated from her for him to judge.

"In some ways, yes."

"You'd hoped to establish some family contact?"

"I thought he might have got in touch if only for my father's sake."

"Because they were brothers?"

Again, she didn't reply directly, merely indicating her answer by a small nod of the head.

"Did you mind?"

Her answer this time was more interesting if only because of its obliqueness.

"I'm used to being alone."

It was said in much the same way as Mr. Barton had voiced the one word "still," with a similar resignation, as if acknowledging a fact of life which had to be accepted, not fought against.

"It can't have been easy," Rudd suggested. For the first time during the interview, he felt a small stirring of compassion for her; not much. She was not the type to invite too positive a reaction, largely because she showed so little herself.

"I've managed," she said.

"Financially?"

She compressed her lips as if the question annoyed her by being none of his business, the only sign of any emotional response she had shown since the interview began.

"I had some money of my own. It's not been easy but I've got by."

"Then," Rudd said with assumed cheerfulness, "you'll no doubt be pleased to hear that your uncle has left you some money in his will. His solicitor, Mr. Gilham, will be getting in touch with you."

"I see. That's very kind of him."

This time she showed nothing, neither pleasure, anticipation nor surprise. Even her answer was ambiguous, not specifying whether she referred to her uncle or the solicitor.

In the same cheerful tone, Rudd continued, "There may be some delay, however, in settling up Mr. Holt's affairs. The inquiries into exactly how your uncle met his death have still to be completed. We're not sure it was from natural causes."

He watched her face carefully, saw her frown slightly and lean forward as if the better to observe him.

"I don't understand," she said flatly.

"Then I'll explain. Your uncle was found dead yesterday morning at the bottom of some steps. It appears," and he stressed the word deliberately, "that he fell and struck his head. We have reason to believe, however, that his death was carefully planned."

Let's see what she makes of that, he thought.

She didn't make a great deal.

"Someone pushed him?" she suggested tentatively.

"Someone hit him on the side of the head with a large stone."

"But that's . . ." she began and then stopped.

"Yes, Mrs. Browning?" Rudd prompted.

She ran her tongue over her lips.

"Murder!"

"Exactly!" Rudd nodded as if pleased at her perspicacity. At the same time, he stood up to indicate the interview was over. This sudden conclusion often worked as a ploy. Out of a mixture of anxiety and surprise, many people could not resist making some last-minute comment, which could be revealing.

In her case, she got up from her chair with the same air of dutiful acquiescence in which she had sat down in it and all she said was "But who could have done it?"

"That's what we intend finding out," Rudd told her, before walking out of the office, followed by Boyce.

Outside, he got into the car, slamming the door in a purposeful manner, hoping Boyce would take the hint.

He didn't.

"If you want my opinion," he remarked, climbing in behind the wheel, "we're barking up the wrong tree. There's no way she could have murdered Rex Holt."

With the feeling that he was arguing for a lost cause, Rudd said, "She has no real alibi. Barton didn't see her on Wednesday evening. He only heard her."

"You mean she could have faked all those noises of doors shutting and the television being turned off?"

If he didn't exactly express the derisive comment "Come off it!" his tone of voice certainly implied it.

"It could be done," Rudd pointed out. "If you're convinced Martin Holt arranged a false alibi with a time-switch connected to the lights in the greenhouse, I don't see why tape-recorders can't be switched on and off in the same way."

"I'll give you that," Boyce conceded magnanimously. "But can you see her doing it? I can't. Besides, she'd not only have to set all that lot up but she'd also have to get over to Martin Holt's place, put his phone out of order and pinch some threads from his jacket. And that's not taking into account the murder itself. She'd still have to make a second trip to Barnsfield Hall to kill Rex Holt and fake the evidence to make it look like Martin Holt was guilty. I don't see how the hell she could have managed it all on her own."

"Why not?" Rudd demanded. He was inclined to agree with the sergeant but not, he suspected, for the same reasons.

"She had no car."

"She could have hired one."

"All right, so she could. But I still don't think she did it."

"Go on," Rudd urged. "Tell me why."

Boyce looked at him sideways, his expression full of a baffled and exasperated embarrassment.

"I can't explain."

"Gut reaction?" Rudd suggested, only half-humorously, remembering Marion Greave's amusement at the same suggestion applied, in that case, to himself.

He wasn't sure why he was playing this game with Boyce although he was aware he was doing it deliberately; as a form of exorcism, perhaps, in order to displace her in his thoughts and to set her image a little further off. It was the only way in which he could reconcile his own high aspirations with the reality of the situation.

Still.

"If you like," Rudd was mumbling. He had turned away to look out of the driver's window, presenting only a closed, sulky profile.

"Not the type?" the chief inspector persisted.

Boyce didn't reply.

"I agree," Rudd said briskly and was gratified by the sergeant's look of astonishment.

"You agree with me?" he asked as if to make quite sure of the chief inspector's attitude.

"Not enough imagination," Rudd explained. "Whoever planned that murder has style and flair and, what's more important, a special kind of inventiveness which she hasn't got."

"So we scrub her off the list?"

"Not yet."

"Why not? If Martin Holt's guilty—"

"I didn't say that."

"But . . ." Boyce broke off.

Rudd humped his shoulders. In the face of Boyce's argumentativeness, his mood suddenly changed from one of rising optimism to a bleak realisation of the task in front of him; not just the case itself but his own personal problem. It wasn't going to be that damned easy after all. He'd struggle on, of course. There wasn't much else he could do. But the thought of having to come to grips with the two areas of his life which meant most to him filled him with an overwhelming sense of desolation and despair.

The view through the windscreen didn't help much either. They were parked at the side of the road, opposite the parade of shops with their ugly, flat façades and the litter accumulated in the gutter outside the fried-fish-and-chip shop. On all sides stretched the streets of little houses, row on row, where people like Barton and Jean Browning lived out their drab lives.

"Let's get out of here," he said.

"Where to?" Boyce asked. "Back to headquarters?"

"No." Rudd came to a sudden decision. "Barnsfield."

As if aware of the chief inspector's mood, Boyce said nothing until they were well clear of the area. Then he asked tentatively, "Any particular reason? For going back to Barnsfield, I mean?"

"We're starting again," Rudd told him.

"Oh, God!" the sergeant muttered under his breath and hardly spoke again for the rest of the journey.

He still didn't have much to say when they arrived at Barnsfield Hall, where Rudd walked round to the back of the house and stood gazing down, hands in pockets, at the sunken rose-garden. The fountain had been switched off and the blinds had been drawn over the glazed doors leading into Rex Holt's room. The house already had the shuttered, deserted air of the place of the dead.

From the terrace they tramped round to the front of the house, past the climbing rose and the clump of hypericum where the threads and the stone had been discovered.

Mrs. Drewett answered the door, looking worried at their unexpected arrival.

"I want to take another look through Mr. Holt's bureau," Rudd announced. "It shouldn't take long. I still have the keys, so there's no need for you to come with us."

As she retreated down the hall towards the kitchen, Boyce plucked up the courage to ask, "What are we looking for?"

"I don't know, Tom," Rudd admitted. "I've just got the feeling we've missed something. So, on the basis of starting again, I'm going over Holt's papers for a second time."

Boyce had the good sense to say nothing in protest, merely standing by, in much the same obedient and slightly apprehensive manner as Mrs. Drewett, as Rudd, unlocking the bureau and letting down the flap, began systematically to examine its contents, compartment by compartment.

Boyce had known the chief inspector in many moods: irritable, jubilant, at times furiously angry. But rarely in this one. There was a con-

centrated aloofness about him which did not invite conversation.
Watching him as he worked his way through the bundles of papers and
documents, Boyce felt unexpectedly in awe of him and aware of qualities about him as a private man which the chief inspector rarely
showed.

God knows what was wrong. It could simply be the investigation.
But Boyce had the uncomfortable feeling that it was something more
than this although he'd probably never know for sure.

Certainly, he'd never seen the chief inspector deal with a mass of
papers with such a fierce and rapid appraisal before, as if he were not
just scanning their contents but eating them up with his eyes.

Most of it was handed back to him to return to the bureau. As Boyce
tucked it back into the compartments, he kept a sharp eye at the same
time on the smaller pile which Rudd had set to one side, documents
concerned mainly with Holt's property, hoping to God he hadn't
missed anything important on the first occasion he'd searched through
the bureau.

Rudd was on the last compartment, that containing the personal
letters, and Boyce began to feel more relaxed. He'd been through those
individually, picking out Trimmer's IOU's and, as far as he could remember, there was nothing else among them which had seemed relevant to the case.

It was then that Rudd struck.

Turning suddenly, a letter in his hand, he demanded, "You didn't
notice this one?"

Boyce looked at it. The envelope, readdressed and with a South
African stamp, looked vaguely familiar but the exact nature of its contents escaped him.

"Wasn't it from the niece, Jean Browning?" he asked. It seemed a
safe enough guess, judging by the postage stamp.

Rudd didn't bother to reply. Stuffing the letter into his pocket and
gathering up the rest of the papers he had set to one side, he relocked
the bureau and crossed to the door, Boyce hurrying to keep up with
him.

"But what's in it?" he asked. "Is it important?"

He felt a similar hollow sensation in the pit of his stomach as he had
experienced years before when, as a young bobby on the beat, he had
been summoned before the superintendent for some dereliction of duty
he had been too raw a recruit to know he had committed.

Rudd's answer, flung back over his shoulder as he rapidly descended the stairs, didn't help.

"I don't know."

He broke off at that point to shout for Mrs. Drewett, who came running out of the kitchen.

In the event, the question the chief inspector asked her didn't seem all that important.

"Who was housekeeper here about four years ago?"

"Miss Moxon, sir," Mrs. Drewett replied hurriedly.

"Doesn't she live in the village? I believe young Mr. Holt went to visit her yesterday?"

"That's right, sir. In the first cottage opposite the school."

"So what's it all about?" Boyce asked as he turned the car out of the gates and headed towards the village.

"I told you, Tom, I don't know." Rudd replied. "And I'm not blaming you. Neither of us had any idea that Mrs. Browning might be involved in Holt's murder yesterday when we looked through the bureau."

"I still don't get it," Boyce replied.

"I'm not sure that I do," Rudd admitted. Feeling in his pocket, he retrieved the letter, which he passed to the sergeant as he parked outside the row of cottages. Boyce read it, keeping his expression blank. He remembered the contents now and recalled having dismissed them as merely a personal communication regarding the death of Rex Holt's brother in South Africa. At the time, he hadn't thought it relevant to the investigation and he saw no reason even now to change his mind.

"Look at the note at the bottom in Holt's handwriting," Rudd added.

Boyce looked but was none the wiser. The scrawled words merely read, "Send acknowledgement and £500."

"Well?" he asked, handing it back.

"Two things occurred to me," Rudd replied. "Firstly, when Jean Browning told me she'd written to Rex Holt to tell him her father had died, she said, 'He sent some money.'"

"The five hundred quid mentioned at the bottom of this letter," Boyce suggested, as if that much were obvious.

"Exactly. But she made no mention of Rex Holt having sent a letter with the money. Yet someone must have written. The note says, 'Send acknowledgement.' So who wrote? Not Rex Holt. It seems more likely that he scribbled those instructions on the bottom for someone else to carry out. But who? Not anyone from the firm either. It was read-dressed from there to Barnsfield Hall. And it wasn't Martin Holt. He'd left home by that time."

"So you think it might have been the housekeeper?"

"It's possible. But if it wasn't her, she'll probably know who it was. I want to see her for another reason. Martin Holt said she'd been work-ing at the Hall for years. In that case, she's likely to know more about the family background than anyone else. And I'd like to find out more about Jean Browning and her father, Rex Holt's brother."

"But I thought you agreed with me that she couldn't have commit-ted the murder," Boyce protested.

"And I haven't really changed my mind," Rudd replied. "At least, I'm still not convinced that she did. What I'm trying to do is to start again with a fresh mind. And that applies to you, Tom, as well as me. No more assumptions. No more gut reactions." His mouth twisted wryly as he said it. "Just a plain, honest-to-God investigation of the facts. So fact number one: Jean Browning's father died in South Africa. What he was doing out there we have yet to find out. But why didn't Rex Holt bother to get in touch personally with his niece when his brother died? He didn't even write to her when she arrived in England. He got his solicitor to acknowledge the card she sent letting him know her address. I want to know why. Fact number two: Jean Browning herself. She stands to inherit ten thousand pounds from her uncle's estate, if not his entire fortune. So I want to find out a great deal more about her, too. What job was she doing out in South Africa? When and why did she get divorced? Exactly when did she arrive in this country? If the housekeeper, Miss Moxon, can't help us, then I propose getting in touch with the South African police and asking for their help."

Biddy watched them come up the long garden path to her front door. Although she guessed they were from the police, she welcomed rather than feared their arrival. The village was full of rumours regard-ing Rex Holt's death, but no one seemed to deny it was murder.

Biddy, who knew some of the facts from Martin, kept her own counsel. But she wanted to know the full truth. She was also desper-ately anxious to find out just how far Martin was implicated. Not that she doubted his innocence. But the gossip touched him as well and couldn't be ignored.

"He'll come in for a fair old bit of money now his father's dead," people said, nodding their heads significantly.

Martin himself hadn't called back again although she knew he'd come as soon as he could; he'd promised.

With the two policemen knocking at her door, Biddy comforted herself with the thought that she might be able to find out from them a little more about Rex Holt's death, at the same time making quite clear to them the fact that Martin had nothing to do with it.

But it was not Rex Holt they seemed interested in when the older of the two men, Detective Chief Inspector Rudd, as he introduced himself, asked his first question.

"Arthur Holt?" Biddy repeated. She had sat them down on the two low armchairs while she herself took her place at the table by the window. That way, she had both of them in view and could see what they got up to. "You're going back a good few years. Well, I don't know much. Mr. Holt never discussed his brother with me. There was talk, of course, especially in Welham, where the family was well known. Arthur Holt quarrelled with his father, don't ask me what about because I don't know. At the time, he and his brother, Rex, Martin's father, were both working in the family firm. It was before the war and the two boys were supposed to run the business as partners when old Mr. Holt retired. It was up on the board over the gate—GEORGE HOLT AND SONS. Anyway, Arthur Holt walked out, taking his share of the family money, and emigrated to South Africa. And that was the last that was heard of him; leastways he never wrote to his father or his brother. His mother used to get a letter once a year, if that. As far as I know, he tried to set up his own business, a printing firm, but it went bankrupt. And that's all I can tell you."

"The prodigal son," Rudd commented.

"But in his case there was no fatted calf," she replied. "He didn't come back."

"But his daughter did," Rudd told her.

"Did she now?" Biddy replied and folded her lips.

"You didn't know?" Rudd asked her.

"No one told me. I don't even know if Arthur Holt's dead or still alive."

"He died in March four years ago," Rudd said. "Were you working then at the Hall as housekeeper?"

"March, you said? Yes, I would be. I didn't retire until I was seventy and that wasn't until the following September."

"Mr. Holt had a letter from his niece, telling him about his brother's death. It seems he got someone else to reply to it. Have you any idea who might have written on his behalf?"

Her answer came without any hesitation.

"Reggie Trimmer. He was always up at the Hall in those days, scrounging drinks and meals. Mr. Holt used to get him to run errands for him into Welham or the village when he couldn't be bothered to go himself. He could type, too; Mr. Trimmer, I mean. So Mr. Holt let Mr. Trimmer deal with some of his letters; not the really important ones, of course. He'd answer those himself or send them on to his solicitor."

"I see. Thank you, Miss Moxon."

The chief inspector had got to his feet. Whether the information satisfied him or not was impossible to tell. Biddy tried to read his expression but his face gave nothing away. He and the broad-shouldered sergeant who accompanied him began edging their way past the chairs towards the door.

She caught them on the door-step.

"I haven't said my piece yet," she told them. "Before you go, I want to know how Mr. Holt died."

"We're still investigating the case," Rudd replied.

His manner, bland, formal, evasive, exasperated her.

"Then let me tell you this," she retorted. "If you think Martin had anything to do with it, then you're bigger fools than you look."

And with that she slammed the door shut on the pair of them.

Boyce waited until they were half-way up the path before beginning to laugh.

"That puts us in our place," he remarked.

"And she could be right," Rudd replied, smiling. He seemed in a better humour as he got into the car. Boyce started the engine.

"Where to? Trimmer's?"

Rudd hesitated before making up his mind.

"No, we'll see Trimmer later. I want to have another talk with Martin Holt again. We missed him yesterday. Let's hope we have better luck today."

CHAPTER THIRTEEN

But their luck wasn't in. When they arrived at the smallholding, the house was locked and there was no sign of Martin Holt anywhere. As he had done before, Rudd peered through the kitchen window and saw the same two cups and teapot on the table.

"Damn!" he said angrily. "Where the hell is he? Whenever we turn up, it seems he's going chasing off somewhere else. See if you can find Webber, Tom. The last time we were here he told us he lives in one of those houses opposite. Ask him if he knows where Holt's gone."

As the sergeant tramped off, Rudd walked to the middle of the yard to survey the larger of the two greenhouses. The light was all wrong, of course. It was late afternoon, not night-time, and the sun still shone on the glass. As a test, therefore, it was hardly fair. But, even so, he could see the heavy leaves pressed close to the glass, obscuring any clear view of the interior.

It would seem Boyce was right. Martin Holt could have faked his alibi. All Webber would have seen was a vague shape and that was easily rigged.

He'd have to check it later under proper conditions, after dark with the lights in the greenhouse turned on, but he already knew what the outcome would be. Whether or not Webber would admit he could have been fooled was another matter.

He walked over to the small shed next, re-examining the loose hasp. As far as that was concerned, he was right. Anyone, even a woman, could have pulled it free and opened the door. It wouldn't have taken much physical strength.

Boyce returned at that moment, announcing, "Holt's gone over to Barnsfield. God knows what for. He didn't tell Webber. We must have passed him on the way."

"Damn," Rudd repeated. "Well, I'm not chasing over there again. We could miss him a second time. We'll bloody well wait for him, Tom."

They had, in fact, passed each other on the outskirts of Welham, neither aware of the presence of the other car travelling in the opposite direction.

Throughout the day, Martin had been thinking of Bea and the last time he had seen her, walking slowly across the lawn towards her daughter and then the two women standing clasped in each other's arms. The memory hadn't exactly haunted him, but he could not get it out of his mind.

He must put it right with Bea, he thought.

Biddy, too, had been in his thoughts. He had promised to go back and see her again. That, too, was something else he ought to do and, at the end of the day, after locking the place up, he set off for Barnsfield.

He went to see Bea first.

Hester opened the door to him as she had done before, her face again expressing that contemptuous dislike as soon as she saw it was Martin on the doorstep.

Well, this time he didn't care.

"I'd like to speak to Bea," he said.

"She won't want to see you. She's resting," Hester retorted.

She seemed about to close the door in his face but he forestalled her by placing the flat of his hand against it.

"I must speak to her," he insisted.

Their raised voices reached Bea, who was sitting in the garden, through the open door at the end of the hall.

"Who is it?" she called.

Hester called back over her shoulder, "Martin Holt," in a voice which dismissed him entirely.

"I want to talk to you, Bea." Martin raised his own voice, thinking how absurd the situation was, thanks to her bloody daughter, who seemed to have taken on the role of keeper.

Bea appeared at the end of the passage, outlined in the open doorway against a background of leafy garden.

"Let him come through, Hester," she said quietly.

Hester grudgingly stood aside to allow him inside the house, following behind him as he walked down the hall and into the garden, where she took her place behind her mother's long cane chair which had been set out on a patch of shaggy lawn under some fruit trees. She evidently had no intention of leaving him and Bea alone to talk.

It couldn't be helped. He'd have to say his piece in front of her but he was very conscious of her presence as she stood, her hands resting on the back of her mother's chair, facing him.

He said, "I've come to say sorry, Bea, for the misunderstanding between us. I didn't intend to distress you. I also wanted to thank you for being so loyal to my father. He had very few real friends."

It sounded terribly phony to his ears, stiff, abrupt, curt; too much as his own father would have sounded had he ever brought himself to make a similar apology.

He saw Bea's face quiver as if she might be close to tears and the sight was too much for him. Before she could speak, he added rapidly, "I'd like us to be friends, too, if that's possible." Then he turned and walked away, striding back through the hall and out of the house.

He had parked the car outside the mill, as he had done before. It didn't seem worth getting into it and driving to Biddy's, which was only a few minutes' walk away. Besides, he wanted to compose himself before arriving at her cottage. He still felt oddly flustered by the interview with Bea, feeling he had handled it badly. If only her bloody daughter hadn't been there, they might have talked properly.

Biddy's delight at seeing him soothed some of his pride; not that she showed it openly but he could tell by the look in her eyes that he was welcome.

Her actual words were "So you've turned up at last."

"I'm sorry, Biddy," he said. "I've had things to do."

"Well, now you're here, sit down, for goodness' sake. Don't stand about, cluttering up the place. I'll make some tea."

She left the kitchen door open so that they could still talk as she filled the kettle and set out cups and saucers.

"I haven't any more news about my father," he told her, raising his voice above the rattle of china. "I haven't seen the police since yesterday."

"Well, I have," she retorted.

Her answer surprised him.

"When was that?"

"Earlier this afternoon."

"What did they ask you about?"

"Your father's brother mostly; the one who went to South Africa."

He was even more astonished.

"Arthur? What on earth did they want to find out about him?"

"Who wrote to his daughter when he died. You knew he was dead, did you?"

"Yes, I found the letter among his papers." He was silent for a moment, remembering the scrawled note at the bottom in his father's handwriting. It was sharp of Rudd to have noticed it although its significance to the police investigation escaped him. "What did you say?"

She brought the tray of tea things through and put it down on the brass-topped table.

"The truth, of course," she told him, giving him a sharp look. "I said if anyone had written on your father's behalf, it was Reggie Trimmer. It was the sort of job your father would get him to do when he couldn't be bothered himself."

"It was more than that, Biddy," Martin replied. "I think it was pride. Guilt as well."

It was better, he thought, that the truth were said, even though his father was dead. There had been too many evasions in the past.

"Stubborn, too." Biddy nodded her head. "Like a brick wall. You knew the niece is living in England now?"

"No, I didn't. Did Rudd tell you that?"

"If that's the shorter of the two, the one whose shoes wanted polishing, yes, he did."

Martin was silent. He could see no possible connection between this information and his father's death.

"Unless, of course," he said out loud, half to himself, "she inherits."

"What are you talking about?" Biddy demanded.

Martin roused himself.

"I was thinking of Jean Browning, Arthur Holt's daughter. She's a relative, of course; my father's niece and my cousin. Never having seen her, I've never thought of her as part of the family before. It crossed my mind that perhaps she benefits under my father's will and that's why Rudd is checking her out."

Biddy was asking with the offhand air she always assumed when the question was important to her, "So you don't know what's in your father's will?"

"No, I don't, Biddy. You know what he was like. He never said anything about his private affairs."

He was anxious to change the subject to the one which was his main reason for coming to see her.

But Biddy wouldn't let it rest.

"You mark my words, money's at the back of it all. It usually is. But I told them, 'If you think Martin had anything to do with it, then you're as big a pair of fools as you look.' "

Her face had flushed up as she spoke and the teacup trembled so much in her hand that she had to put it down on the table.

He said quickly, aware of her distress under the outburst of anger, "Biddy, you weren't worried on my account, were you?"

"*I* knew you hadn't done it," she replied. "But it wasn't what *I* thought that bothered me. It was what was going on in their heads, the fools."

She nodded her head towards the window, indicating the world outside; not just the police but the whole of local opinion.

Martin took her hands in his, moved by her concern and yet exasperated at the same time by the fact that neither of them had yet voiced the word "murder." It was time that that evasion, too, was finished with.

"I didn't murder him," he said.

"I know that," she broke in.

"And Rudd knows it, too. Charlie Webber, the man who works at the smallholding for me, saw me on the night my father was killed. So I'm in the clear as far as the police are concerned."

She pulled away her hands to dab under her eyes.

"Thank God for that. That inspector could have told me, though; going on about Arthur Holt and not a word about you. I shall tell him, too, if ever I see him again."

Indignation had dried her tears and he smiled.

"You do that, Biddy." He paused for a moment before adding, "Will you tell *me* something?"

"It depends what it is," she replied warily.

Getting to his feet, he went to stand in front of the fireplace, his back to her as he looked at the photograph of his mother on the mantelpiece. Still without turning round, he continued, "It's about my mother and Edward Voyte. Did you know that he broke off the affair after he returned to Oxford?"

She was silent for so long that he wondered if she had heard him.

"Who told you that?" she asked at last.

"His mother. I went to see her yesterday. According to her, the relationship was nothing more than a flirtation."

"On his part maybe." Biddy's voice sounded bitter.

"But she knew it was over?" he persisted. "Tell me, Biddy. I need to know the truth."

"Why? They're both dead now and anyway it was over and done with years ago. Why is it so important to you?"

It was impossible to explain the reason to her. He wasn't even sure of it himself. Part of it was the need to have this lie, too, finally exorcised.

But above all, he felt that knowing the truth would better equip himself in the future. He had relied for too long on an adolescent dream of love, the falseness of which had not occurred to him before. What he wanted to remember was Bea's hand resting on his father's in that gesture of tenderness and loving acceptance.

He heard Biddy rise to her feet behind him and cross the room. When he turned round, she was standing in front of the sideboard, opening the little sandalwood box and taking from it an envelope which she passed to him.

"Here," she said. "You'd better read that. I nearly gave it to you on Wednesday when you called and then changed my mind. Perhaps I should have let you read it then." As he opened the envelope and took out the sheet of paper it contained, both scented with the fragrance of the wood, she continued, "Your mother kept it in her bureau, along with the other letters he sent her. When she was dying, she made me take it out and promise I'd burn it after her death." The colour was high in her cheeks again. "I don't know why I didn't. It just seemed wrong somehow to destroy it when he'd meant so much to her. It would have been like her dying all over again."

He knew exactly what she meant. He had experienced a similar feeling when his father had slammed the drawer shut on the other letters and poems from Edward Voyte.

The letter, headed simply with the name of his college and the date, "September 14th 1939," read:

> My dear Elizabeth, I should have told you the truth before I left Hatton to return here but I couldn't find either the words or the courage. Now that war is declared and I shall be leaving soon to join the RAF, I feel I must be totally honest with you. Like the summer, the time for self-deception is over.
>
> You were part of that peacetime and a dream of love which at the time was very sweet. But it is now over.
>
> My dear girl, I wish it could be otherwise but the events of the past few days have made me face up to reality.
>
> I don't know if I'll survive this war. Whether I do or not, I shall always remember you and our brief summertime of loving.
>
> Please don't write to me again. Try to remember me, if at all, without regret. Edward.

So that was where she found the quotation for her gravestone, Martin thought. Even in death, she hadn't given him up.

"Well?" Biddy was saying.

"He still didn't tell her the truth," Martin replied. "It wasn't just the war which made him break with her although that's the impression he's trying to give. I don't know if he lacked the courage or, to give him the benefit of the doubt, was trying to spare her feelings. But there was another girl, the sister of a friend of his. If he hadn't been killed, they were planning to get engaged on her twenty-first birthday."

"I see." Biddy pressed her lips together before bursting out, "I wish now I'd burnt the wretched thing! It brought so much unhappiness."

"Yes," Martin agreed quietly. "And none of it was really necessary. If Edward Voyte had told her the truth in this last letter, she might have come to terms with it."

Although as he said it, he doubted it.

"What will you do with it?" she asked, seeing him slip it into his pocket.

"I'm not sure," he admitted. "I may burn it, as she wanted. Perhaps I ought to. I don't know."

He still felt too close to the situation to come to any positive decision.

"I must go, Biddy," he added, stooping down to kiss her cheek. "But I'll come again as soon as I can."

She was anxious to keep him, the first time this had happened. Placing a hand on his arm to detain him, she asked, "What will you do, Martin, when everything's all right again?" He knew what she meant— when the murderer of his father had been found and he could come into his inheritance although he doubted himself if anything would ever be quite the same again. "Will you move into the Hall?"

That was an easy decision.

"No, Biddy. I shall sell it. I don't think I should want to live there. It's too big and besides . . ."

He didn't like to add that, however much he loved it, it held too many painful memories of the past for him ever to feel at home in it again.

She said, "You know your father owned other property round here as well?"

"The fields behind the mill?" he asked. "Yes, I saw a copy of the deeds in his bureau. He also owned some cottages in Welham."

"And the mill itself," she added.

He stopped, surprised, in the doorway.

"Did he? I didn't know that. When did he buy it?"

"About eighteen months ago when that couple who were running it as a pottery sold up. It's not generally known because he got his solicitor to act for him. He was going to have it done up as a house and then resell but he had that stroke and seemed to lose interest. He asked me not to say anything and I wouldn't have done except . . ."

Except he's now dead, Martin finished the sentence silently for her.

"It'd make a nice house," Biddy said offhandedly and, having planted the idea, she was content to let him go.

He needed no encouragement from her, however. The place had fascinated him for years and, as he walked back to where his car was parked on the forecourt, he stood surveying it as he had done before but this time with a new sense of potential ownership.

As far as property was concerned, he had to admire his father. If nothing else, he had a feeling for bricks and mortar and stone which matched his own.

Peering through the slats of wood which covered the dusty windows, he saw again with increasing pleasure and excitement details which he had forgotten—the broad oak planks of the floor, the heavy beams which supported the upper storeys.

Walking round to the back of the building, he looked about him again.

The layout couldn't have been better. The huge, overgrown, cobbled yard backed directly onto the fields which were also his father's property and were probably the reason which had prompted him to buy the mill itself. It made, in his father's own words which Martin remembered his using on occasions, "a nice little parcel of real estate."

Although, unlike his father, he had no desire to own more than he could use or occupy, he had to live somewhere and earn his living. Restoring the mill and working these fields would satisfy that desire, which Biddy must have been aware of, to put down roots again.

Not only that but he'd inherit more than enough to pay Charlie a pension. So money had its uses, after all, Martin thought wryly.

A voice behind him startled him out of his reverie.

Turning, he saw Hester Chilton coming towards him across the yard, picking her way through the discarded machinery and the clumps of tall nettles.

"I saw your car," she explained. "I thought I'd look round while I waited for you. I didn't know you were already here."

"Yes," he said and waited. He saw no reason why he should give her any encouragement or make it easier for her to say whatever it was she had quite clearly on her mind.

She stood awkwardly in front of him, the colour high in her face, her fists jammed down tightly into the pockets of a loose denim jacket she was wearing over jeans.

"I came to say I'm sorry," she said, lifting her chin. "I think I've been unfair to you. No, not think. I *know* I have. I also want to thank you for coming to see my mother."

"I see," he said. He would have left it there, unsure how to continue and too embarrassed by her awkwardness to think of anything further to say, had not the expression on her face reminded him of Bea's when she had turned away after explaining about his father's will and, anxious not to repeat the same mistake, he added quickly, "Thank you for coming to tell me that. I'm fond of Bea and I don't want her hurt any more. My father's death was bad enough."

"She loved him, you know," Hester said with a defiant air.

It no longer exasperated him. He could understand the reason for it now. It arose out of the same sense of self-protection which, in his case, took the form of silence and withdrawal.

"I know," he said. "I realised that on Wednesday when I saw them together. They were good for each other. It's a pity they never married."

"Do you mean that?"

"Yes, I do."

"Wouldn't you have minded?"

"A few weeks ago I might have done. But I didn't understand how much they meant to each other then."

Her chin went up again.

"*I* would have minded. I didn't like him."

If she were trying to anger him, she didn't succeed.

He merely said, "My father? I didn't like him much either, although I'm beginning to understand him better now. That's why I'm grateful that Bea loved him. She was the only person who ever did. You knew about him and my mother?"

She must know, he thought. Bea would have told her.

"Yes," she said and added awkwardly, "I'm sorry."

"She's dead," he said flatly. It was more than a mere statement of the fact although that was all he intended telling her. For himself, it meant far more—an end to the past and to the bitterness and regret which had surrounded it.

He knew now what he would do with Voyte's last letter: burn the bloody thing. It was what she had wanted and it was about time her wish was carried out.

To change the subject, he indicated the mill.

"Biddy's just told me my father bought it some time ago. I shall move in when his will's proved. I thought I'd sell my smallholding and set up here."

"It'll need a lot doing to it," she remarked. As they were speaking, they had begun walking towards the building. "But it's beautiful," she added. "It would make a splendid house."

"It's sound." To prove it, he banged his fist on the flint wall. "It's the interior that will need the most renovation although I shall keep the beams and the old floors."

"So you'll be near my mother," she remarked. "Would you . . . ?"

She broke off as if too embarrassed to complete the sentence although he knew what she meant.

"Of course," he replied although that consideration had not occurred to him until that moment. It had been Biddy he had been thinking of and his own return to his roots. "I want to keep in touch with her."

The look she gave him reminded him again of Bea. Bea's face, too, had worn that same expression when they had met outside Barnsfield Hall on Wednesday morning, tentative, appealing and yet ready to be withdrawn should he not respond to her. He saw, too, how attractive, in fact, she was.

"I ought to be going," she said.

He could have left it there. It was too soon to make any kind of commitment even on the most casual level.

All the same, he called out as she crossed the yard, "I shall see you again at Bea's?"

For a moment, he didn't think she'd heard him. She continued walking and it was not until she reached the corner of the building that she turned to call back, "Of course! I shall look forward to it, Martin."

And then she had gone.

So that was that.

God alone knew how the relationship would develop. That was in the future but it offered as bright a prospect, it seemed to him, standing alone in the yard, as all the other expectations that the place promised him.

Before he left, there was one small gesture to the past which he knew he must complete and which it seemed right to make in that place.

Breaking through the hedge into the field beyond, he walked a few yards and then stood looking about him. From that position, he could see, on his left, the mill itself, its high gable end rising above the trees, and, to his right, the meadows stretching down towards the river and its line of willows, their leaves glistening in the sun.

This was the view from Fair Mile Hill seen at close quarters, his own particular piece of the landscape which he had loved since childhood.

He had come home at last.

With the heel of his shoe he dug out a tussock of grass, revealing the earth beneath. It was dry in the July heat but still friable.

His land, he thought, crumbling it between his fingers.

He laid Voyte's letter in the small hollow left by the roots of the grass and then, striking a match, applied it to one corner of the paper.

The flame, invisible in the bright sunlight, ran quickly across it, consuming the words in the sloping handwriting.

Remember me, if at all, without regret.

When the letter was reduced to nothing more than a blackened, buckled mass, he scattered the earth over it and then walked away.

CHAPTER FOURTEEN

"Here he comes," Rudd said as Martin Holt's car turned into the yard.

"And about bloody time, too," Boyce muttered.

They had been sitting on a couple of empty boxes in the shade of the outbuildings, awaiting his arrival, for the past two hours, Rudd with more equanimity than the sergeant, who seemed to consider Holt's absence as a deliberate conspiracy on his part to pervert the course of justice, an opinion which he had expressed several times to Rudd's exasperation. So it was with relief that the chief inspector got to his feet.

"Waiting for me?" Holt asked pleasantly through the open driver's window as Rudd strolled towards him.

The man seemed more relaxed, Rudd thought. Less wary and on the defensive. He wondered what had happened to bring about this change.

"We wanted another talk with you," the chief inspector replied in the same easy manner.

"Then come inside," Holt said, unlocking the back door and ushering the two men into the kitchen. "I'll make some tea."

Even Boyce cheered up at this offer.

They sat down at the plain deal table which took up the centre of the room. As Martin Holt put the kettle on, Rudd looked about him covertly. In contrast to Barnsfield Hall, the place was small and minimally furnished. Unlike his father, Holt appeared to have no desire for possessions although, remembering the serviceable television trolley and the worn leather slippers on the dead man's feet, Rudd wondered if both men, father and son, had not shared a basic simplicity of taste which, in Rex Holt's case, had been superseded by the need to live up to the reputation of a rich man.

Holt placed the three mugs on the table and sat down facing the chief inspector and the sergeant.

"Well?" he said with a touch of his former irony, as if their presence amused him.

In the same light manner, Rudd remarked, "You're very elusive, Mr. Holt. Whenever we've called, you've been out."

"I've been following an inquiry of my own," Martin Holt replied.

"And is it satisfactorily concluded?"

"Yes; as far as these things ever are. Shall we say, I've finally laid it to rest."

"I wish I could say the same about my own inquiries."

Rudd made the remark deliberately, aware that they were fencing verbally with each other, a game which Martin Holt, for some reason of his own, wished to play and in which the chief inspector was prepared to join if only to see where it led.

"But your inquiries are real," Martin Holt replied, his voice more serious. "Mine turned out to be nothing more than an illusion."

"Perhaps mine are, too," Rudd remarked. He was thinking specifically of Holt's alibi. Was that nothing more than a trick? Face to face with him again, he saw that Holt was much more capable of planning a murder than Jean Browning, who lacked, as he explained to Boyce, the imagination.

He had the feeling, too, that, like most tricks, there was some quite simple explanation which, once he had grasped it, he would kick himself for not having seen before.

"Your case?" Martin Holt was asking. "You think my father's murder was some kind of an illusion?"

"Only in the sense that the evidence might not be all it seems. Isn't that the way you'd define an illusion, Mr. Holt? Something that appears other than it really is?"

Holt was watching him closely, aware that the initiative had passed into the chief inspector's hands.

"It seems as good a definition as any other," he replied. "But how does that relate to me? I assume you're here to interview me about the case?"

"Your alibi intrigues me," Rudd replied.

"I thought that had been cleared up. Didn't Charlie tell you he'd seen me?"

"But did he really? Or was it all an illusion, a trick, quite literally, of the light?"

"A time-switch," Boyce put in heavily, feeling that, as the idea had been his, he wasn't going to let Rudd steal his thunder. "You could have rigged up some kind of dummy figure in the greenhouse and then turned off the lights by means of a timing device."

Rudd nodded as if in complete agreement with this statement.

Martin Holt stared at the chief inspector in utter astonishment before bursting out laughing.

"It's ridiculous!" he cried.

"I agree," Rudd said equably, surprising Boyce this time. "But a lot of things would appear to be ridiculous until they're proved otherwise. People once thought the sun revolved round the earth. Galileo's idea that it was the other way round seemed quite absurd."

"That was proved," Martin Holt retorted. "There was scientific evidence."

"Point taken," Rudd said and smiled as if pleased with Holt's quick-wittedness. "Which brings me to my own evidence."

"What evidence?" Martin Holt demanded.

Rudd avoided answering directly. Instead, he asked a question of his own.

"You don't happen to own a green tweed jacket, do you?"

Martin Holt frowned.

"No, I don't think so."

"Not hanging up, say, in one of the outhouses?" Rudd persisted with artful ingenuousness.

Holt stared him straight in the eyes for a moment as if trying to read his thoughts and then, getting up so abruptly from the table that he startled both Rudd and Boyce, he flung out of the room and they saw him striding across the yard towards the shed, the door of which he wrenched open.

He was back within a few moments, the coat over his arm.

"This, you mean?" he asked and, as Rudd leant forward to examine it as if for the first time, he added angrily, "I'm not stupid enough to imagine you haven't been snooping around here while I've been out. I don't know what this jacket has to do with my father's murder or what evidence it's supposed to represent, but I haven't worn it since last spring. I'd even forgotten I'd left it hanging up in the outhouse. Anyone could have taken it."

"Exactly!"

Rudd was beaming.

Martin threw the coat down on the table.

"I don't know what damned game you're playing—" he began.

"It's not my game," Rudd replied. "But someone set it up although, to be frank with you, Mr. Holt, I've no idea at the moment who's at the back of it."

As he said it, he heard Boyce clear his throat in disapproval of the turn the interview was taking, but he ignored him.

Orthodox technique had got him nowhere and yet he felt he was circling round the perimeter of the solution, most of the clues already in his grasp. All that was lacking was either a little more evidence or the wit to reassemble what he already knew into a different pattern.

So, if orthodoxy hadn't supplied him with the answers, he was prepared to try a less conventional approach, to shake up the pieces of evidence, in other words, and, by tossing them down on the table, to see if they wouldn't form a new pattern.

He chose a piece at random; a minor piece it was true but one which had some link with the case and which he had been discussing with Miss Moxon only that afternoon.

"Tell me about Mr. Trimmer."

"Reggie? What more do you want to know about him apart from what you found out from Biddy this afternoon?" Martin asked.

So Holt had been to see her, Rudd thought, and had presumably discussed his visit with her.

"She told me it was likely that Trimmer had written the letter to Mrs. Browning, forwarding some money when her father died. Apart from that, I found out very little. But I'm curious to know more. What sort of a man is he? How long had he known your father?"

Rudd leaned back in his chair, his expression friendly, inviting Martin to talk.

He seemed a little nonplussed by the situation and began hesitantly.

"They'd been friendly for years, even before my father moved into

Barnsfield Hall. Trimmer lived in the village and it was he who let my father know when the Hall came up for sale. He had a small estate agent's in Welham, that's how he knew about the property market. He used to carry out minor business deals for my father as well—collect the rents on some of his property, for example. After they both retired, Trimmer used to call more often at the house, as a guest ostensibly, although I think my father still found his services useful."

"You don't like him much?" Rudd suggested. That much was apparent from Martin Holt's ironic tone.

"I think he's an inquisitive man and a gossip. It was one of the reasons why my father didn't entrust him with anything important."

"One of the reasons?" Rudd picked up the remark.

Martin Holt smiled sardonically.

"When it came to anything really important to do with money or property, my father trusted no one but himself."

It seemed a dead end, Rudd thought. He had learned little more than he already knew or might have guessed for himself.

Again, almost at random, he picked another piece to try although Martin Holt's reference to Miss Moxon—Biddy as he called her—had given him the idea.

"What was your reason for calling at Miss Moxon's this afternoon?"

"It was a private visit which had nothing to do with my father's death although while I was there I tried to set her mind at rest."

"About what?"

"Funnily enough, about my alibi." The corners of Martin Holt's mouth lifted wryly. "She'd heard gossip about me which had distressed her. I told her, as far as the police were concerned, I was in the clear. I had an alibi which you now tell me I could have faked. Ironic, isn't it? But the main purpose of my seeing her was about a private matter. Which reminds me, I'd like the Voyte papers back if you've finished with them."

His last remark suggested the reason behind Holt's visit to Barnsfield. It was connected in some way with Edward Voyte, about whom Rudd had learned a little from Holt himself and, although it could have no possible bearing on the case that he could see, he was intrigued by the manner in which the dead poet's name had cropped up yet again in his inquiries. Even Holt's reference at the beginning of the interview to the inquiry which he himself had been making and which had turned out to be nothing more than an illusion which he had finally laid to rest could also indicate the same theme.

Even Rudd himself had been drawn into it and he remembered with painful clarity, sitting there in Martin Holt's ugly little kitchen, in the glare of the early evening sun, setting like a conflagration behind the outhouses, the evening before spent in Marion Greave's lamp-lit drawing-room, discussing Voyte's poems.

Hadn't he, too, been chasing after a dream which had, after all, been nothing more than an illusion? But, unlike Martin Holt, he could not state with the same assurance that it had finally been laid to rest.

The Voyte papers were, in fact, in his brief-case on the back seat of the car parked outside in the yard. It would have been a simple matter to fetch them and hand them over.

But he felt suddenly for no reason that he could explain that he didn't want to part with them yet although as evidence they seemed to have no bearing on the case.

He said, looking contrite, "I'm sorry, Mr. Holt. I've left them in the office. I'll have to return them to you another time."

Martin Holt shrugged.

"It doesn't really matter. I'd promised to let Hurst have the letters for the book on Voyte he's writing. It'll be a good excuse not to hand them over. I wasn't very keen on him using them anyway although I suppose, in the interests of scholarship, he should at least see them."

"I'll try to get them back to you before Hurst leaves the country," Rudd promised him. "I understand he's going up to London tomorrow and then flies back to the States next Friday."

"You've seen him?" Martin Holt asked with little more than polite curiosity.

"Routine inquiries," Rudd replied, feeling there was no need to add any further information. More to distract Holt's attention from such official business, he added, "How good do you think Voyte's poems are?"

Martin Holt considered the question seriously, perhaps out of relief that the subject had shifted away from the investigation into his father's death.

"It's difficult for me to judge. Hurst himself admits that he's a minor poet but seems to feel he's worth the research, all the same. Personally, I think he's more fascinated by the story—the young poet turned airman, cut down in the flower of his youth. It had some romantic appeal for him, like an Arthurian legend. In fact, he spoke of it being like a pilgrimage for him." He smiled briefly. "Part of the illusion, of course.

But he waxed quite lyrical on Wednesday afternoon over the bottle of whisky he opened."

Rudd looked blank.

"Opened?" he repeated as if he hadn't heard properly. "You mean he started a new bottle?"

He heard Boyce shift slightly in his chair but not enough to distract Holt's attention, who was looking at the chief inspector with a puzzled expression.

"Yes; he got it out of a small fridge built in under the dressing-table unit in his room. Is it important?"

"And you had a few drinks together while you discussed Voyte?" Rudd suggested in a jocular manner.

Martin Holt looked annoyed at the question.

"No, we didn't. I was driving home and it was too early in the day, anyway, for me to drink much. I still don't get the point."

"There isn't one," Rudd replied. "At least, only a very minor one which you needn't bother with. About your phone," he continued, changing the subject adroitly, "is it back in action?"

"Yes, it is. And I don't see the point of that question either," Martin Holt replied. "Is that all?" he added, as Rudd and Boyce rose to their feet.

"For the moment," Rudd said.

They were almost at the door before Martin Holt called out, "You've forgotten the jacket!" at which Boyce, looking flustered, turned back briefly to collect it, meeting Holt's sardonic glance as he did so and colouring up bright red.

"My God!" said Rudd in disbelief as they got into the car, where Boyce slung the jacket onto the back seat. "Lawrence Hurst!"

The pieces had fallen into an entirely unexpected pattern and, what surprised him most, without any attempt on his part to rearrange them. It was all down to sheer bloody good luck! For some reason this pleased him, as if the gods, for once, were on his side.

Boyce said, more cautiously, "It's not much to go on."

"I agree," Rudd replied. "But it's a start. If Hurst opened a new bottle of whisky, say, at four o'clock on Wednesday afternoon, then what in God's name was he doing ordering another one six hours later at around ten? Go on," he continued, seeing Boyce open his mouth, "you tell me the objections."

As you usually do, he added silently to himself.

"Well, first off," the sergeant said, "he could have drunk the first bottle himself."

"Unlikely," Rudd pointed out. "There's nothing to suggest he's a heavy drinker, not like Trimmer."

"Okay," Boyce conceded that point. "Then he could have broken it or had people in for drinks."

"Point taken. We'll check on that, of course, but we're going to find the answer to both questions is no."

"But why are you so sure? After all, the man's got an alibi."

"It's because of his alibi that I'm convinced he's guilty."

"But the manager saw him!" Boyce protested.

"Did he? I'm beginning to wonder. All Benson said was Hurst opened the door and told him to put the bottle of whisky on the table. Why *told*, Tom? Why didn't Hurst take it himself?"

"But if Hurst wasn't there, who the hell opened the door?"

"That's what I propose finding out," Rudd replied.

"I still don't get it," Boyce said heavily. "Why should you think Hurst is guilty because he has an alibi?"

"Because Rex Holt's watch was broken at eight minutes past ten," Rudd explained. "Supposing it was smashed deliberately, not to alter the time the murder was committed but to confirm it because Rex Holt's killer had an alibi to cover that time?"

As he said it, he was aware of a sense of guilt in passing off Marion Greave's theory as his own, not that he could see any way out of the situation except by letting Boyce know that he still met her, an admission he was unwilling to make. At the same time, the guilt was diminished by a stronger emotion—relief. The image he had had of her earlier, during the interview with Martin Holt, of her sitting in the armchair in the lamplight, had receded; only a little, it was true, but enough for him to be able to contemplate it more equably.

"And that's why," he continued, "I'm convinced Holt is not the murderer. None of the other suspects have an alibi with the exception of Martin Holt and, if we go along with the supposition that Holt would have done a better job of making it look like an accident, then there's only one other person who fits that particular theory—Lawrence Hurst. He had the opportunity, too, to look Barnsfield Hall over when he called on Rex Holt that morning and, as Holt knew him, it would have been easy enough for Hurst to persuade him to join him on the terrace that evening. He had only to say he'd called back because there was some detail regarding Voyte he wanted clarified. Holt would have been surprised but not deeply suspicious."

"Yes, I can see that." All the same, Boyce sounded puzzled. "But what about Voyte? Where does he fit in with all this?"

"What about Voyte indeed!" Rudd exclaimed. "I could kick myself for not asking that question earlier. A minor poet hardly heard of in this country! And yet Hurst knew not just about him but about an even more obscure teenage love affair he'd had with Martin Holt's mother before the war. He could have found it out through research, I admit; that is if he's a genuine scholar, which I doubt. But there was a much easier method which I think he used and one we can prove by asking a few simple questions. And once we've got the answers to those, I think we shall be able to pin a motive on him as well."

Trimmer began by denying anything. They interviewed him in his sitting-room, where he had been eating a snack supper on a tray in front of the television, a glass and a bottle of whisky on the floor beside him.

"I don't know what you're talking about!" Trimmer protested.

"Letters," Rudd reminded him quietly.

Looking at him, he was convinced Trimmer was lying. The man possessed a natural predilection for gossip which, in the chief inspector's opinion, more often than not arose out of malice, and he could see about him plenty of evidence of Trimmer's pathetic attempt to copy Rex Holt's life-style which suggested envy of the man.

"Supposing I told you," Rudd continued, trusting to Trimmer's stupidity, "that I have the necessary evidence?"

Trimmer's defences collapsed as Rudd hoped they might.

"I don't see I did anything wrong!" he asserted. "When Rex asked me to write to his niece when his brother died and send that money, I had no idea she'd write back!"

"And so a correspondence developed," Rudd suggested, "in which you let Jean Browning into quite a few family secrets?" He refrained from glancing at Boyce, who, pen poised over his notebook, seemed absorbed in the task of taking down Trimmer's statements, his expression quite inscrutable. And yet only half an hour earlier, he had been protesting volubly that any connection between Hurst and Jean Browning was too far-fetched to be considered.

"Show me one good reason why I should believe you," he had said.

Well, there it was, Rudd thought, not without a pleasurable sensation of having been proved right.

"She was naturally interested in the family background," Trimmer was saying with an innocent air although the manner in which he fingered the silk scarf tucked into the open neck of his shirt suggested that he was more aware of his betrayal than he was willing to admit.

"Including the unhappy relationship between Rex Holt and his wife," Rudd continued. "And I've no doubt you explained the reason for it. You had an estate agent's business in Welham before the war, didn't you? So you would have heard the gossip. Then, of course, once you got to know Rex Holt more intimately, it wouldn't have taken you long to pick up more information from a remark here and there which, added together, made a fairly detailed picture of Mrs. Holt's unhappy marriage and the reason behind it—a love affair with a young Oxford student called Edward Voyte who wrote poetry and was killed in the war."

"I may have mentioned it," Trimmer conceded unwillingly. "Now I come to think of it, I believe I did happen to refer in one of my letters —only in passing, mind you—to Mrs. Holt and Edward Voyte. It was no great secret. She kept his photograph and letters in her bureau when she was alive, which—"

He broke off, aware of what he was about to say.

"Which you came across one day and read?" Rudd finished the sentence for him.

Trimmer began to bluster.

"I had no intention of snooping. The bureau was moved upstairs after Mrs. Holt died. Rex used to keep some of his papers in it. One day he asked me to fetch a document he wanted. The letters from Voyte were tucked in with it and, in replacing them, I just happened to glance at them, that's all."

Rudd refrained from pointing out that, as the letters from Voyte were inside envelopes, Trimmer could hardly have "happened" to glance at them, as he had said. He had found out what he came for. There was no point in pushing Trimmer into a further confession of prying into the Holt family affairs.

His expression blank, he merely said, "I shall need a statement from you, Mr. Trimmer. In the meantime, I'd prefer that you didn't discuss this interview with anyone. It could be a serious matter."

The threat, although spoken in an even, formal voice, wasn't lost on the man. He looked genuinely apprehensive as he watched them leave, his pale blue eyes milky with anxiety and awareness of Rudd's unspoken contempt.

"Where now?" Boyce asked, as Rudd climbed into the passenger seat beside him.

For his own reasons, he didn't want to refer to Trimmer any more than the chief inspector although Boyce's silence on the subject was more out of a need to protect his own self-esteem. He had been proved wrong and he didn't want to give the chief inspector the opportunity of saying so.

"The Red Lion," Rudd said briskly. "And we're going to have to go about the next interview more carefully. I don't want to tip Hurst off before we're good and ready. We'll ring Benson first from a call-box in Welham just to make sure the coast's clear."

Their luck was in. Hurst had gone out for the day—to Suffolk, as the manager explained when, a few minutes later, he ushered them both into his office.

"Some research for the book he's writing, I believe," he added. "He left soon after breakfast but he's booked in for a late dinner this evening if you wish to see him."

"No, I don't," Rudd replied, silently applauding Hurst's intelligence in keeping up his pretended interest in Voyte at this late stage of the game. "And I don't want the fact that I've called here today to be made known to him. Is that quite clear, Mr. Benson?"

"I understand, Chief Inspector," he replied. "Nothing will be said, I assure you. Now, how can I help you?"

"I want to check again on Mr. Hurst's movements on Wednesday evening. You said he dined here and then went to his room, where you later delivered a bottle of whisky he'd ordered. Will you tell me exactly what happened—in detail, this time, please?"

"Well, as I told you before, he rang down at about five to ten and I took the bottle upstairs myself, as the staff were busy. I knocked and he let me in—"

"So you saw him?" Boyce put in, exchanging a brief glance with Rudd.

"No, not exactly. He was in the shower. He called out to me to wait a moment and then unlocked the door so that I could come in."

So that was how the trick was worked, Rudd thought.

"And the bathroom is just inside the door, I believe?" he asked, trying to recall the layout of Hurst's room.

"Yes, that's right," Mr. Benson replied.

"Go on," Rudd said. "When you entered the room, what was Mr. Hurst doing?"

"He was in the bathroom with the door ajar. He called out, 'Thanks. Could you put the bottle on the table, please?' I set it down next to his typewriter and then left, saying goodnight to him, but I don't think he heard because of the water running in the shower."

"I see." Rudd stood up, Boyce getting to his feet at the same time, neither of them so much as glancing in the other's direction.

"Is that all?" the manager was asking.

"Not quite," Rudd replied. "You have a passkey, Mr. Benson? I'd like to examine Mr. Hurst's room. No, not to search it," he added as the man seemed on the point of protesting, "I just want to check the position of the bathroom. We shall be only a few minutes."

Despite the chief inspector's assurance, Benson handed the key over reluctantly and accompanied them into the foyer, where he watched them go up the stairs.

It took only the few minutes that Rudd had promised, long enough for him to position himself in the bathroom, where he waited for Boyce to knock at the door. Then it was simply a matter of reaching an arm round the bathroom door to unfasten the catch. By the time Boyce entered the room, Rudd was out of sight, the bathroom door half-closed.

"Child's play!" as Rudd himself pointed out.

Boyce merely grunted in reply.

"There's just one more detail to check," Rudd continued as the two men emerged into the passage. "There must be a fire exit on this floor somewhere. Safety regulations would insist on one."

They found it round the turn of the passage—a heavy metal door, appropriately labelled, opening onto a small balcony with a flight of iron steps leading down into the backyard behind the hotel kitchens with a gate giving access to the car-park which lay beyond.

"Convenient?" he asked Boyce. He was determined to provoke some response from the sergeant, who had kept uncharacteristically silent since the interview with Trimmer.

"All right," Boyce conceded grudgingly. "But it's still only a theory."

"But a good one," Rudd replied. "It hangs together; better than the case against Martin Holt. Hurst and Jean Browning worked together, he committing the murder and she providing him with an alibi. She must have rung down to reception, using a tape-recording of Hurst's voice, to order the bottle of whisky and then hid in the bathroom with the tape-recorder, which she switched on and off at the right moment when she let the manager in. Clever stuff, eh? Shows imagination. That's what makes me think it was Hurst who planned it all. She lacks the style although it was she who provided the motive—as Rex Holt's heir once Martin Holt had been disposed of. Meanwhile, Hurst slipped out of the hotel by way of this fire exit and carried out the murder, taking care to make it look like a clumsy attempt to fake an accident. That's why Holt's watch had to be smashed. It had to show the time the murder was committed, too soon after Hurst had ordered the bottle of whisky for him to be thought guilty even if we considered him a suspect and checked up on him. It was all part of the illusion."

He chose the word deliberately, remembering Martin Holt's use of it earlier that evening.

Boyce said, "But how are you going to prove the connection between Hurst and Jean Browning? After all, it sounds unlikely. She's South African, he's American. They couldn't have come from more different parts of the world if they'd planned it."

"Perhaps they did," Rudd said lightly. "That's something we can check through our liaison officer at the Yard's Interpol bureau. Meanwhile, we're going to set up our own little illusion."

"How?" Boyce asked.

"You'll see," Rudd said infuriatingly. "It won't be difficult, providing we make good use of our own sound effects. Come on, Tom," he added, glancing at his watch, "we ought to be pushing off. Hurst could be arriving any minute and I don't want him to find us snooping round the hotel. Besides, I want a last word with the manager."

Mr. Benson was co-operative. Yes, he agreed, he'd make sure the receptionist asked Mr. Hurst for a forwarding address before he checked out of the hotel the following morning, which he would pass on to the chief inspector.

"So that's that for the moment," Rudd said as they crossed the hotel car-park.

He felt in a jubilant mood at the way the investigation was going. All the pieces were dropping very satisfactorily into place.

To his added gratification, Hurst's hired Ford turned into the car-park just as Boyce started the engine and Rudd put out a hand to delay the sergeant from driving off.

There was no chance the man could see them. It was now dusk and the car-park was dimly lit.

They watched in silence as Hurst got out, locked the car door and walked briskly towards the hotel entrance, Rudd's eyes fixed on his retreating figure with the suppressed excitement of a Labrador scenting game.

If Martin Holt's quest was over, he thought, he could at last see an end to his own.

And with the lifting of his professional spirits came the easing of the weight of personal regret which had hung heavily about his heart.

CHAPTER FIFTEEN

The hotel was a small, comfortable establishment just off Baker Street, converted from four tall terrace houses and managing to maintain, despite the alterations, some of the qualities of those original, elegant, family residences. The foyer was overlooked by the manager's office, through a window behind the receptionist's desk just inside the entrance and, by discreetly positioning himself inside this room, Rudd was able to watch the comings and goings of the guests and staff without being seen himself.

To his left, he had an oblique view of the stairs and the small lift which ran beside it; to his right, the revolving door which led into the street and which from time to time gave out the faint shirring noise of rubber whenever anyone arrived or left. Straight ahead, a pair of swing-doors led into the bar, its interior clearly visible through the glass panels.

To any casual observer, the foyer presented the quite normal appearance of any hotel reception area. The girl behind the desk, a pretty, plain-clothes WPC, wearing a pink blouse and a grey skirt, looked the part: DC Turner, in the porter's uniform, borrowed for the occasion, stood just inside the revolving door ready to welcome any new arrivals while Kyle, acting as assistant barman, seemed quite at home serving drinks to the assorted plain-clothes men and women who, together with genuine guests, occupied the bar lounge.

The time was ten minutes to eight.

Outside, the London dusk was turning a purple pink, lit by the neon sign over the revolving doors, beyond which the street lamps marched away into the distance in a diminishing perspective of lights towards the brighter dazzle and subdued roar of the traffic along Baker Street.

Meanwhile, Hurst was upstairs packing in readiness for his departure the following morning, as the chambermaid, another WPC in hotel uniform, had reported half an hour earlier, having entered his room on the pretext of checking that his bed had been turned down for the night.

Everything seemed ready. The hook was baited and there was nothing Rudd could do except wait for the fish to rise to it. Which was a good metaphor, he thought, sitting relaxed in a corner of the manager's office and remembering the hours spent as a boy on a river bank, watching with the same sense of pleasurable anticipation the end of his float resting gently on the surface of the water.

Boyce had evidently not shared such an experience. He was clearly on edge although trying not to show it, folding and unfolding his arms and shifting about on the chair next to Rudd's with a bored expression on his face as if to show an eagerness for action rather than the tension of waiting. As for the manager, he made no attempt to hide his anxiety. An affable man under normal circumstances, he had given up any pretence of doing the hotel accounts and had retired to the far side of the office, out of sight of the foyer, where he paced up and down, smoking cigarettes which he crushed out before they were half-finished.

"Are you sure everything's going to be all right?" he asked for what must have been the twentieth time.

God knows what he was expecting. A shoot-out, perhaps, in his lemon and white foyer, blood spattered on the French wallpaper and corpses stretched out on the fitted carpet.

"My men know what they're doing," Rudd assured him yet again. "There won't be any trouble."

Touch wood, he added silently to himself.

So far, their luck had been in. The telephone call made to Jean Browning at work earlier that afternoon, carefully timed at exactly 5:25 P.M. to catch her just before the supermarket closed and conducted over a particularly bad line, the sound effects pre-recorded and fed into the receiver, had seemed to work. At least, she hadn't, as far as Rudd could ascertain, listening in on an extension, shown any signs of suspicion, accepting the voice, only partly heard, it was true, over the accompanying crackle, as Hurst's although the young sergeant on loan from the Met on account of his ability to mimic voices and accents had been careful to keep the conversation to the minimum.

"Listen, Jean," he had said, "I can't stop long. Something's turned up—nothing really serious but I must see you before I leave tomorrow.

Can you come to the hotel tonight at eight o'clock. You know where it is?"

"Yes, of course. What's happened?" she had replied.

"I told you; nothing serious."

She had tried to question him further but the sergeant, with a quickness of mind Rudd later congratulated him on, simply said before hanging up, "Sorry, I can't hear you, the line's so bad. I'll see you tonight at eight, then?"

She hadn't attempted to telephone him back although, if she had, the WPC acting as receptionist had been instructed to inform anyone putting in a call for Mr. Hurst that there wasn't any answer from his room.

So far so good.

The hands of the gilt clock facing the chief inspector across the foyer, a minute and a quarter fast according to his watch, showed exactly two minutes to eight. She could arrive at any minute.

Like a stage director checking the set and actors just before the curtain goes up, Rudd glanced to left and right of him again. The WPC was typing something out below the reception counter, Turner was standing, hands clasped behind his back, at the door, Kyle was serving a fair-haired man, DC Barney, in fact, with a whisky and soda while a young couple, dressed for an evening out at a night-club, perhaps, had drifted out on cue from the bar into the foyer and were chatting together as if waiting for a taxi or friends to join them.

As Rudd checked their positions, he heard the faint flapping sound of the revolving door and, turning his head quickly, saw a woman enter.

For a moment he did not recognise her as Jean Browning. The mental picture he had been carrying in his mind of a passive, ordinary-looking nonentity, wearing the supermarket's checked nylon overall, in no way corresponded to the slim figure, discreetly but smartly dressed in blue summer suit, her brown hair loose on her shoulders, who was approaching the reception desk with an air of quiet assurance.

It was only when he saw her profile with that stubborn chin, so like Martin Holt's and surely an inherited family feature, that he realised who she was and picked up the internal telephone which connected with the reception desk.

"Go ahead," he said briefly when the WPC answered it. Replacing the receiver, she put up one hand to a gold-stud ear-ring, as if it had become dislodged during the brief call, smiling as she did so at Jean Browning, who was now standing in front of the desk.

It was a tiny signal, too small to be noticed except by those looking for it, but it was passed quickly along the chain of plain-clothes men and women who were waiting for it—to Turner, who moved unobtrusively in front of the revolving door and from him to the three men who had been strolling along the street outside and who now turned towards the hotel entrance.

Inside the hotel foyer, the man in evening dress waiting with his woman companion straightened his tie, a signal to those inside the bar.

Rudd took it all in with one rapid glance before turning his attention back to the reception desk, where the WPC was now speaking on the telephone—to Hurst, who would no doubt be surprised to hear that a Mrs. Browning was waiting downstairs in reception.

It was one of the tricky moments in the plan.

Would Hurst become suspicious and make a bolt for it? Rudd hoped not. If possible, he wanted to make the arrest after the couple had met, thereby establishing without any doubt the connection between them. But in case the man's suspicions were roused, he had men posted behind the hotel and also at the foot of the emergency stairs leading down from the upper floors.

He came, the lift doors opening to reveal him standing inside its small, brightly lit interior, where he remained for a few seconds, his eyes searching the foyer, even his head tipped slightly backwards as if he were snuffing the air for the least scent of danger.

For those few seconds, he ignored even Jean Browning, who was standing at the reception desk, smiling nervously and clearly wondering why he hadn't stepped forward to greet her.

The next moment, Hurst walked out of the lift and crossed the foyer.

Insulated inside the manager's office, Rudd could only guess what Hurst was saying by the look on his face, no longer the pleasant, affable expression he normally presented but frowning with displeasure.

"What the hell are you doing here?"

Her answer, too, could be surmised by her astonished reaction.

"But you phoned me and told me to come!"

Looking back later on the events which followed, Rudd estimated that it took about half a second before the significance of her reply struck Hurst. At the time, it seemed that there was a longer interval while they stood confronting each other before Hurst reacted, during which Rudd wondered why the tell Turner and the others didn't move in to make the arrest.

All of them seemed trapped motionless inside a bubble of time, frozen into the attitudes they had assumed at the moment of the meeting between Hurst and Jean Browning.

Then, as he himself made his first step towards the office door, the bubble broke. Hurst was off and the foyer erupted into action.

In that half-second, he must have realised he was cornered and had worked out an escape route. The door into the street was blocked by Turner and Hurst turned instead towards the bar, using his shoulder to thrust the plain-clothes man in evening dress against his woman companion.

"Christ!" Rudd heard himself yelling as, with Boyce behind him, he flung open the office door and set off in pursuit.

It was like witnessing a speeded-up film or a video tape. There was Hurst ahead of him, storming through the bar, Kyle vaulting over the counter, Barney flung against it, another DC, Maynard, running, arm outstretched, a few inches only from Hurst's shoulders while the real guests leapt to their feet, screaming and shouting, a reaction which was repeated seconds later as Hurst and the others burst through the swing-doors into the dining-room.

Rudd, pounding a few feet behind the main action, had confused images of tables laid for dinner, a woman guest shrieking and clutching a glass of wine, a waiter flattened against a pillar, the sounds of a crashing tray and breaking china.

He felt the shards crunch briefly under his feet as he followed the others through a second pair of swing-doors leading into the kitchen, where he paused momentarily to take in the scene.

Maynard and the young DC who had been guarding the back door had Hurst trapped between them and he knew it.

He had halted in the narrow gangway between the banks of stoves on one side and a long preparation table on the other, where he stood at bay, turning his head this way and that.

As Rudd's glance took in the chef, backed up against one of his own stoves and a waiter, crushed in behind the swing-doors by the press of men who had crowded in, he was aware that it wasn't quite over. Not yet.

If Hurst chose to make a fight for it, he still had time to pick up any of the weapons which lay too close at hand. Within inches of him, a meat cleaver lay horribly exposed on top of the preparation table, while on his other side and also within easy grasp a saucepan of soup stood simmering on one of the stoves. Either, if flung at one of the DC's who confronted him, could be lethal.

Almost without making any conscious decision, Rudd stepped forward, calling out, "Give in, Stolley! It's all over, man!"

He used the name deliberately rather than the alias, Hurst, by which the man had been known throughout the investigation, hoping it might surprise him.

The trick worked. Rudd saw him glance over his shoulder in astonished recognition and, in that same brief moment, Maynard closed with him, wrenching his arms behind his back.

It was, as Rudd had said, all over.

What followed was a literal as well as a professional clearing up. Apologies were made to guests and staff, plain-clothes men and women, no longer needed on the case, helping to set the bar and the dining-room to rights, where the damage turned out to be minimal.

Hurst, or rather Stolley, was sent back to headquarters in Chelmsford under escort for later questioning.

Which left Jean Browning.

Rudd interviewed her in the manager's office, where she had been temporarily held until Stolley's arrrest, dismissing the WPC who stood guard at the door as he and Boyce entered.

She had assumed the same passive attitude which she had taken up at the first interview, sitting with her hands clasped in her lap, her face expressionless. But the Holt chin was set and Rudd realised, as he sat down opposite her, that it was not going to be easy to persuade her to admit to anything.

He began in a relaxed, conversational manner, hoping to break her by sympathy and kindness.

"Lawrence Hurst, or to give him his real name, James Stolley, has been arrested, Mrs. Browning, and will be charged with the murder of your uncle, Rex Holt. Do you have anything to say?"

She shook her head although the name, James Stolley, clearly affected her. Rudd saw a look of alarm in her eyes.

"Very well," Rudd resumed, acknowledging her silence, "then let me tell you what I know about you both and the relationship between you."

Some of it, as he was only too aware himself, would have to be bluff. The facts he had managed to discover in the short time available didn't cover the whole story but he was hoping that, by convincing her he knew everything, he could persuade her to confess.

"You met James Stolley three years ago in South Africa, where you were working as a secretary for a local Johannesburg newspaper. Stolley was a Canadian, a free-lance journalist and something of a drifter, who was working his way through Africa, covering any news story which he could sell to one of the agencies willing to buy his material. You met and had an affair in consequence of which your husband divorced you, citing Stolley as co-respondent."

That much at least was fact, turned up by the South African police in the records. Stolley's background had been given to him by the editor of the newspaper, whom Rudd had telephoned personally.

"Stolley didn't want to marry you, however, although when he heard a particular story you had to tell, he stayed around, didn't he? And that story, Mrs. Browning, concerned a rich uncle of yours in England who'd sent you five hundred pounds when you wrote to tell him of your father's death. He hadn't written to you himself but a friend of his had, Reggie Trimmer. Trimmer enjoyed passing on titbits of information about Rex Holt and his family. He's naturally a gossip, with a sharp nose for other people's business. Envy and malice played a part, too. He couldn't run Rex Holt down to his face, so he used you as a convenient means of expressing that malice by letting you know some of the less successful aspects of Rex Holt's life—his unhappy marriage, his disappointment in his only son, Martin.

"As for you, you had your own problems, a failed marriage and a lover who didn't appear to want to marry you. But more important still, you had a lifetime of bitterness inherited from your father, who had turned his back on the family business but, instead of making his fortune, had died a bankrupt."

Rudd was guessing again. He had no evidence to support such a statement except for the impression he had gained of the Holt family with its stubbornness, pride and inability to forgive, passed down from father to son or, in this case, from father to daughter.

"A lifetime of bitterness," he repeated softly.

It made a good motive for murder.

He waited for her to respond but her eyes remained fixed on the neutral space between them.

"But," he continued, "through the correspondence with Trimmer, you learned quite a lot about your uncle, Rex Holt, including the reason for his unhappy marriage—his wife's love affair with Edward Voyte, a young poet who had been killed in the war but whom she had never forgotten. She had even kept his letters and the poems he had sent her all those years before. I don't know why you passed the story on to Stolley. Was it simply for something to talk about, Mrs. Browning? Or did you hope to persuade him with this account of undying love of the seriousness of your own feelings towards him? One thing I'm certain of, though, you wanted to impress him with the fact that, despite your own poverty, you had a rich relative in England who might leave you something in his will."

She still didn't reply although Rudd thought he could glimpse the glitter of tears under her lids.

"And Stolley was impressed. He likes money, doesn't he? And the story gave him an idea. With his background as a Canadian journalist, he could pass himself off as an American researcher, inquiring into Voyte's background for a book he was writing. This would give him access to Rex Holt and the means to discover his routine and the layout of the house. Because what he planned was to murder Rex Holt and, by incriminating the son, to get him disinherited. Then you, as the next direct heir, would benefit from everything Rex Holt possessed, which should have been his. How much persuading did you need, Mrs. Browning? Some, I imagine. Unlike Stolley, I don't think you're ruthless. You wouldn't willingly kill for gain. But Stolley held a very powerful card in his hand. Come in with me, he said, and I'll marry you."

This, too, was guesswork but he had scored. He saw a tremor run across her face.

"It wasn't an easy plan to carry out, however. Stolley had to provide himself with a new identity. As a Canadian citizen he had no problem returning to Canada and from there crossing into the States, where he set himself up in New York in a small apartment, earning a living under his real name, James Stolley, by writing articles for Canadian and American magazines and newspapers."

That much Rudd had established through the immigration authorities and inquiries carried out by the New York police on his behalf.

He waited again for her response before giving her the last piece of information, which he had held back until that moment, hoping that she might break and, by making a statement, supply him with the missing information he needed to complete his case.

But she made no sign. Indeed, her withdrawal was now total, for she had retreated even from the space between them and sat, looking down at her clasped hands.

Taking out his notebook to impress her with the authenticity of his next statement, he said, "The New York police inform me that he wasn't alone. He shared the apartment with a woman—"

"That isn't true!" she cried, throwing back her head.

Rudd held the page of his notebook towards her.

"It's all there, Mrs. Browning, taken down during a telephone call to New York. If you still don't believe me, I can show you the telex I received this morning, confirming the information. The woman's name is Sharon Mary Hunter. She's twenty-five, a divorcée and works in a department store. She moved in with Stolley not long after he arrived in New York. The neighbours know her as Mrs. Stolley although there wasn't, in fact, a legal marriage. He was saving that particular bargaining point for you, wasn't he, because that was the only way he could guarantee getting his hands on Rex Holt's money?"

She wept then, but not passionately. Over the years, Rudd had seen many women crying, angrily, bitterly, but rarely with the utter dreariness and defeat with which the tears slid out of Jean Browning's eyes. She made no sound or movement, not even attempting to brush them away, simply letting them fall as if she had blanked off the emotion which had inspired them.

Rudd waited until she stopped weeping, watching her with a close and yet compassionate attentiveness, hoping that the other Holt quality she had inherited, pride, embittered by the account of her lover's unfaithfulness, would at last persuade her to talk.

He said, "How did Stolley arrange to get hold of a passport in the name of Lawrence Hurst?"

It was one aspect of the case which he hadn't yet been able to uncover.

She didn't reply for a few seconds and Rudd was about to abandon the interview, postponing the rest of the cross-examination until later when she, too, like Stolley, had been taken back to headquarters.

And then, without any preliminary, she began to speak in a rapid voice, without raising her eyes.

"About a year ago, he covered a story for a newspaper—a suicide; a man named Lawrence Hurst who'd shot himself. Hurst was about his age and Jimmy was able, through his contacts with the police, to find out about his background. Hurst had no friends and no immediate family. He'd never applied for a passport either. The story didn't make more than a couple of lines, so Jimmy thought it was safe to use his identity. He applied for a passport in Hurst's name, using his date of birth and other background details. He also set up another address as

Hurst on the other side of town, well away from the district where he was living. He even wrote some articles under Hurst's name. He thought if the police checked up, they wouldn't go much further back than a year. At the same time, he started the Voyte research, by writing to his Oxford college and the RAF."

"Which you'd heard about from Trimmer?" Rudd put in.

"Yes; he'd mentioned a few details about Voyte's background, not much, but enough to give Jimmy a start. From the RAF, he got the names of some of the men who had been in Voyte's squadron, while the Oxford college put him in touch with a few of his fellow undergraduates. He wrote to them and one of them gave him the address of Voyte's mother, so he was able to write to her. The research had to be authentic, you see, in case anyone checked up."

"But no one mentioned Mrs. Holt?"

"No and it worried Jimmy. He really needed someone else other than just Reggie Trimmer who knew about Voyte's love affair with Martin's mother but no one mentioned it."

"All the same, he decided to risk it?" Rudd suggested.

She looked up briefly.

"He thought it wouldn't occur to anyone to ask about it," she replied.

And he was right, too, Rudd thought grimly. It hadn't.

"Then, last spring, he decided to come to England. He'd done enough research to make the trip possible."

"Meanwhile, you had already moved here?" Rudd asked.

"Yes. The plan was that I'd be living in London well before Jimmy arrived. I was to let Uncle Rex know of my address but make no other attempt to get in touch with him. Jimmy didn't think he'd contact me himself. I was to get a job and keep in the background as much as possible."

Orders which she'd carried out to the letter, Rudd thought as he nodded to her to continue.

"Jimmy had already written to several Voyte contacts including Uncle Rex, arranging interviews with them which would make his cover-story seem genuine if anyone checked up on him."

"So Hurst, or rather Stolley, arrived in England about a fortnight ago," Rudd said, picking up the thread of her narrative, "his intention being to carry out the murder of Rex Holt. Did he intend meeting Martin Holt last Wednesday?"

"No, that was a mistake," she replied. "Jimmy had arranged an interview with Uncle Rex to look at the Voyte papers. He had no idea, until he arrived at the house, that Martin had been invited to lunch. As part of the plan had already been set up, there was nothing Jimmy could do about postponing it."

"You mean putting Martin Holt's phone out of action?"

"Yes. He'd already done that on Tuesday night. Jimmy had found out Martin's address through Reggie Trimmer and kept a watch on the place for several evenings, so he knew Martin lived alone and had few visitors. Once the phone was dead, he wouldn't be able to make or receive any calls on Wednesday evening. At the same time, he wanted to find something at Martin's place which he could plant as evidence against him."

"Which he did," Rudd put in. "He discovered an old coat hanging up in an outhouse and took some of the threads, which later he left on a rose-bush near the scene of the murder. And on Wednesday, of course, he was able to see for himself the layout of Barnsfield Hall and chose the best place to carry out the killing."

He kept his voice and features bland, expressing no more than a dispassionate interest in what they were discussing but, all the same, he touched some response in her.

"I don't know any details," she said quickly. "Jimmy didn't want to tell me too much. He said it would be safer. And . . ."

She broke off.

"You yourself preferred not to know." Rudd completed the sentence for her.

"All he said when he came back to the hotel on Wednesday night was everything was all right."

All right! Good God! Rudd thought. Just how far had she managed to blank out her emotions in order to come out with a statement like that? Rex Holt, her own uncle, had been murdered in cold blood, evidence planted to incriminate a totally innocent person, his son, who, if found guilty on a charge of parricide, could have served a long prison sentence, and yet she could accept Stolley's assurance that everything was all right!

At some point she'd have to face up to the truth—that Stolley had lured Rex Holt out onto the terrace, where he'd struck him down at the top of the steps with a stone and had then, by smashing his head on the bottom ledge, guaranteed that a murder inquiry would be started. He had even gone to the extent of replacing Holt's watch on his wrist before smashing that, too, in order to cover his alibi. Which brought him back to the interview with Jean Browning.

"I take it you'd arrived at the hotel earlier?" he asked.

"Yes; I'd left the house by the back way. There's a gate in the fence which leads into a lane behind the house. Jimmy had driven down early that morning, at about two o'clock, to set up an alibi for me."

"Tape-recorders and time-switches?" Rudd suggested pleasantly. "So that your neighbour, Mr. Barton, would hear the usual noises of doors shutting and the television playing and would be prepared, if asked, to state that you had been at home that evening?" When she nodded, he continued, "Because, of course, you were needed at the hotel to set up an alibi for Stolley? How did you get down to Welham?"

"Jimmy had hired a car for me, which he'd left in a side turning a few streets away. The idea was I'd have a drink in the hotel bar and then go upstairs to the ladies' cloakroom, which was on the first floor. No one noticed me. There was a party going on and there were lots of people about. Jimmy had left his door unlocked and I let myself into his room when the corridor was empty."

"What time was this?" It was Boyce who put the question.

"About nine o'clock. That gave Jimmy plenty of time to drive over to Barnsfield by half past nine. He knew Uncle Rex went to bed fairly early."

"How?" Boyce asked, raising his head from his notebook.

"From Reggie Trimmer. We were still writing to one another and Jimmy got me to ask questions about Uncle Rex, as if I were naturally interested in him and his way of life. So we knew he lived alone and that the servants went off duty at seven o'clock."

"Yes, I see," Rudd said blankly. "And he left the hotel, I assume, by the fire-escape, the same way he'd slipped out in the early hours of Wednesday morning to drive up to London and fix up your alibi? Meanwhile, on Wednesday evening, you were to establish his by a similar method, a tape-recording of Stolley's voice, ordering a bottle of whisky to be sent up to his room over the telephone. You then hid in the bathroom with the shower running and, when the manager knocked at the door, you simply leaned out to let him in, at the same time switching on the tape-recording of Stolley, or rather Hurst, as the hotel staff knew him, telling whoever delivered the bottle to put it on the table?"

"Yes," she replied. "Jimmy told me to keep the shower running; then the waiter wouldn't be suspicious if Jimmy didn't answer if he spoke to him. It would be assumed he hadn't heard because of the noise of the water."

"And then you left the hotel after Stolley returned to the hotel by the same way he'd left, up the fire-escape?"

"Yes, by the main entrance and then I drove back to London. After work the following day, I returned the car to the hire firm. It was on the other side of Streatham and we didn't think you'd trace it. I got a bus home."

"And what were the long-term plans, Mrs. Browning?" Rudd asked pleasantly. "I imagine those had been set up?"

"Jimmy was to return to the States and keep up the Hurst identity for a few months. Then, when everything had quietened down, he was to go back to Canada on his own passport. When the will had been proved, he would have joined me in the Bahamas."

"Once you'd inherited and had sold off what you could of Rex Holt's estate?"

"Yes; he was going to find me a good lawyer in London to handle everything and arrange for the transfer of the money bit by bit so that it wouldn't look suspicious. Once the major part had been paid over, we were going to get married."

For a moment, she seemed on the point of tears again and then that Holt chin was raised and she looked directly at Rudd. "I loved him," she continued. "Why couldn't he be faithful to me? I was to him. I did everything he asked."

She had inherited, Rudd thought wryly, all the family qualities of tenacity, stubbornness and pride and he could only hope, for her sake, that they would help her through the long prison sentence she was going to face.

Only one question remained, a minor one but he wanted it cleared up all the same because it was on this point that he had first become aware of Stolley's involvement in the case.

"Tell me," he said, "why did Stolley invite Martin Holt up to his room on Wednesday afternoon?"

"He was worried about meeting Martin that morning. There had been some family quarrel about the Voyte papers and Jimmy wanted to make sure Martin accepted his story about the research. He felt that, if Martin believed it, he'd make it seem acceptable to the police when he talked about it."

Which was, in fact, what had happened. Martin Holt had shown no suspicion regarding Stolley's cover as an American researcher interested in Voyte, an attitude which had persuaded Rudd to accept his authenticity.

Remembering this, he couldn't resist replying, "That was clever of him, Mrs. Browning, but a mistake all the same. You see, he opened a new bottle of whisky in order to offer Martin Holt a drink, which made me suspicious of the alibi he so carefully set up a few hours later."

She smiled for the first time—a strange little smile, bitter and yet oddly triumphant, as if she, too, were pleased at Stolley's error, a reaction which the chief inspector could understand even though he could not sympathise with it. As she had said, she had done everything asked of her; it was he who had been disloyal. It must have been a source of ironic satisfaction to her that it was he who had blundered. But cold comfort, all the same.

Even after she had been led away to the car by a uniformed woman sergeant and a WPC to be driven to headquarters, it left a bitter flavour in his mouth, as if he could taste on his tongue the ashes of a love consumed by hatred.

His own car was waiting, Boyce at the wheel but, on a sudden impulse, he signalled to him to wait and, turning back into the hotel, let himself into the tiny telephone-box by the staircase.

Marion Greave's voice came to him like a draught of pure, clean water.

"The case is over," he said, "and you were right about the inheritance. Can we meet? I want to thank you by taking you out to dinner."

She hesitated for a moment only.

"Of course. Could you be free tomorrow night?"

"Yes," he replied. He'd make damn sure he was. "Shall I pick you up at half past seven?"

"I'll be ready." She paused before adding, "As a friend, Jack?"

"As a friend," he repeated with more assurance than he really felt.

JUNE THOMSON was brought up in an Essex village, in a background very much like the setting of her novels. She was educated at London University. She makes her living as a teacher, and in her spare time has written the eleven Inspector Rudd novels which had brought her a wide following in both England and the United States. Her most recent novels are *Sound Evidence, Portrait of Lilith,* and *Shadow of a Doubt.* She lives in Hertfordshire with her two sons.